Fiona Cooper lives in Nor[...]
Heartbreak on the High Si[...] *Swiss Family Robinson* and *The Empress of the Seven Oceans. Jay Loves Lucy, I Believe in Angels, Rotary Spokes* and *A Skyhook in the Midnight Sun* are also published by Serpent's Tail.

Blossom at the Mention of Your Name

·····················

Fiona Cooper

Library of Congress Catalog Card Number: 95–69750

A catalogue record for this book can be obtained from the British
Library on request

The right of Fiona Cooper to be acknowledged as author of
this work has been asserted by her in accordance with the
Copyright, Designs and Patents Act 1988

Copyright © 1995 Fiona Cooper

First published in 1995 by
Serpent's Tail, 4 Blackstock Mews, London N4
and 180 Varick Street, New York, NY 10014

Phototypeset by Intype, London
Printed in Great Britain by Cox & Wyman Ltd., Reading, Berks.

Love, always to Jean and Winston

in memory of Ray, the unforgettably Divine Miss M.
for Callum, wherever you are,
and all the fairies – I believe in you

with thanks to:

Zsarday, Yee Chuan, Tony, Tommy, Tom, Teresa, Tenebris,
Shena, Sheanagh, Sarah, Sandra Hush, Mr Rosen,
Rosemarie, Rose, Her Imperial Highness the Grand Duchess
Regina Fong, Auntie Phyllis, Pete, Patience Agbabi,
Octavia, Noël Coward, Neil, Monika, Misdemeanours,
Millie, Melina, Mavis, Mary, Maltese Joe, Lisa, Lily Savage,
Kris Kirk, Kitty, Julia, John, Janet, Jack, Hylton, Hugh,
Hollis Maclaren, Graham, Future Tense, Fenella, Esther,
Ellen, Edith, Ed Heath, Dot, Dolly, Divine, Patrick Dennis,
Dee, Christie, Chrissie, Cathy, Caroline, Camp David, Brian,
Betty Bourne, Bloolips, Bet, Barry, Andy, Andre Adore,
Alma, Adrella.

thanks also to the Society of Authors for fiscal lifeblood via
the K. Blundell Award.

Part one

....

Fairyland

1

Callum had studied every book he could find on the ancient lore and craft of earth magic and when he could find no more words on paper, he'd distilled sage, bathed in it, drunk it in and wandered in every wild place he could find, seeking wisdom.

He was so soft of voice and step that rabbits didn't even pause in mid-nibble when he came to where they were. A stalking heron would take his form as simply a part of the riverbank world and swivel her eye back to the stream for the elusive silver flick of a fish.

When he dived into the ocean, sea anemones carried on combing the water, hermit crabs do-si-do-ed in his shadow. If he lay in a pool, see-through shrimps skedaddled along his skin and fish the size of staples grazed the pores of his body.

In the summer, he was a creature of the shore and his wavy hair went white blond like a child's with the salt and sunshine. His skin became the colour of wild honey and his blue eyes matched the sky at dawn. He loved life, he loved men. And he loved dancing. Dancing in The Powerhouse on a Saturday night, he was Queen Astarte of the Seven Veils, She on whom all men gaze and lose their reason. So he joked, so he hoped.

Gerth worked in The Great Outdoors, a sportswear company which had offices in the city: he had snappy suits and ties and a crocodile-skin wallet. One Saturday night him and the lads, his mates, dared each other to go in The Powerhouse and take the piss out of the poofs.

In Gerth's world, men were hard and tough. If their jobs didn't involve muscular effort, they went to a gym and played football at the weekends. Gerth had muscles like lumps of steel. He dreamed of Versace and Armani, but on a Saturday night he wore heavy boots and thick denim and a leather jacket. The way he walked made his clothes look like armour.

In The Powerhouse, Gerth felt like an astronaut with his head in a helmet that distorted both speech and vision. A spaceman landed among aliens with his oxygen tanks running low. The dance floor was bright as a full moon and the creatures dancing were ethereal and weightless. Only his heavy boots kept his feet on the floor as he gawped. Callum was the lightest and brightest of all the dancers. It would take at least a space suit on his slender-shouldered liquid-hipped body to give him the shape of a real man like Gerth and his mates.

Bloody hell, Gerth thought, glowing neon under the disco strobe. For a moment, he felt himself rise like a helium balloon – even the studded soles and steel toe-caps weren't enough to pin him down. His head beat with blood.

He was in a group of his mates, bunched together and bristling with booze and contempt, all geared up for queer-baiting until chucking-out time. Callum wore sandals for chrissakes, Jesus sandals made of turquoise plastic, sandals and loose silky trousers with mickey mouse braces, and pink flamingo earrings.

And Gerth couldn't stop staring at him.

He was dancing, this will o' the wisp beauty, dancing by himself in the strobe lights like a fairy, *a fucking fairy in a glen*, Gerth snarled inside. So why did he want to hold him in his arms and stroke that silky hair and run his hands over that slender body? Who did he think he was, that poof, fucking Tinkerbelle?

'Mine's a fucking pint,' he told his friends. 'I got to piss.'

'Watch your back, Gerth!' they told him.

He shoved his hands in his pockets and shoved his shoulders through the dance floor. The bog. His zip. Piss. Zip again and turn round who should be there but Tinkerbelle for chrissake, peering in the mirror and fluffing up his hair.

'It's so *hot*,' he told Gerth. 'So *hot*! How can you wear that leather?'

Gerth's fists itched, but his heartbeat softened them into hands that wanted only to reach out and touch . . .

. . . a friggin' *fairy*?

'Not that it doesn't look good,' the fairy was saying. 'In fact it looks wonderful.'

Gerth was speechless. The fairy was waiting for his reply.

'Leather's for real men,' he said.

'Oh, real men,' the fairy said, sighing. 'Real men are hard to find these days.'

'Yeah?' Gerth's chin turned to steel.

'Oh, yes,' the fairy said, his mad blue eyes twinkling with laughter.

'I gotta go,' Gerth shouted, stomping towards the door.

'Au revoir . . .' Callum wagged his slender fingers.

Gerth raged through the pastel carnival of dancers and slouched back to the can-toting Marlboro-smoking Men.

'Where you been, Gerth, mate? Have a nice time?'

'Fucking great, mate. Pint,' Gerth said, and pint again until he passed out.

Next afternoon, shaving to go down the pub for Sunday piss and pool, he found a pink card in his pocket. A card with a phone number and the words 'ring me?' His heart lurched. Ring who?

He couldn't resist.

Well, the voice was definitely Tinkerbelle. 'Hello' with rising levels of amused irritation as he put down the phone without speaking time and time again. Then Tinkerbelle said:

'I don't know who you are and if you wish to run up your phone bill on silence, that is your choice, of course. But I think I know you. Let's just say there's a lot more to being a real man than wearing leather. I think you understand me.'

Gerth slammed the phone down and just made it to the pub for last orders. Sharing a leer with his mates over the barmaid made him feel normal again. But everything jarred: her harsh blonde curls, her curvy bum, his mates' third-rate second-hand fantasies about her. Usually, they went back to his flat or someone else's and watched blue movies on a Sunday. This Sunday he found he was watching the blond male stud.

That night he picked up the first slag who smiled at him and took her home and gave her a bloody good seeing to.

'Think you're bloody Rambo?' she said, laughing. 'Or is it Guinness Book of Records time?'

'Don't talk,' he said. 'Turn over.'

'Oh, Christ,' she said. 'I might have known you'd got something to prove. Your type always does. I hope you've got some vaseline.'

2

'Hello, this is Callum. Please leave a message, because if you don't, how will I ever know you called? Bye!'

Callum. He had a name.

Where the hell was he? Gerth had been ringing him for a week now and always the same three rings, a click and the gentle mockery of his message. He rang in the morning, mid-morning, lunchtime, afternoon, evening; he rang well after the pubs were shut. He was fucked if he'd leave a message, the bloody fairy probably handed out cards like confetti. The bloody machine was probably only on because of him ringing and hanging up. Sometimes when he punched the number his heart beat faster, sometimes he'd pressed redial so often he just felt numb.

Every day he thought he saw the fairy in town but it turned out to be some student tramp, some ethnic right-on bird, some hippy schoolboy. That week, the streets were full of blond fluffy-headed people, Jesus, where did they all come from? It was like an alien invasion.

The worst thing was not being able to say anything to anyone. No 'got me eye on this bit of stuff, bird, tart, bint, she's begging for it', no returned nudge and belly laugh, no 'good luck mate tell us what she's like'. He felt as if he was constantly running on the spot, heartbeat racing nowhere. The Sunday night tart had kept them all quiet so far, they saw her in the bar and went whoo! and she laughed and flipped the bird at them and said *ooh, it's my kinky stud* whenever Gerth went anywhere near her. Just like normal.

Gerth went shopping and bought a new shirt, OK it was a smudged navy just the same as new denim, but it was silk, soft as swansdown and the pocket and buttonholes were embroidered. It hung in his wardrobe and taunted him every time he opened the door. He bought white trousers that clung to the arse and the muscles of his thighs. They glowed on the hanger beside the shirt. Soon he hooked a calfskin belt over the hanger, a soft tan with a gold buckle in the shape of King Neptune. A real woofter give-away – the words died with the vision of dippy skippy Callum dancing like a houri, smiling like a Pre-Raphaelite angel.

Gerth started to take long baths, soaking in foam and scrubbing his skin smooth. He was fanatically clean, and every day since he'd had his flat, he'd showered two or three times, scalding then ice-cold water driving at his skin, driving the smells of pine forests and musk into every pore with soaps and gels and sprays. Now he wanted just to smell green, a light spring forest green.

There was no way he could joke the lads into The Powerhouse that Saturday, dead obvious if he even mentioned it. He spent the evening on the Tuxedo Princess, a sweaty dry dock meat market for the sexually challenged. His mates and him fetched up with a mini-skirted gang of post-pubescent talent and since he wasn't interested, the best-looking one made a huge play for him. To jeers and cat-calls, he took her phone number.

'You could score there, Gerth, she's hot for it!'

'Treat 'em mean, keep 'em keen,' he said automatically.

A taxi took him home alone and he shredded her number out of the window: all the booze in the world couldn't shift him from sober.

The late movie was *My Beautiful Launderette* and he watched wide-eyed, flicked channels when it finished, wide awake and almost hysterical with tension: the early morning movie was *Sebastiane*. Men again, men touching and smiling and kissing like it was going out of style. His whole world was upside down and inside out: since he'd seen Callum it was as if he'd walked through a door where no door should be, into a world where nothing depended on what he'd known all his life. Like Alice down the rabbit hole, arse over tip into loony land.

Three o'clock in the morning. A moon nearly full outside his window. Everyone in the whole world was asleep except him.

He rang Callum and gasped when there was no click, no hum, just a real voice saying:

'Hello?'

And then into his silence,

'Hello. I heard you gasp. So you're not just a fault on the line. Why not talk to me – go on?'

'Hello,' Gerth said.

'Oh, it *is* you,' Callum said warmly. 'I sort of hoped it was. I sort of hoped you might come to The Powerhouse tonight, then I thought no, he wouldn't. Well, what can I do you for?'

'Dunno,' Gerth said. 'Feel a real prat. Dunno why I called.'

'Would you like to see me?' Callum sounded patient.

'I suppose . . .'

'Don't fall over yourself with enthusiasm,' Callum sighed. 'Can we try that again? Would you like to see me?'

'Yes,' Gerth said. 'Would you like to see me?'

'Oh yes,' Callum said.

'Well, when?' Gerth said. Christ, was any of this real?

'How about . . . mm . . .' Callum hummed for a second or two, 'Now?'

'It's three o'clock in the morning!' Gerth said, fumbling for brakes on a roller-coaster ride.

'So it is,' Callum said. 'You can see the church clock from my window. It's a lovely night. Shall I come to you? Would you like to come to me?'

'Yes,' Gerth said. 'Yes.'

'Well, which?' Callum said, 'You're not being very decisive.'

'I'll come to you,' Gerth said.

'I think you'll need the address,' Callum was laughing at him.

'Right,' Gerth said. 'I'll be with you as soon as I can get a taxi.'

'Until then,' Callum said. 'And don't worry.'

'I'm not worried,' Gerth said.

'Well, that's all right then,' said Callum.

3

Callum's instinct when he met people like Gerth was to freeze with fear, sheer physical terror which he masked with a display of manners so perfect they were dazzling. *Never talk to strangers, never walk alone anywhere in the city, never make eye contact.* Excellent manners and an oil slick of camp when he was among his own kind. It was all very well to feel aroused by hard muscular energy – put those strong arms around me, honey, hold me tight, and hold me *now* . . . and for ever? The reality of real men was fists against ribs and skull, bootcaps carving their own shape into soft flesh and crumpled jaws.

Since when had he slipped his phone number into anyone's pocket, let alone a leather pocket belonging to a total stranger slumped on the floor, paralysed with drink?

So what was Gerth – a walk on the wild side?

Callum had his phone programmed so that hitting memory and button seven would ring in Wol's house. Wol would answer, and, hearing nothing, ring all the emergency services at once. It was a mutual arrangement: Wol was a silky skimpy fairy, just like him, only he lived in a housing association terrace in the West End of the city. Callum's flat was seven floors up in Garstone Towers, you could see the river and four bridges from his window. He called it his eerie eyrie.

Perhaps he should look exactly the same as he had in The Powerhouse, even though that was his Queen Astarte drag and he only ever wore it on a Saturday night. Yes: that was what Gerth knew of him, that's what he'd seen, that's why he'd called and that's why he was coming over.

He was coming over. And now was neither the tail end of Saturday nor the beginning of Sunday. He was in the time-warp of three a.m., walking on a concrete floor in mid-air, waiting for a dark stranger to buzz his intercom and burst into his life.

'This could be the biggest mistake you've ever made,' Callum told his mirror.

However.

What sort of music was right?

He looked at his tapes: *Rhythms from the Rainforests, Mother Earth Calypso, Songs from Ocean, Air Symphony, Zodiac Suite, Echoes of an Enchanted Evening.* He pictured Gerth listening and rocked back on his heels. Any of them would get all that macho energy riled and confused.

Blessed be Wol! Last Samhain, he'd given him a tape full of jazz band schmaltz. Callum pressed buttons.

> *When the moon shines bright over Wyoming*
> *That's when I long to be right in your arms*
> *When the stars are bright over Wyoming*
> *That's when I long to see your heavenly charms*

Well, Garstone Towers wasn't Wyoming, but it would do very well. And as the singer warbled about cabin doors and ever mores and loving hearts that never part, Callum flitted around the room lighting candles and scattering pinches of crumbled herbs on the melting wax. He ought to have wine – he ought to have food, but there was no point even pretending to look.

Then he sat and waited, eyes closed on a fantasy as familiar as a favourite home movie: Mrs Callum Ordinary with a wonderful meal in the oven. A baby asleep in a pink and white nursery. A key turning in the lock and a man without a face coming in with a bunch of flowers and sweeping him off his feet. Mr Ordinary had Gerth's shoulders and he was smiling. Callum opened his eyes. Did Gerth smile like that?

The intercom buzzed.

4

You wouldn't expect a fairy to live anywhere else really, Gerth thought, lurking in the dark doorway. Garstone Towers – a high-rise hangover from the seventies, giro city, a standing joke under constant threat of demolition, peopled by students and hippies and OAPs. He felt his brand-new white trousers loud as a leper's bell. The soft caress of silk on his back and chest and arms was like the magical touch of his first woman. The first time he'd been naked with another human being. Just like then, he hadn't a clue what to do.

Callum's voice came through a steel oblong beside the door. 'Hello?'

'Hello,' Gerth said, his hand sweating round the glass neck of the bottle.

'Come in,' said the steel oblong, 'There's a lift straight ahead of you. Come up to the seventh floor and turn right. Pass seventeen doors and then knock on mine and I'll let you in. Have you got that?'

'Yeah,' said Gerth.

'I'll buzz you in,' said the steel oblong.

Moonwalking couldn't feel as strange as this, Gerth thought, swimming into the smell of new paint, and pressing the recessed lift button. Wheels hummed and steel ropes ground along pulleys. He looked around, totally confused: the walls were a clean minty green, the skirting board was glossy jade. He'd been brought up in a council house on the outskirts of the city, but these days he thought of council as dead-end, and in the city, a place where sick and piss and graffiti were shrugged off as standard. Council meant you were stuck. This hallway was elegant: round the corner from the lift there was even a welcome mat outside a front door.

The steel doors of the lift opened and he walked into the seven-foot metal cube. At the back was a deep square hole level with the floor. He didn't know that it was for coffins. He pressed a button with the number seven dimpled like braille and the doors shut.

Going up!

Maybe the lift would stick between floors.

It didn't.

He stepped out when the doors opened and stood amazed at the vista of city lights at his feet. Turn right. Callum's instructions had programmed him like a robot, and he walked obediently, counting doors. His feet slowed when he reached sixteen. Christ, this was real do-your-head-in stuff, this was. Seventeen.

He knocked at Callum's door.

A rustle. Soft footsteps. Windchimes. Keys turning.

Callum stood there – no, he swayed, he leaned, even with his feet still, Callum was dancing. Callum, just the way he'd been only a week ago: all the fluffy blond people who'd turned his head in a dozen nameless streets in town vanished from his mind. In Gerth's memory, Callum was as insubstantial as the Cottingley fairies – sepia-tint cut-outs of yesteryear, fake or real, no-one would ever know. But this fairy was flesh and blood, his hair glowing like a halo, his eyes dancing with mischief and mascara.

'Come in,' Callum said, flattening himself into the wall.

Gerth passed him and he locked the door, eyebrows and lips twitching a smile: look at the lad, done up to the nines, he thought, all ironed and pressed and smelling like a spring forest, and all for me!

'Straight ahead and turn right,' he said.

Gerth's mind was already blown: no-one he knew had a flat like this. The corridor was hung with windchimes: a spiral of frosted glass bells, their lips turquoise and pink and primrose yellow, an airy pagoda of paper-thin copper birds, a cascade of shell discs, luminous silver like dried honesty. The floor had stepping stones of carpet, pink, turquoise, yellow, so pale they were almost white. Paint trees grew up the walls and their fine branches met overhead in a ceiling of sky blue. The trees continued into the wall ahead, and he felt he could walk through them, as if plaster and brick were an illusion.

The open door faced a wall-length mirror, framed with branches and leaves so that he saw himself, him and his new clothes and his ice-cold bottle, stepping from a forest glade into a living room . . .

Like no living room he'd ever seen.

A bookshelf and a drawing board were the only things rising more than two feet from the floor. Callum had four makeshift tables like islands studded with junk – Gerth didn't know that these were altars and each pile of junk was treasure celebrating the elements. There were no chairs, just cushions and pillows wrapped in bright blankets. Records and tapes skirted the length of a whole wall. The walls were alive with trees, waves, coral caves, mountains and each painted dreamscape was decorated with glossy magazine cut-outs. Birds, fish, butterflies, laughing faces with painted haloes floating around a mountain, a shiny paper bunch of bananas hanging from a ragged hem of emerald and jungle green.

'Have a seat,' Callum said.

'I brought this,' Gerth said, holding out his bottle of wine.

'How kind,' Callum said. 'You must be psychic: this is one of my Mother Hubbard periods. I'll open it.'

In the kitchen he dithered: he had some glasses, but Wol had brought them from Poland and they were precious, hand-blown with fragile twisted stems. He liked to use them for rituals. Only he and Wol had ever drunk from them. It would impress – good heavens! – whatever his name was next door, but just suppose *things* turned flat or unpleasant and the glasses held the contamination? The thing was, it was them or cups and he picked one up, looking at the galloping bunnies on the rim and Peter Rabbit eternally nibbling his carrot under the glaze.

Gerth stood for a moment, watching the night: it was a starscape, riverscape, cityscape, where the moon shone as bright as day and the picture window was too high to need curtains. He sat on a rainbow blanket with a cushion behind his back, and looked up at the ceiling. Lilac with a silver star straddling the central light-fitting, its five points linked by a circle and a constellation of symbols. Oh, the fairy was into astrology, was he? Gerth couldn't even remember his star sign. He noticed the music, it was nothing he knew, schmaltzy crooning like his auntie played at Christmas. He thought of sickly sweet sherry and mince pies, and lit a cigarette, looking for ashtrays.

'Here we are,' Callum said. 'And I've realised I don't know your name.'

'Gerth,' he said, taking a bunny cup – a bunny cup, for chrissake! – 'Cheers!'

'Well, Gerth,' Callum sat facing him, cross-legged, 'Cheers.'

Gerth gulped, needing the sting of alcohol to shift his numbness. Callum sipped, for wine spun dizzily to capture his head and set his tongue dancing like a dervish. Gerth was everything he and Wol had ever dreamed about and longed for, tall, dark, handsome and strong, in *a one to one situation* with a bottle of wine way after midnight. It was a fantasy they chanted by heart on wish evenings, when a rainbow rings the full moon and anything can happen. But he seemed bewildered, this Real Man, shy, as if he didn't have a clue why he was there or what to do. Perhaps twenty questions was the best approach. Callum knew it was necessary to keep his head. There must be no false moves.

'So what do you do, Gerth?'

Bunny cups and polite conversation? Gerth's idea of meeting Callum hadn't held any of this. The sub-hippy tat he'd expected, only nothing so beautiful and extreme. Smoking a bit of shit maybe, low lights and fumbling around, fighting for flesh, just like any one-nighter.

'I work,' he said. 'Boring stuff, I suppose, distribution down at the sportswear shop, ski-suits mainly. Lots of paperwork. A bit of travel.'

Like down to Leeds for a sales conference and piss-up every few months. Bradford ditto, once even as far as Milton Keynes. Next month he was going to Cardiff, spearheading the shake-up of a new branch. What had they said in his interview: 'This isn't a job in any sense of the word, Mr Machen, it's a career.' Now he had a company car which devoured motorways with an eight-valve roar and he was introduced as a rising/thrusting/dynamic young executive. He knew that such sure-fire bird-pullers were unlikely to impress Callum.

'What about you?' he said.

Callum giggled.

'Well, I don't work as such,' he said. 'I'm one of the chronically unemployable. Sometimes I do washing up and a bit of cooking at Gauchos Pacificos. I worked in the parks for a while. And in the wholefood shop. I seem to have a problem keeping jobs. Someone like me can wear denim and a perfectly ordinary shirt and still look like a girl. What people think of as a girl. All flowery and delicate. A pansy. A pensée, a little thought. But pansies can survive the hardest frost, which is fortunate.'

So Gerth wasn't going to do the apeman stunt, me Man, you fairy, shut up and get fucked. That was a relief. Callum didn't like getting fucked, as he liked to be courted and he liked to make love.

'Go on,' he said, twinkling. 'Tell me what you think of the decor.'

'It's different,' Gerth said, then he laughed, 'OK, Callum, I think it's weird. It's so frigging weird I don't know what I think. It's the sort of thing you see in films. And I mean weird films. I think I like it . . .'

'But would you let your sister marry it?' Callum said. 'It isn't finished, I don't know if it ever will be. It seems complete and then the light changes or I find another picture. And then there's the seasons so maybe it'll never be finished. What's your place like?'

Gerth waved an arm.

'Um.'

'You live on your own?'

'Yeah. It's – well, it seems really dark, looking at here. I like wood. I do carpentry and there's shelves. Tables. It's sort of – brown. Grey. White. I mean, I've got pictures, but in frames, sort of.'

He wanted to say: all the wood is painted Salamanca, my walls are apricot white, I've got an airbrushed print of Hugh Hefner's 16–valve OHC customised De Santos Wolverine over the mantelpiece and a scale-model De Lorean by my bed. I tiled my kitchen myself, just like when I went to Gran Canaria. I've got a Wharfedale mega-blaster with diamond speakers in every room. My bathroom is black and white and silver. It all seemed spartan, even sterile, compared with here.

'You'll be one of these marvellous people who doesn't have clutter,' Callum said. 'A few treasured *objets d'art*, all very sophisticated. This must be strange for you.'

The tape stopped and Callum flowed over to change it.

'What sort of music do you like?'

'Anything,' Gerth said. 'It doesn't matter.'

'Oh, but it does matter,' Callum said, looking at him very seriously. 'Why don't you have a rummage and I'll top you up?'

He lingered in the kitchen, half wishing he'd used the glasses. Then he heard the music. Gerth had chosen *South Pacific*, which he'd forgotten he owned.

'Cheers.'

Gerth's job, his joblessness, his decor, Gerth's flat. He had eighteen questions left. They could be condensed into one: what do you want with me? Perhaps he should leave the next question to Gerth. He sipped a little more wine, but Gerth said nothing.

'I haven't seen you in The Powerhouse before last week,'

Callum said. 'I don't know if you go there often, as they say, but I'm sure I wouldn't have missed you.'

'I'd never been before,' Gerth said.

He wanted to tell Callum everything. Me and the lads were pissed, we came to take the piss. And then I saw you and I've never felt this way about anyone. Only now he was in fairyland and what if fairies turn to goblins?

Callum felt he was wading through setting cement, blindfold. Try again!

'It *was* you ringing me and not speaking? I thought so. Just that it happens quite a lot and it can be alarming, living on my own. As I do.'

'I'm sorry about that,' Gerth said. 'I sort of bottled out, I didn't know what to say.'

'Hello would have done,' Callum said. 'It doesn't matter. You finally gasped and spoke and here you are, Gerth. You don't look the nervous type.'

Gerth smiled – a curve of the lips straight from fantasy island!

'Real men get shy as well,' he said, then tough and casual: 'I suppose I want to go to bed with you. Do you want to?'

'I think I *probably* do,' Callum said. 'Only I want more talk. I don't even know who you are. Not that anyone ever knows anyone else, but desire is only a part of it, do you think?'

Gerth hadn't thought.

'Dunno. Seems good enough to me,' he said, wondering about just leaping on the fairy.

'Oh, for a one-night stand I dare say,' Callum said. 'Only I don't do one-night stands. I'm a true believer at the altar of love, Gerth. I'm a marrying sort of queen.'

Well, what happened to the rampant lust poofs were supposed to have? Gerth and his mates knew that they did it all the time, all over the place and with anyone. They had quite a lot to say about it; one of his mates thought AIDS was punishment for doing it. He didn't. He didn't like to think about terminal diseases, although he generally used condoms rather than a wish and a prayer the morning after. You never knew what slag you were sleeping with after all. And you couldn't be too careful these days, not with the CSA.

'Marrying?' he said and gulped more wine.

'Yes,' Callum said. 'Along the lines of life not being a rehearsal. Like music. It matters what you put into your life, it matters even more who. Everyone's done the one-night bit, but what's a moment's pleasure? I want a lifetime's ecstasy.'

Gerth felt slapped.

'I think sex is fun,' he said. 'You know, fun?'

'Oh, it's fun,' Callum said. 'I was sounding a bit serious there, wasn't I? I suppose it's my dream, marrying someone who loves me. I'm very serious about my dreams. Tell me your dreams. If you like.'

The room became a moored boat rocking in the darkness. Callum changed the music to an up-beat South American mountain band and sat down again.

Gerth stood and started pacing around. He wished he was wearing his usual clothes, the reassuring bite of leather at his wrists and neck, the rough denim on his skin.

'You know,' he said. 'I've never done this before. I feel a total prat.'

'Which bit?' Callum said, suddenly thinking, *oh my God, he's straight*.

'You,' Gerth said, sitting again. 'You. I've never – you know, with a man. Never wanted to. Only – you! I don't know. I don't bloody know.'

'You've never been with a man?' Callum said. 'Am I a bet? I'd rather know.'

'No,' Gerth said. 'Don't you see? I haven't told anyone about you.'

'You don't know anything about me to tell,' Callum said.

'All right. Christ. I mean, I haven't told anyone what I feel about you. They don't even know I've got your phone number. They haven't a clue that I've rung you. They didn't even see that I spoke to you. No way are you a bet, Callum. I'm not a bloody saint but I'm not a total bastard.'

'Calm down,' Callum said. 'Let me see if I've got you right.

You came to The Powerhouse with your friends – who are all straight. Straight men in a gay nightclub usually means trouble, but never mind that for the moment. While you were there, you saw me, we chatted in the boys' room and you went back to your friends and ignored me for the rest of the evening. Yes, you did. You passed out and I found a piece of card and put my number on it and put it in your pocket. Which I may say I've never done before. You woke up the next day and started ringing me.'

'Yes,' Gerth said. 'I had to.'

'You were so struck by my beauty and presence that you couldn't speak?' Callum laughed harshly and it sounded strange. 'You've never been with a man before. So what do you want with me? You see, the bet theory does fit.'

'It isn't,' Gerth said, what the hell. 'I think I've fallen for you. How do I know? You're not a bet, believe me.'

'Fallen in love?' Callum, whisper soft. 'Do you mean that?'

'Yeah,' Gerth said. 'Whatever.'

'And what do you want to do about it?' Callum said.

'I don't know,' Gerth said. 'You tell me.'

'Oh no,' Callum said. 'I can only tell you what I want. There's all the desire in the world bubbling round this room this night. That's no problem. But I want courtship, Gerth, I want marriage. *Probably* with you. We'll see.'

'What do we do now?' Gerth felt drained.

'Kiss me.' Callum said gently. 'I'd like that.'

5

'One moment, please!'

Callum pushed Gerth from on top of him and sat up, smiling.

'Sorry,' Gerth said, amazed how easy it was to kiss Callum; he was soft as a woman and his strength came as a surprise. But maybe men didn't . . .

'Is there something wrong?'

Callum smiled and drew his knees up to his chin.

'Nothing at all,' he said. 'Only there's no need to be so hasty. I mean, I think we were getting a bit wham bam, thank you ma'am, and it's a shame to tear along a motorway when the scenic route is so beautiful. You don't know what I'm on about, do you?'

Gerth shook his head, he was totally confused. You did it or you didn't. Who's to say fairies didn't prick-tease just like women?

'Let's have another glass of wine and talk,' Callum said.

You didn't.

'Take your clothes off,' Callum said, slipping his robe to the ground.

Gerth was embarrassed by his easy nakedness. You did?

'Now,' Callum said. 'I'm not a one-night-stand queen. I have, actually, been celibate for almost three years. Apart from the sheer pleasure of taking the slow scenic intergalactic route – we have to discuss sexually transmitted diseases. AIDS?'

Gerth blushed.

'You see, you handsome hunk,' Callum breathed, 'your community still believes it's a plague from Almighty God sent down to exterminate "queers". Honestly, to hear the average het male, they think immunity is their birthright. It isn't.'

'You think I've got AIDS?' Gerth looked down.

'I don't think anything,' Callum said. 'I imagine you've been behaving in a way that didn't take AIDS into account. Rather like a woman who has a pee after sex and hopes she's not pregnant. Dangerous. HIV is a virus. A virus knows no morals. A virus's purpose in life is to survive and multiply – HIV is simply very successful. Its success involves damaging our immune system. Hence AIDS. It's no judgement, Gerth, it's something we have to discuss.'

Gerth had had nightmares about AIDS after a week of TV documentaries involving tombstones and glaciers and silhouetted confessional voice-overs. He hadn't slept with anyone for at least a month. Then Rock Hudson and Liberace and some Russian ballet dancer and Freddie Mercury were all dying of AIDS and he relaxed. It wasn't something that he ever talked about these days.

'Even if you were positive,' Callum said, 'safe sex can be even more of a turn-on, from what my friends say. Hasn't it occurred to you that I might be what they call a risk?'

Gerth looked at him and shook his head.

'As it happens, I'm not,' Callum said. 'I've been for the tests and I aim to stay negative. Play safe. But you?'

'I've got no signs,' Gerth said.

'Neither had Magic Johnson,' Callum said. 'All I'm saying is, I would very much like to make love with you. It's hurting me having to stop and talk like this. But I don't just want a one-night stand and I certainly don't go for unsafe sex.'

'Got to pee,' Gerth said.

His head was reeling with words and wine, his body was trembling with shackled desire. His brand-new silky shirt stuck to his spine and armpits, his bright white trousers were scored with creases. He looked at his prick while he was peeing. Surely to God he hadn't got AIDS? Callum was so matter of fact about it. His blood ran cold.

6

Gerth woke with his head on Callum's belly, Callum's fingers in his hair. He kept his eyes shut for a few minutes, registering the rise and fall of Callum's breath, the warmth of hairy thighs under his forearm. The last thing he could remember was standing in the toilet peeing. Lost hours were nothing new to Gerth and his mates.

But this morning after was like no other. No mates for him to check it out with, just Callum, sprawled out like Lady Godiva and sleeping sweet as a baby.

He edged away from the strange warm skin and went to the bathroom. Snatches of their conversation came into his mind. Love. Marriage. AIDS. Standing peeing and thinking, have I got AIDS? Suddenly it was vital to get dressed and get out, away from this hippy Santa's grotto and the mad fairy who called it home.

He picked up his crumpled clothes and swore. Dead give-away, both the pansy clothes and the state of them. And Rixie lived up the way, Big Dan stayed with his mum over the High Road, the tart from the bar worked on the buses. Someone was sure to spot him. It'd have to be a taxi.

As he wet his hair and pushed it into place, Callum's face appeared, smiling in the mirror.

'Good morning, Gerth,' he said.

Gerth's neck tightened and he clenched his fists and mumbled at the sink. Callum slipped his arms round his waist and kissed his shoulder. In broad daylight.

'Oh dear,' Callum said, dropping his arms. 'What's wrong?'

'Well, I dunno, Callum,' he said, pushing past him into the living room, 'I'd best be off.'

'Just like that?'

'Well, I mean, I've a job to get to, like.'

'The hiking ski-ing fraternity require your services on Sundays? I had no idea they were quite so demanding.'

Gerth glanced at him, oh shit, those blue eyes were guarded, on the edge of pain, and everything in him wanted to just grab hold of the loony fairy, pink silk kimono and all, and stay.

'I'd forgotten it's Sunday,' he said. 'Don't know where the time goes.'

'I don't want to keep you, of course, if you're dying to escape,' Callum said, each word dropped neat as a rabbit turd, 'but it hardly seems good manners to leave without saying goodbye.'

And if you try to, I shall have hysterics and faint, he thought.

'Well, I just didn't know . . .'

'Sit down, for goodness sake,' Callum said. 'I'll make tea. Coffee if you prefer?'

'Coffee,' Gerth said, sitting. 'Please.'

'Put some music on if you like,' Callum said and vanished into the kitchen.

He filled the kettle and breathed deeply. Hang on, he thought, the hunk is new to all this. Virgo intacta in fairyland. No doubt his usual night-time activities end in slipping away without a word, leaving some drunken stranger asleep. He wanted to fling himself at Gerth's feet and plead, but that would never do. Act as if the sun is shining and the clouds have no choice but to leave or look ridiculous. Be mistressful!

He went back to the living room, smiling.

'You must have been very tired,' he said. 'You went to the smallest room in the house, my dear, came back, sat down beside me, held my hand and I was talking to you. Then your hand went all soft in mine and you were fast asleep. Is it all very strange to you?'

Gerth melted and looked up from under his eyebrows.

'Weird as fuck, Tinkerbelle,' he said.

'Tinkerbelle?' Callum's eyebrows shot up. 'Is that how you think of me? I'm flattered – *Peter Pan* is my favourite film.'

Gerth blushed as he left the room. *Peter Pan*, for chrissakes, a bairns' film. He wanted something familiar – be seeing you, I'll call you, any old half-truth to get away. Even a row would do.

Callum started singing in the kitchen. Not humming, or half dum de dum phrases, but a proper song with all the words. Gerth curled up with embarrassment, for his voice was sweet and lovely, he was singing 'touch me in the morning' as if he was on stage.

He rustled back into the room and slid a tray on to the floor, bunny cups again and a teapot shaped like a can-can dancer. On his knees, he crossed to the stereo and put on music Gerth had never heard before. Classical.

'Morning maniac music,' he said, pouring tea. 'A little Chopin. Gone Chopin, Bach in five minuets . . . don't mind me. Milk? Sugar?'

'Yeah,' Gerth said. 'Thanks.'

He spilled coffee on his shirt – Callum whisked it off his back and rinsed it. He took out a cigarette and Callum lit it before he could find his lighter. Callum snuggled back on the cushions and drew a cover up to his neck.

'You're very welcome to join me,' he said. 'You do realise it's only quarter to seven?'

'No,' Gerth said. 'Ta. Quarter to seven, is it, I'm sorry. That's the middle of the night on a weekend.'

Callum smiled.

What a beautiful back Gerth had! The line of his neck, the curve of his jaw: Callum sipped tea and watched him. This moment was his and always would be.

'No,' Gerth said, 'I'd better get home and change.'

'Don't change a hair for *me*,' Callum said.

'About last night,' Gerth said, blushing.

'Oh dear,' Callum said. 'This sounds sinister.'

'Well, like I said, Callum, it's all weird. You know.'

'Sorry, I don't.'

'I thought I knew what I felt,' Gerth said. 'What I wanted. Only it's all so weird. I don't know now.'

'Would you like to swing on a star?' Callum asked. 'Or carry moonbeams home in a jar? Or would you rather be a fish? The choice is yours.'

'That's it,' Gerth shouted. 'You're doing my head in.'

Surely that would spark a row – but no. Callum knelt behind him and started to massage his neck and shoulders. Once more, Gerth was surprised by the strength in his hands, man strength where everything else was girly, cissy, soft. Stupid. He shrugged furiously, because it felt so good and he wanted to hate it, how he wanted to hate it.

'I think,' Callum said, mentally crossing every finger and toe as he played his last card, 'I think that perhaps it's not a good idea. I'd hate to feel responsible for you being unhappy. Perhaps we should just say goodbye and forget it.'

Gerth's heart raced. How dare the fairy give him permission to go?

'Maybe we should,' he sneered.

'If that's what you want,' Callum said smoothly, digging his thumbs into the iron tension at the base of Gerth's neck so that he jumped.

'I don't know what I want,' he growled.

'Perhaps you'd like some time and space. As they say,' Callum said, giggling and gouging his knuckles all the way down his spine.

'Where I come from,' Gerth said, 'they don't talk like that, man, Callum. Time and space, geet posh. We talk plain.'

'Lovely,' Callum said, pounding his shoulders. 'Well, talk plain to me.'

'There you go again,' Gerth said. 'Listen, Callum, I'm going. Right? I need to go.'

Callum knelt back on his heels. Gerth towered over him.

'I'm off,' he said.

Callum shrugged.

'Aren't you going to kiss me goodbye?' he said.

7

Gerth looked down into Callum's blue eyes and felt dizzy, as if he was at the edge of a high diving-board with the siren lure of bright blue water way down below. He clenched his toes inside his hard leather shoes, clenched them until they cramped. He thrust his hands into his pockets, for a wild pulse exploded through every finger, but the flesh of his thighs throbbed with the same beat, so loud and so much heat that he was drunk with it, deaf with it.

He let his toes spread again and crouched on his heels in front of Callum. His hands flew out to hold Callum's face, and his knees collapsed as they drew close.

Diving into Callum's mouth, oh God, his tongue running along their clinging lips, his hands working into Gerth's thick hair, Callum's fingers on his back. They pressed close until their naked flesh pulsed as one.

'Are you sure about this?' Callum whispered.

Gerth forced him backwards on the cushions and tore at the stiff metal button on his jeans. He had Callum's hands pinned above his head and his legs weighting down the rest of his body. Yeah, Gerth thought, I'm going to fuck you, fairy boy, you with all the words and your sweet goddam reason.

'I'm going to fuck you till you scream,' he gasped, kicking his legs free from the white cloth that bound them.

Through the scarlet tide raging in his head, he saw Callum's face so close below him, and his eyes were flashing grey. Suddenly, he was catapulted on to his back, with Callum sitting astride him, pinning his wrists against the cushions.

And Callum was laughing at him and shaking his fluffy blond head.

'Dear Gerth, it doesn't have to be this way,' he said calmly.

He dropped his head to Gerth's chest, dragging his tongue across both nipples so slowly that Gerth broke into a sweat and moaned. His thighs moved against Gerth's body, and he took one hand away from Gerth's wrists and stroked his belly softly, drew his fingers briefly over Gerth's prick and sunk them hard into his thighs.

Gerth raised his free hand in a fist, but Callum's eyes hypnotised him and he let his arm drop, weak as a puppet. Callum loosened his other wrist and nodded slowly. He stuck one finger in Gerth's mouth and Gerth found himself sucking it, biting his palm, his eyes welded to Callum, groaning with ecstasy. Now Callum was rocking one hand down his thigh, his mouth darting a lightning kiss/bite to Gerth's navel, then smooching tongue and teeth along the other thigh. Gerth spread his fingers and tore at the air, he drove one hand into Callum's hair and pushed his face into his prick.

'So impatient!' Callum said, throwing his arm aside.

Jesus, where did he get strength like this? Gerth was paralysed and helpless.

Callum crouched over him, tongueing his ankles, working his lips against the arches of his feet. Gerth felt his strong hands smooth along his calves and the weight of his arms as he held his thighs down. Callum took one toe in his mouth and his tongue flickered around it like wildfire: Gerth felt his whole body become this toe, and then the next; he lived only in his toes, sheer pleasure whirling through every cell and sending him flying. His skin only existed where Callum touched him; he couldn't feel his hands or arms and his face was numb as he gasped deep breaths into lungs that fizzed a million deep space novas where he used to have eyes.

The mad fairy was all over his calves, the back of his knees, his tongue traced the soft curve at the top of his thighs and his hand stroked Gerth's bum, soft as a breeze, harder, then kneading his solid flesh like a baker rolls his dough.

'No!' Gerth gasped, turning his head; he could feel his arse tighten and his buttocks clamp together against Callum's magical fingers.

'No?' Callum said. 'No what, I wonder.'

The full weight of him covered Gerth's back and his sly tongue rippled over Gerth's neck and his ears, his toes curled around Gerth's feet and he rocked his body as easy as a child on a swing.

'What am I doing?' Gerth thought. It would have been so easy if he'd come, but Callum didn't seem remotely interested in making him come, he was just playing with every inch of him, turning every cell of his body to molten lava.

Callum slipped one finger between his buttocks and rubbed the tip of it deep into the cleft.

'No,' said Gerth. 'No.'

Callum's hand stopped moving and he nuzzled into Gerth's neck.

'No?' he teased. 'Not even one little pinkie, Gerth?'

He bit the pillow and Callum took his hand away. Gerth felt his buttocks relax, and at once, Callum's hand was back, insistent, sure, undeniable. Gerth didn't want to think about what he was doing, as his finger slipped past the tight muscle, up and down, slow and strong, deeper in every time, then almost out. He loved the feeling, blocked what it meant, surfaced from bliss knowing Callum had lied, this wasn't *one little pinkie* for chrissakes! He tossed his head from side to side like a maniac, because he loved it.

It was so weird, his head raged against what was happening, his body craved more and more.

'Yes,' he whimpered. 'Just do it, just do it.'

Callum laughed and eased his body so he was lying spread-eagled on Gerth's back.

'Non non, chéri,' he said. 'Let's make love, Gerth, I'll show you how.'

It was like when he was a teenager and you were supposed to know what to do with girls. Once, a girl had taken over his inexpert fumblings, put her hand over his and worked his fingers and palm against her until she was gasping with pleasure. She'd worked on him with the same impatience, and he saw her the next night and the next, though they hardly spoke. The fourth time she had Durex in her handbag, although two of them split. She was in control, her face became a mask of purpose, she knew just when to guide him into her, and she rode on top of him until they both screamed yes, yes, yes. What had happened to her? He'd stopped seeing her after his name and hers appeared on the school toilet walls.

'All right?' Callum breathed into his ear.

'Yes,' he whispered.

Peace filled him as Callum finger-fucked him, slowly, gently, every move brought a wave of delirium and he started to move with him, sweat filling his eyes.

Callum rolled over so he was lying beside him.

'Beautiful man,' he said, holding Gerth's face, kissing him, folding his arms round him. Gerth felt like a boat in mid-ocean, and Callum was the wind and the waves and his whole body could do nothing but obey him.

Callum started to eat his hand, finger by finger and Gerth's arm became immortal, every muscle was pure light, and he forced his other arm to touch Callum, to run his fingers over those smooth shoulders.

His palm curved over Callum's bum, the feel of that flesh blew his mind and he sunk his mouth into Callum's neck, feeling a down of stubble on his chin; his tongue shivered into Callum's ear and he lapped at the lobe like a kid with an ice-cream. Callum liked that and Gerth felt so proud of the wonderful animal noises he was making.

And then he was a rag doll again as Callum placed his arms back on the cushion and sat astride his shaking belly.

'You're lookin' good, Houston,' he drawled, a crazy smile lighting his face. 'You have a lovely body.'

'Do I?' Gerth said, Jesus, he usually said that – well, to women – he'd sort of had the idea he'd be saying the same to Callum, and here was Callum, totally in control, like a high priest at an esoteric ritual. He gazed up at him and Callum drew his head back, his smile floating like a soaring bird whose wings are translucent against the sun.

Callum anointed him with oil and their skins slipped against each other until heat and desire made them one, Gerth's head thundered and he drew Callum down to him, devouring his smile, kissing his eyes, burying his soft hair in his neck.

Callum snuggled beside him, slipped down his body, caressed his belly, set him on fire. His fingertips and tongue caressed his prick, and Gerth thought, I am your creature, I am yours, you can do what you want with me, I am, I am, I

can't hold on much

longer

Catherine wheels spun in his head and his body was a torrent of shooting stars, the fifth of November, the fourth of July, he was a sky lit with exploding brilliant sparks.

And then he was floating in darkness, in a warmth that filled him and covered him and his body registered Callum again, always Callum, his soft skin, the sweet male smell of him, his laughing eyes huge and deep blue.

Gerth always wanted to leap up and wash himself after he came, now more than ever, but his body refused to move: he was perfect just the way he was, perfect and perfectly happy.

Callum breathed out a gentle breeze and giggled as he dabbled his fingertips on his sticky belly. He took two candy coloured cigarettes from a box on the floor. He lit both and handed one to Gerth.

'Have a cigar,' he said lightly. 'How're you doing?'

Gerth closed his eyes and drew in smoke. Suddenly his body started to shake with laughter.

'I'm doing fine, Tinkerbelle,' he said, ruffling Callum's hair. 'You?'

'Never finer,' Callum said dreamily. 'You have such a cute bum. A cute belly-button, cute pecs, even cuter toes, Gerth, you're irresistible.'

'I haven't done much,' Gerth said, 'yet. Have to find your erogenous zones, Callum.'

'When one is in love,' Callum said, 'one's whole body is an erogenous zone. Let me put on some music.'

'I mean I can't just take,' Gerth said.

'Well, who's taking?' Callum said, 'Do you think I've been anywhere other than on cloud nine? Anyway, we've got all day and a lifetime, if you like. I'd like.'

They stared into each other's eyes. Gerth felt tears coming and buried his head in Callum's chest.

It was midnight before he rang for a taxi.

8

Rixie gulped Scotch and roared away down the road, dodging juggernauts that screamed up out of nowhere, swerving around a flock of thirty-mile-an-hour grannies clogging up two lanes. The cones – he'd forgotten the cones, and his brakes screamed – too late. Metal on metal, rubber on skid and his car exploded in the ditch.

He could hear ambulance sirens and a triumphant metallic voice.

''Ello, 'ello, 'ello, driving a bit fast, was we, sir, a bit over the limit, speedwise and breathwise, if I'm not much mistaken. You're nicked!'

The screen went blank. Bugger it! Rixie groped in his pockets for change and fed it into the machine. He stood, hips thrust forward on a level with the controls.

'Have you beat the bastard?' Dave put two pints on top of Motorway Maniac, the newest electronic bandit in The Shoulder of Mutton.

'Naw,' Rixie said. His fingers flew over the knobs.

'That's it, man!' Dave said, stabbing at the screen.

Rixie's car went up in a fireball.

'There's got to be a way,' Dave said, watching simulated flames fill the screen.

'There's Gerth! Look at the sly bugger, grinning all over his ugly face. Gerth, you bastard! Get 'em in, mine's a pint, and Dave's too.'

Gerth ordered.

'What's this pansy drink, then, or is it pure vodka?' Rixie skitted him.

'Spritzer,' Gerth said, 'For the rising young executive.'

'Jeez, have you seen his neck?' Rixie dragged at his shirt collar. 'Was she trying to murder you or what? Look at this, Dave!'

'Piss off,' Gerth said, 'There's nowt wrong with a bit of enthusiasm.'

'A bit of enthusiasm, listen to it!' Dave punched his ribs. 'Looks more like Invasion Of The Rat People to me, like.'

'What I'd like to know,' Rixie said, 'is this. Is your lady friend in casualty? And if she's not, is she one of them – you know – Miss Whiplash like? We've heard you're a bit kinky, man, and I'd like to see under your shirt, Gerth!'

'Ooh, Betty,' lisped Dave. 'People will talk, dear!'

'We're just friends,' Rixie piped, falsetto.

'Cheers,' Gerth said. How the hell could he tell them? Like he'd been building up to all day, a quiet, serious chat, if you don't like it, well, that's tough. He'd rehearsed it the way Callum talked, all earnest and gentle. And here he was, shouting against eighties rock-fuck guitar, flashing machines blaring electronic threats and promises, men in grey black navy and pinstripe suits bragging about super deals and wheels. Younger men with dark jackets draped on their shoulders, the only colours in the place were inch-wide strips of bright trendy ties. After Callum's flat, it was all so drab.

If Mac had been here it would have been easier. Mac had mellowed since Trish, he could talk to Mac and know that between you and me stayed that way. He'd hinted around that Sunday tart a few weeks back, what did Mac think of different sorts of sex and Mac laughed and said that whatever you did it was all right so long as you both enjoyed it.

Around lunchtime he'd thought of calling Trish, even. They'd all been surprised at Trish, she wasn't exactly a dolly bird type, quite dumpy, not beautiful, but they could see how happy Mac was. No-one could miss the light in their eyes; Mac and Trish were friends and in love and it was canny being round them. Gerth had decided he'd talk to Trish if he hadn't got the bottle to talk to Mac. She'd know how to tell Rixie and Dave – or even if he should tell them. Tonight his secret would have to stay that way; he'd fence with Rixie and Dave, keep them guessing and just make sure they didn't follow him home. To Callum's flat.

Home.

'Well, you're still on your feet, man,' Dave said, inspecting Gerth's knees, 'Was she good, was she?'

'I'm saying nowt,' Gerth said. 'How's the Motorway Maniac, Rixie?'

'Terrible, man,' Rixie said. 'Wait till he's had a few, Dave, and he'll sing like a friggin' canary. It's the cones, Gerth, the cones and the car-transporter and the daft ould cunts in their morrie minors.'

'Out of my road,' Gerth said and fed the machine.

His feet tapped to 'Don't You Want Me, Baby' and he flicked switches and buttons deft as a cat.

'Look at the smug bastard,' Rixie said. 'Shite! That's it, Dave. Trust Casanova! You race up to the grannies and there's your first Get In Lane. Past the first, and the second, and drop in between the third and the fourth.'

'Aye,' Dave said.

'It's a clever bastard,' Rixie said. 'Like the bastard playing it.'

The screen dazzled for a second.

'Any faster and you'd crash there,' Dave said. 'Not this smart fella. He's got the technique.'

'Working on it,' Gerth said. 'Practice makes perfect.'

'Mr Perfect,' Dave said. 'I'll get 'em in.'

He winked at Rixie.

'Aye, Dave, it's your round.'

'And you can keep the bloody vodka out of my spritzer,' Gerth said, 'I know you bastards.'

'Would we, Rixie, would we?'

'You would,' Gerth said, spinning his car past the last cone and putting his foot down for the road ahead.

He was on his fourth replay, flashing past every record on the scoreboard, half listening to Dave and Rixie, when he checked his watch and crashed into the safety barrier.

''Ello, 'ello, 'ello . . .'

'You take over,' he said to Dave, 'I'm thirsty with all that road.'

He sipped his drink.

The jukebox said:

Oh, yes, I'm the great pretender . . .

Maybe that was a way in. They'd worked out a Freddie Mercury routine years before, drunk enough to be sure of their talent. Then Freddie died and they couldn't bear to even think about it, let alone talk about it. I mean, Liberace was one thing, but Rock Hudson and then King Freddie? Gerth realised they never talked about gay unless it was taking the piss. Suddenly, in his world, with his mates, Gerth felt like a Martian.

'One for the road?' he said.

'Divven talk to me about roads!' Rixie said, kicking the machine. 'Are you off soon, like?'

'Yes,' Gerth said, itching to be with Callum again in the extravagant colours of his mad eyrie. He wanted to throw off the shackles of his suit and sprawl naked on hippy cushions . . .

'Are you seeing her tonight?'

'Well, I just might be,' he swaggered.

'Is this the real thing, Gerth?' Rixie belched.

'Maybe it is,' he said. 'It'll do me.'

'The lad's not with us tonight,' Dave said. 'We've lost him altogether.'

'Aye,' Rixie said. 'We'll not see this lad again till she blows him out.'

'Aw, piss off, Rixie,' Gerth said. 'I came, didn't I?'

'I'd hope you did!' Rixie said. 'Hey, Dave, did you hear that, he says he came!'

'You enjoy it, man,' Dave said paternally. 'He'll tell us it all when it's over. Give it a week?'

'No, it's serious,' Rixie said. 'I'd put odds on a month. Fiver?'

'I go for six weeks,' Dave said.

They spat and slapped each other's hands.

'Are you in this bet, Gerth?' Dave said, laughing.

'Try for ever,' Gerth said. 'All me money on it.'

He leaned back against the taxi seat and watched the twinkling lights of the river. When he was a lad, he'd dreamed of sailing down the Tyne, sailing away to a land no-one knew about, finding gold in the streams and diamonds on the trees and sailing home like a hero, like a king. The only time he'd ever been on the river was on the Shields ferry or the Tuxedo Princess. No-one ever told you what it would really be like when you were grown up.

Especially now.

9

'The longest day,' Callum said after they'd hugged and staggered into the living room and collapsed in each other's arms – *I can't stand up while you're holding me!*

'How were the boys?'

'All right,' Gerth said, tugging his tie loose.

'It's very strange,' Callum said. 'I've been trying to picture them, and all I can see is muscly hunks and do you know, Gerth, I think I'm just a tad jealous.'

'You're never serious!' Gerth kissed him passionately.

Callum's eyes flickered with pleasure, but he kept his face severe.

'Serious,' he said. 'Yes. You have no idea – I'm starting to live and breathe you. I'm jealous of your work, Gerth, I'm jealous of your suit. I walked around this morning holding your pillow – I'm jealous of your sleep. This may drive you mad, but I feel you should know what sort of queen you're marrying.'

'It doesn't drive me mad,' Gerth said. 'I like it, it's just – bloody weird. I've missed you too, you know.'

'So what was it like, then, seeing the boys?'

'Aw, average. Rixie's getting serious about this Motorway Maniac machine in The Shoulder. He's crackers, man, I think you'd like him. Dave's full of the usual shite. Ah, you'd like him as well.'

'But would they like me?' Callum said softly. 'Never mind. What do they look like? What did you talk about? Isn't there

someone else you usually hang round with – you said you
were the four musketeers.'

'Well, there's Mac, only he's with Trish – he's not out every
night.'

'Did you tell them?'

'I thought about it all day,' Gerth squeezed him tight. 'You
can't talk in a pub, Callum, not talk. Properly. I think I'd be
best telling Mac first. He's, like, my oldest mate. We were at
school together, me and Mac. It'd be like you – and what's
his daft name, Wol – we're close.'

Callum relaxed a little.

'Sorry,' he said. 'It's just after you rang, I thought you'd
go out with them and change your mind about me. About
us. It's so much easier being straight. No-one looks at you
twice, you can go where you want. It's an easier freedom.'

'How do you mean?' Gerth was astonished. Free? No bastard on this planet was free unless he was filthy rich.

'I have to fight – or at least make a stand daily for my
freedom,' Callum said. 'It's second nature to me now, like
breathing out and breathing in. I don't think you know about
that.'

'Say more,' Gerth said, frowning. If any bastard picked on
Callum, he'd put their lights out.

'It's not so much the violence,' Callum said, picking up his
thoughts. 'You just have to be sensible. No dark alleys alone
and wear a dark coat over your clothes if you're clubbing. Cab
fare in your shoe. The sort of things women have to do, really.
It's more the looks and comments. I ignore them most of the
time, but there are days when I'll forget and feel happy and
relaxed and someone will say something disgusting about me,
as if I don't exist. Shirt-lifter. Arse bandit. You know. And it
hurts. Am I not fragrant? Do I not bleed?'

Gerth was silent. He'd said things, him and the boys, Christ,
that was how he'd first met Callum, *up that bent club to take
the piss out of the poofters.* Everybody did it.

'You've got us thinking,' he said. 'It's awful, Callum.
Couldn't you – you know – dress different? Act a bit? We all

put it on, me and the lads, the mouths is tough as shite, but you'd not meet better friends than Mac and Rixie and Dave.'

'But why should I?' Callum said. 'I think suits are ridiculous, but I'm better mannered than to go around shouting about it. I hate those sub-military haircuts and heavy shoes Men seem to have, but it's none of my business. They make me their business. I just want to be alone, like dear Miss Garbo, well, not so. I want to be safe wherever I go – it's a basic human need, if not a right.'

'Ah, don't worry,' Gerth said. 'You've got me, man, Callum, and I'm crackers about you. I don't give a shite what they say.'

'Be hoped it stays that way,' Callum said. 'And enough of Miss Serious! Hardly the way to conduct a honeymoon! I've made your tea. Are you hungry?'

'I am,' Gerth said. 'You don't have to cook for me, man, I thought we'd get a take-away – if you wanted.'

'Oh, I've enjoyed cooking for us. I love being Dame Fanny Crackpot,' Callum said. 'Your job, as the man of the house, is to pour wine and attend to the music.'

He flitted into the kitchen.

'I bought a couple of tapes,' Gerth said. 'Shall I put them on?'

'Lovely!' Callum called.

Gerth hung his jacket up and took the tapes from his pocket. He'd spent his lunchtime in Virgin, wondering what Callum liked, wanting music that said it all. Nostalgia, Blues, Rock, New Age, Musicals. He didn't know where to begin, and one of the assistants came over and said did he need help?

He'd blushed.

'Well, I am,' he said. 'Only I don't know what. It's, like, for a friend.'

'What sort of atmosphere do you want to create?' The assistant had been brisk and maternal.

'Well, I . . .'

'Romance?'

'Yes,' he'd said – did it show?

'You can't fail with Ella Fitzgerald,' the assistant said. 'Or Dakota Staton. Or Dinah Washington. At the risk of being racist, *no-one* sings better than the grande dames of black jazz.'

'Isn't it a bit – old-fashioned?' Gerth said. He'd never heard of any of them.

'Slip into that booth,' the assistant waved his ringed hand. 'Let me tease your ears.'

He heard 'Misty', he heard 'Someone's Rockin' my Dreamboat', and he heard 'Love For Sale'.

'Well?'

'The first two, he said.

'Miss Staton and Miss Fitzgerald,' the assistant said. 'How wise.'

He pressed start. Three bars in, Callum came in and kissed him.

'How wonderful,' he said. 'I adore Dakota Staton. Where did you find her?'

'In Virgin,' Gerth said.

'Virgin?' Callum giggled. 'My friend Bella works there, I wonder if she served you.'

'Naw,' Gerth said. 'It was a fella served me.'

'Bella's a fella,' Callum said.

'Uh?'

'Oh, she's a slut, dear, a positive slut. She'll have made a beeline for *you*. I shall have to get you a ring. Or a ball and chain. Hands off – he's mine! Now sit and read your paper or have a cigarette, whatever relaxes you. Dinner's in five minutes. A drink?'

'That's my department,' Gerth said. 'What do you think I've got in my briefcase, like?'

'I love champagne,' Callum said. 'This is perfect.'

They clinked glasses.

'Callum,' Gerth said. 'Why d'you call him Bella? Why d'you call him she? I mean, I know gays call each other she, just why?'

Callum's eyes widened.

'Historical,' he said. 'It's only been legal to be bent since

1967, and even then, not until the age of twenty-one. Although, we're only allowed to at 18 – what a victory that isn't! Prior to that, what could one do socially? Ask about the boyfriend? It was a code, I suppose. She for he. Give him a girl's name, call him the wife and you can speak freely. It carries on, everyone's got a girl's name, just about. It's just a bit of camp.'

'But how can you tell who's gay?'

Callum threw back his head and laughed.

'Sweetheart!' he said, kissing Gerth's hair. 'It's an instinct. For example, you are, and your friends who came to The Powerhouse aren't. Historically, if you weren't sure, because you just could NOT be faintly camp, they talked about the friends of Dorothy. Do you know Dorothy? Are you one of Dorothy's friends? I assume it came from a passion for the divine Miss Garland. *The Wizard of Oz*. My favourite film.'

'I thought that was *Peter Pan*!'

'Oh, but it is,' Callum said. 'And *Sunset Boulevard*. And *Sextette*. I have dozens of favourite films. Why restrict yourself to one of anything? Apart from one's husband, of course. There is only one of you.'

'Girls' names,' Gerth said. 'What's yours?'

'We-ell,' Callum considered. 'Wol calls me Cassandra when I'm feeling moody and prophetic. There is my manifestation (lovely word, makes me feel surrounded by men) as Queen Astarte of the Seven Veils: that's how you first came upon me. For a while, I was Aphra, after the prolific and underrated Miss Behn. I used to write dreadful plays.'

Callum was off. Gerth refilled their glasses.

'What would I be?' he asked.

'Oh, let me think! Bella is Albert, Bert – then Bella, you see? Wol is William, Will, Winifred for his wondrous keyboard talents, and then Wol because he's so wise. Gerth. Obviously Gertrude, and that makes me Alice. Stein and Toklas? No? Literary monogamous dykes of yesteryear, a shining example to us all.'

Gerth wondered if he'd ever get half of what Callum said.

Not that it mattered. Bugger the details when the feeling was so high and right and mighty and the champagne bubbles teased his throat and nose against a backdrop of music soft and rich as cream.

'I've gone coarse,' Callum said, whisking in with a tray. 'Four course. This is an entrée, adapted and meatless but otherwise courtesy of Mrs Beeton. A real lady.'

'I've heard of Mrs Beeton,' Gerth said. 'Me mam was a great one for cooking. Do you not eat meat, like?'

'No,' Callum said. 'Not since I was nine. We drove past a slaughterhouse and my father found it necessary to tell me all about it. My eminent pappa believed in education.'

'Aye, it's not nice when you think about it,' Gerth said. 'Mac's Trish, she's vegetarian, and we've had a canny few meals there.'

One bridge I don't have to cross, thought Callum, grateful to Trish. It was odd, being in love with a virgin caveman. Maybe that's why he'd gone through agonies of jealousy all day. Part of him simply didn't believe Gerth could love him – and, after all, he'd never actually said so, and Callum was too proud – or wise? – to ask. Yet.

'This food's great,' Gerth said.

Callum smiled.

'I aim for perfect domesticity,' he said. 'As defined by Saint Zsa-Zsa: A cordon-bleu queen in the kitchen and a whore in bed.'

'I go for that,' Gerth said.

They ate with their eyes on each other and soon they'd had enough food. It was hours later with their bodies crying out for sleep that they knew they'd never have enough of each other.

10

'I'm going away, like,' Gerth said, later in the week. 'It's business.'

'Going away?' Callum collapsed on the bed, his pink kimono dying around him like a parachute.

'You daft bugger,' Gerth said. 'Not like that. I've just got to go to Cardiff over the weekend. Friday and Saturday. I'll be back on Sunday.'

'It's a lifetime!' Callum whispered.

'Get away with you,' Gerth said, knotting his tie. 'It's part of the job. Keeps us in take-aways and champagne.'

'I'd trade them for your time,' Callum said, digging his chin into his knees. He gazed at Gerth without blinking.

'Now what?' Gerth smiled at him.

'Just fixing you in my mind,' Callum said.

'I'll be back on Sunday, man!'

'Will you?'

'Of course I will. Howay, Callum, man, don't. I wouldn't go if I didn't have to. I'd rather be with you, you know it. Don't you?'

'I can't help it. There's traffic for a start. The roads. And you'll probably get drunk after you've had your meetings and meet someone and go to bed with them and not come back. Or come back and lie to me. Don't.'

'What? Lie to you?'

'Any of it,' Callum said. 'It's important. You're important.'

Well, this was something, wasn't it, not a week together and a list of don'ts. Gerth was about to bluster, then he thought, well, fair enough. He was flattered as hell: no-one had ever bothered asking for his fidelity before. No-one had ever proposed to him before. If Callum had looked pathetic and pleading, he'd have despised him, but he didn't. The steel of his eyes was serious, searching. Gerth was deeply moved. *It matters. I matter.*

And Callum was right. Most times he travelled, he did get drunk and if he slept alone it wasn't for want of trying. The Russian roulette of strong drink and the chance locking of eyes. It was all expenses, anyway, and what else was there to do in a strange town. Who cares?

Callum cares, he thought.

He remembered the last one-night stand and realised it could have been the one before. Shit.

'You see?' Callum said. 'I *know* you. Apart from my feelings, and my galaxy where you're the brightest star if not the sun and moon rolled into one, you're a very attractive man. To women and men. I'm not just saying it. You know you are.'

'Get away!' Gerth felt like he was in the head teacher's office, getting rollocked in that quiet, superior tone that was worse than shouting. Time to turn the tables.

'What about you?' he said. 'Two nights without me – I bet you'll be giving it rock all in The Powerhouse Saturday night, and who's to say some tall dark handsome stranger doesn't sweep you off your feet?'

'My feet,' Callum said, 'are thoroughly air-bound with you. I only go to The Powerhouse to dance. You're the only pick-up, to put it crudely, that I've ever made on the scene.'

'Keep it that way,' Gerth said, looking down.

'Oh, I will,' Callum said. 'Anyway, it's summer solstice on Saturday, so Wol and I will probably be down on the beach.'

'That's the day,' Gerth said. 'There's all the wicked night as well. And you notice I don't go light about Wol.'

'We're blood brothers,' Callum said. 'And for solstice, we'll be up all night. I wish you could be there.'

'Not my scene,' Gerth said. 'Ye knaa. I'd feel daft with singing and chanting and dancing around.'

'You'd love it,' Callum said. 'But never mind. It's not to be – and we have all the solstices in the world left.'

'So that's your Saturday,' Gerth said, sitting and putting an arm round him. 'What about Friday? I'll ring, you know.'

'I'm going to Wol's,' Callum said. 'He wants to know all about you. Frou-frou girly chat. While you're chewing fat cigars and clinching multi-million deals, you can rest assured that my only conversational topic will be you. You. You. Like the beat beat beat of the tom tom. You're in my heart.'

He held Gerth's palm over his heartbeat.

'Can you feel it?'

'Ah, don't start me off again,' Gerth said, desire surging in his blood. 'Look at the time, Callum!'

'Only got eyes for you, ducky,' Callum affected a camp whine. 'Go on, hunk of my life. Piss off. Abandon me.'

'I'll be back,' Gerth said.

'You'd better be,' Callum said. 'Now go, will you. Go on, before I ruin my mascara.'

'You're a head case,' Gerth said. 'And, Callum . . .'

'Mm?'

'I love you.'

After he'd gone, Callum tiptoed back into the living room where the three words hung in a holographic rainbow all over the room. He started to sing.

11

Callum and Wol rose at dawn. There was much to do. Callum was making a boat, and he'd been collecting wood debris from skips and back lanes for weeks. A torn blue window frame, ripped bamboo shelves, jagged off-cuts from a kitchen worktop, warped spindles from a discarded staircase. The shape of the boat came to him in a dream just before he woke. It was a Viking ship seen through the haze of dawn, proud, ghostly and destined to go far. Last year, the boat was a canoe, old chintz cushion covers stiff with varnish on a frame of splintered garden canes.

He used raffia to lash the wood together and smiled as it took shape and the blue-painted sticks rose like a tipi at the prow.

Wol lay on the floor painting the sail, thick advertising paper dumped next to a hoarding. The bright colours had grabbed him from across the street, and two words: 'fresh' in scarlet letters, pink letters reading 'reach'. The background was flowers and a butterfly's wing which separated into a billion rainbow dots close to. There was half a scarlet cartoon smile as well, and Wol knew that this paper had been sent for him, and was meant for the ship of solstice. Fresh Reach.

He'd rolled it carefully and carried it home, smiling, while his neighbours tutted and nudged from their doorways.

Most years, they'd taken roses and burned them but last June it simply didn't feel right. Everywhere they went for months afterwards, there were rose-bushes in full bloom, some even in November. Seasons weren't clear-cut like they remembered from childhood, and they wondered if it ever had been that way, or if it was just stories – snowy cards for Christmas, bunnies and daffodils for Easter – nostalgia? Maybe it was the mathematically accurate calendar the world ran by, flying in the sweet face of the moon with its thirties and thirty-ones and leap years trying to catch up by lopping one rogue day.

Global warming? Callum said it looked like the earth shouting from every verge and field – I'm here! Between pavement slabs, through acres of dry gravel, over miles of land torn up for housing and industry, dandelions and hogweed and thistles and grass like gauze rocketed into being the minute the soil was left alone.

They walked a lot, Wol and Callum, paid bus fare when they had it to take them beyond the city limits and walked all day, all night. Walking and wondering, once they'd come upon a dual carriageway whose islands and verges had been planted and tended like gardens.

'Must be a royal visit,' Callum said, spot on.

'How awful to bloom among the fumes,' Wol said. 'And they won't bother caring for them once the pennoned Daimlers have gone past!'

So one winter midnight, they'd found that road again and brought rose-bushes home with them, digging in the darkness, crouching against the occasional set of headlights. These roses were as tough as weeds and bred to flower constantly in the worst conditions. With Wol's love and care – water, good earth, music, laughter – his small back yard was a cloud of soft-scented pink. And he'd planted one bush in a pot so they could take it to the ritual of summer and bring it home again to live.

'Paper roses, paper roses,' Callum trilled, shaping the ragged rattan shelf into a throne. 'Wol! Paper roses?'

'Of course!' Wol said, finishing a sea of spirals on the hem of the sail.

'What we need is a discarded hat,' Callum said. 'You know? A sort of shiny straw affair with red satin roses, the sort of thing camp peasants dress their donkeys in. Only I don't know any camp peasants . . .'

'Not in Fenham,' Wol said. 'Apart from me, and I don't have a donkey. But I've also been collecting dead heads. Doesn't that sound ghoulish? My gran used to do that. Dead head the roses. I thought it was a really grisly way of saying it, but then there's always pot pourri.'

Callum smiled.

'You see?' he said, 'A travelling rose-bush, paper-roses and a raid on your pot pourri mountain – we never needed to burn real live ones at all.'

Wol's phone rang.

'It's the man in my life,' Callum said.

'Are you sure?'

'Oh, I'm sure,' Callum said and picked up the phone.

He said:

'*I love you. Well, come back then, you're always welcome back. No, I didn't – just some cider – did you? See, you don't need to. Up to the beach. Oh you should see this boat! No, it'll be gone by then. I miss you every second. Just come back. We don't need it, Gerth, we'll manage. Well, I always have. I need a photograph if you're going to keep this sort of thing up. Oh, never! Well, maybe. He's fine, he's lovely. He likes the sound of you. He says I look good on you. He wants to meet you. Whenever. Make it soon. I know. OK, put the phone down. Yes, I love you. I adore you. I'll see you – it can never be soon enough for me. Bye. Bye. Bye.*'

He cradled the silent phone.

'Brother,' Wol said, squeezing his shoulder. 'I'm so happy for you. Is he coming back in time for tonight?'

'Oh, I don't think so,' Callum said. 'He's done mega-brill with his sales and they want to take him out for dinner. He's away with it, Wol, he just loves it. He wants me to have driving lessons, I don't know where that came from, but I can't see me at the wheel. He's mad, Wol, just barmy. I swear he'd get me a mink coat and diamonds if I asked him.'

'He's your angel,' Wol said. 'Does he have *any* faults? I just don't want you splattering against the flame of love, again.'

'No more singed wings,' Callum said. 'This is sunshine not

candlelight. Faults? OK. I guess there's two things which could be a problem. One: his mates. The boys. He doesn't know if he can tell them. I don't wish to be the cause of him dropping them. There are few things worse than an *affaire de coeur* which one cannot shout from the hilltops. That I have to leave in his wonderful hands.'

'Fancy getting a virgin!' Wol handed the joint back. 'Tricky, but such a privilege. For both of you. What else?'

'Well, it's money,' Callum said. 'He really likes it. He earns a lot of it and he likes to buy things. You know me, Wol, I just don't, I never have, and he's talking about washing machines and washing-up machines and mega stereo systems. And he has a thing about cars – his flat's full of pictures of dream-machines – you know, Dolly Parton meets Arnold Schwarzenegger in spectacular chrome! It's a bit odd, I mean, if I want something, I'll do the skips or have a swap. It's a bit frightening.'

'Enjoy it,' Wol said.

'Oh, I'm cheap to please,' Callum said. 'I only want him and his time, not the things him selling his time can get. And he'll be there tonight, living in my heart, my every cell, my soul.'

'We'd better get a move on,' Wol said. 'The light's no guide to time today. I'll put some rice on.'

12

There is no nightfall on the longest day of the year, but when shadows lengthened and shrunk back into themselves so far as to vanish, it was time. Callum and Wol loaded Wol's bull-nosed Morris hybrid, packing blankets around the boat, the rose, the bells, the drum. Most fragile was a willow wand figure and this lay crosswise near the roof, wrapped in a red velvet curtain.

They parked behind the dunes at the far end of the seven-mile bay and made a camp above the high-tide line, inches from the shimmer of damp sand. The rose-bush stood in a cairn beyond where sparks and heat could hurt it, near enough to see and smell.

'Boy scout,' Wol said lovingly, as Callum sparked a fire from wood shavings and straw, feeding in twigs and sticks and dry branches. Soon they'd drag out the old elm root stashed in the sand and it would last until the sun actually rose on a new day.

'Between the worlds,' Callum said, sitting by the flames.

'Food for the journey,' Wol said, breaking bread and spearing three chunks on twigs to warm on the fireside stones.

'Drink for the journey,' Callum said, uncorking a bottle of rosy liquid.

A scent of fruit and flowers rose from the neck and drifted through the flames. This wine was distilled from wild fruits and petals collected from the summer before. Sometimes it was cloudy, or bitter, sometimes so sweet it could only be sipped. Wol loved it because it could never be predicted or repeated; Callum said it was magic – water, berries, petals and

yeast confined behind glass. Add a few months and hey presto!
– summer wine.

He poured two glasses and tossed a third on to the toasting
bread.

'Are you ready in your heart for the journey?' Callum asked.

'Are you ready in your mind for the journey?' Wol answered
him.

'Are you ready in your flesh for the journey?' they said
together.

'I am ready in my heart and my mind and my flesh for the
journey,' they chanted and smiled long and slow.

'Then let us pledge,' Callum said and picked up his silver
knife.

He nicked his palm and watched blood well from the cut,
growing along the lines of his palm like roots. Wol took the
knife and did the same. They clasped hands, bloody palm to
palm and gripped until their hands were white.

'So may we travel,' Callum said. 'My blood is your blood
and my heart beats with yours, brother.'

'So may we travel,' Wol repeated. 'My blood is your blood
and my heart beats with yours, brother.'

They had first done this after the glorious double negative
on HIV blood tests twelve months apart. Negative, negative,
they left the hospital on wings, as if reborn. Wandering in the
park, they couldn't find words for it – ducks, flowers, a lily
pond, crawling babies, trees alive with summer, it was all
marvellous and wonderful and so precious.

Words came after many hours when they sat in Callum's
flat, eyes alive with the sparkle of candle-flames and the river
lights beyond the window.

'Let's be blood brothers,' Wol said, 'to mark this day. It's
so easy to go, oh fuck it and play Russian roulette with yourself, but I'd never hurt you.'

'Night and the beautiful strangers,' Callum said. 'I know.
Even without this disease, it kills your spirit. Ta – fucket –
fucketa fucketa – fuck off!'

'It's the needles with me,' Wol said. 'I know where they

can take you, sew you a coat of many magic colours and keep you warm against it all. If I think of your blood flowing there, under my skin, it's sacred. I won't poison it.'

They'd first met in Credsworth, a rural loony bin. The inmates called themselves knackers. Wol was glassy-eyed and emaciated with smack, Callum dumb and wretched with smack, rocking around a heart broken once too often by one careless stranger too many. Hadn't he got a home to go to? The doctors asked, but he shook his head. Better be here than back in the well-heeled strait-jacket of his ever-loving family. Tranks and methadone for Callum to numb him through the agony of healing, methadone for Wol to keep the horrors at bay. Knowing the drugs and insomnia and despair, they had a way of eyes meeting and tears or laughter flowing between them. The shorthand of shared nightmares.

People who haven't been in the pits don't know what it's like, and how it's hard to stay out in the world sometimes. Wol and Callum both knew the welcome safety of a tiny room off a grey corridor, institution hours and meals and locked doors that take away dangerous choices. Without each other, they'd maybe never have left Credsworth, certainly they'd never have lived so well on the outside, knowing the other was just a phone call away. Callum would rather be stick-insect thin than have his phone cut off; he and Wol made each other gifts of phone stamps, necessary as air.

Every year they renewed the promise of blood between them. This year of Gerth, as Callum had begun to call it, was the seventh letting and sharing of blood. Wol had wondered if Callum could still be sure, and Callum knew how strong the lure of dull brown liquid in a syringe was for both of them. They smiled as they bandaged each other's hands in red silk. They'd kept the faith for yet another thirteen turnings of the moon.

'All that is and will be is ours,' Callum chanted.

'Now and always,' Wol said. 'I'm so happy.'

'We've come a long way,' Callum said. 'And there's a million star miles to go. I'm happy, too. That's me and you, happy.'

It didn't need to be said, do you remember. Callum remembered Wol's face white and sheened with sweat, fingers biting into his arms, feet kicking each step on the waxed floors. Wol remembered Callum's perch on the windowsill, rocking on bone-thin buttocks, washing all the light from his eyes with tears enough to float the ark.

Happy. Now.

They ate hot bread and nudged the third piece into the flames.

'The sea's very calm tonight,' Wol said, setting his drum between his knees. 'Let's drum up some travelling waves.'

'Drum with the waves that are travelling,' Callum said softly. 'We mustn't play with it, brother.'

Wol grinned. This was Callum as no-one else ever saw him, touching base, he called it, his legs crossed like the branches of an old tree, the sides of his feet finding their own shape in the sand. From weeping willow to wise old oak. He said:

'We're here to praise it and know it, not to impose.'

He wandered light as a sea-bird along the shore, picking up pebbles, choosing shells whorled like fingertips, shells smooth as an old-fashioned razor. He arranged them round the hot stone circle like a child's picture of the sun. The fire was sinking down.

Wol dug in a dune and hauled out the elm root, one of a dozen he'd found when disease petrified swathes of elms across the face of Europe. Callum scooped hot ash and embers into a bronze bowl, ash-rich from the wine-soaked bread. Wol put the hyena-striped root into the circle. Soon there were flames.

Now it was time to dress the wicker figure in paper roses and paper vines and wrap the raffia-tied wrists in the red silk from their left palms. They laid it in the boat and Wol hoisted the sail, its scarlet and pink letters flapping in the breeze, the light from over the horizon picking out the gold-painted spirals and runes for safe voyaging. They hauled the boat to the edge of the waves, and Callum poured glowing ash from the bronze bowl on to the figure's chest. Knee-deep in water, they waited until sparks fizzed on the wicker and a curl of flame grew from the wicker heart.

'Go soon and safely,' Callum called, wading deeper. 'Safely and soon and as far as the ocean takes you!'

Soon the icy waves slapped their chins and their free hands drew them out deeper and deeper until they were past the breakers.

'Love go with you as she stays with us,' Callum sang and the waves took the Fresh Reach from their hands. She sailed away into the bright night-time, the wicker man blazing to ashes.

For a while they trod water, then clasped hands for a second before swimming for the shore, racing up the sand and stripping off their clothes beside the fire.

'To life!' Callum said, handing Wol his glass of wine.

'Life!' Wol said and they downed the first of the summer wine.

Soon their blood knew the filtered abundance of the summer gone by, and flames told their skin to stop peaking and shivering. They lay like ancient clay statues – *Young Men at Rest* – as still as the sand itself. All around them the tang of ocean air, wood-smoke for incense and the bright pink perfume of roses.

Part two

·························

Mazeland

13

'By crummy, that was a cracking sales meeting, young Machen! Expansion, that's the watchword!' Hal Bagwig confided in Gerth, summoning the waiter to refill their glasses. 'Another of these, young man!'

The waiter was in his late sixties, but then, so was Hal Bagwig, founder and controller of Gerth's firm, The Great Outdoors. He was canny, coarse and rich as Croesus, riding his monogrammed Rolls Royce with its numberplate HAL 1, on the crest of every rags to riches cliché in the book. He liked to think he'd kept the common touch, and always talked loudly to waiters and chauffeurs and doormen.

Life had given him wealth and a wife and three daughters whose education made them strangers to him. Their marriages widened the gap and some thirty years down the line, he was baffled by a God who'd presented him only with granddaughters.

None of his sons-in-law were remotely interested in The Great Outdoors, and on his sixtieth birthday, Hal looked around the dinner table and realised that he was the last of his line. There wouldn't be another Bagwig – ever – and this lot? Well, they'd sell The Great Outdoors the minute he turned his toes up. He lost sleep over it, combing his empire for young men – even one young man – who'd got what it takes.

Gerth had caught his eye at the first sales conference he'd attended. Not so much Gerth as his tie, a good old-fashioned tweed lying on crisp white cotton. It stood out among the silky flowers and pastel abstracts that made Hal Bagwig twitch. Fashion, he supposed, but it looked bloody pansy to him.

Thanks to his mother and Marks and Sparks, Gerth's suit and mirror-sheened brogues spoke of Hal Bagwig's own youth, when hard graft and respect and tradition were the only way. Everything about Gerth was as rare and welcome as finding proper Yorkshire pudding in the plague of bistros and pizzerias that infected late twentieth-century England.

'I like that chap, Gerth Machen,' he told the Newcastle manager over the phone. 'By jingo, you did well hiring him. He's a credit to TGO and to you. Keep me informed about the lad.'

Three years later, Gerth was well along the path of success as defined by Hal Bagwig OBE. He was solid, Hal said, solid, the sort of chap Hal would have welcomed as a son-in-law.

Tonight in Cardiff Gerth was sitting at a dinner table with five men old enough to be father or uncles to him, all of them deferring to Mighty Hal, a little suspicious of Gerth's youth and charm, but thoroughly in awe of his sales figures. 'The old man's taken to you,' his manager said. 'You'll go far.'

Dinner with the top brass! It was a dream, and Gerth sat there, suddenly wondering, what on earth would Hal Bagwig make of Callum? He gulped his wine to drown a crazy grin.

'Expansion, Gerth,' Hal said loudly. 'What say you?'

He leaned back like a veteran ringmaster, sure of his protégé.

'Consolidation,' Gerth said after a pause. 'I think that's something I've learned in the relatively short time I've been with TGO. Define your market, build up and consolidate. You can only expand on very firm foundations. I feel that TGO has laid these foundations nationwide. Consolidation and investment. As an example, in Newcastle alone, we used to be 63, Sailmarket. Now we're 57 to 71 Sailmarket.'

'Go on lad,' Hal said, nodding.

'Now there's Europe,' Gerth said. 'We may not like it, but it's here and it's not the flash in a pan we thought it might be. Our branch has secured the contract for Italiatrek Himalaya – and, to digress a little, but it is relevant, this is because of our hand-finishing. We resisted phasing it out, and although it raises costs, it's been proven to be well worth it. Nowhere else can offer it any more. I have to say I thought it was a daft idea at first, but Mr Norton is the boss, and now I can see why.'

Mr Norton smiled. Young Machen was getting the idea.

'New brooms may sweep clean, Gerth,' he said, 'but their heads tend to drop off and so do their bristles.'

Hal Bagwig laughed.

'By crummy, yes, Norton,' he said. 'It's something that gets forgotten these days. I'm well pleased with your operation. I'll be sending some of the fellows from here to have a look at you. See if we can't put a bit of northern backbone into these valley boyos. Eh?'

David Hughes smiled agreement. Valley boyos – the old bastard! Old Bagwig had refused point-blank to let them diversify into leisurewear – *we're ski, Hughes, not bloody après-ski!* – and it had taken some very skilful fiscal cuisine to disguise the sweeteners he'd already lavished on Giulio d'Acosta, the temperamental fashion genius who occupied his heart and home. TGO was one big family, according to Hal, and tonight David should have been entertaining the party at his house. But Giulio had refused point-blank to go out. Neither would he stay, dressed down and shut up – and as for hiding any of the rococo homo-erotica scattered in every room? Don't even ask! David pleaded decorators and plumbers and booked the most expensive restaurant in Cardiff. Hal Bagwig raised his eyebrows – TGO was in a mess of over-expansion in Wales, and his manager could afford home improvements? And a restaurant whose thick parchment menus scorned basics like English dishes and prices? Hal glared at David Hughes. A man of forty who dressed like a bloody fashion plate, spending thousands on interior decoration when he didn't even have a wife . . . By the great god Bingo, it would have to be looked into!

Port and cigars brought a promise of new directions for the next sales conference – to be held in Newcastle, and David Hughes's heart sank as the party broke up and he taxi-ed home alone. It was well known that Hal invited the chosen few to his hotel suite for a snifter of something special, and the uninvited, sooner or later, would be dropped.

Damn Gerth Machen and his schoolboy eagerness! No doubt he'd have a safe girlfriend in a semi *oop North*. A comfortable bosom and child-bearing hips, sporting a diamond engagement ring, her life's ambition to be Mrs Gerth Machen, hostess and mother. David tugged his tie loose and shrugged. As far as TGO went, he was history – sooner or later and all because of Giulio, but then, Giulio was the only thing he'd ever valued in the whole of his life. He closed his eyes and dreamed of Brazil.

14

'I hope Mac didn't mind,' Gerth said, sitting next to Trish in Humph's cocktail bar. 'There's your Purple People Beater – I don't know how you can drink that stuff.'

'It's Mac's fault,' Trish said, giggling. 'When we were first together, I said I liked liqueurs and I came home one day and found half a bloody off-licence on the kitchen table. I mean, all colours you know, not just like Tia Maria and Cointreau. He's so over the top. I tried everything and I've got hooked on Parfait Amour – that's the purple one. It's French for perfect love, isn't that cute?'

'You're really happy together, aren't you,' Gerth said; maybe Callum would like Parfait Amour. He'd love the name and the colour anyway.

'Yes, we are, Gerth,' Trish said. 'I mean, you've got to work at it, you know, but then it wouldn't be worth having without. Would it?'

'I suppose,' Gerth said, sipping his Rambo Rampage, wishing it wasn't all frothy pink with umbrellas.

'So what's the trouble?' Trish said. 'And no, Mac doesn't mind, you're his mate, if he thought for one minute you were chatting me up, he'd break your back.'

'Howay,' Gerth said. 'It's nothing like that.'

Trish picked a green cherry out of her glass and bit it in two.

'Go on then,' she said. 'What is it?'

'I've got to know it'll stay private,' Gerth said.

'Don't even think of it,' Trish said. 'I told Mac, look, I

said to him, there's no point me coming home and you going: go on tell me, cuz I won't if he doesn't want me to.'

'Sorry,' Gerth said. 'Just I don't know where to start.'

'Well, it's got to be money or sex,' Trish said. 'You're going to be a millionaire before you're thirty, Mac says. So unless you've got a secret account at a bookie's or drugs or something, it isn't that.'

'I'm not snorting my millions up my nose,' Gerth said. 'And I've never seen a millionaire in a bookie's.'

'So it's sex,' Trish said. 'And that can be anything. I know you lot; that's never a problem going on what you say. Say, mind, I'm not daft, I know you lads, got to be Casanova in front of each other. Nothing you say can shock me, either, Gerth, I'm broad-minded.'

'I'll get us another drink,' Gerth said. 'Dutch courage.'

She watched him go to the bar and smiled. He had that strut in his walk, just like Mac, just like all of them, his suit like armour, wallet like a baby's cuddly, expensive tab like a dummy, the heavy gold at his wrist saying I AM SOMEONE. Underneath, he cried just like anyone, worried sick about putting on weight and losing his hair, honestly, *men*, thought Trish.

Gerth went through three Slow Comfortable Screws – champagne effect wine, three kinds of brandy and lemonade – while Trish drained her fourth Purple People Beater. She wondered if he'd got one of those nasty little infections. A social disease? He was tongue-tied, but he seemed happy enough. She'd have to give him an opening. Mac was the same. Ask to talk to you then spend ages doing anything but.

'Well, Gerth,' she said, chewing a slice of pineapple. 'You've got to say something soon, else I'll pass out and Mac won't be too impressed!' Her face was open and concerned and he wondered how she'd look at him once he told her.

'Sex,' he said, well, it was a start, 'like you said, but it isn't the sex, Trish, I'm in love.'

'Well that wasn't so hard, was it?' Trish said. 'It's lovely. Being in love, you just want to tell the world. Is she nice?'

'That's just it, Trish,' Gerth said, what the hell. 'It's a fella.'

'Christ,' Trish said, 'I wasn't expecting that.'

'What do you think,' Gerth said.

'I think I'll go and do my lipstick,' Trish said. 'Then I'll buy you a drink. Then I might have something to say. Just drink your drink and don't worry. I'll be back.'

Gerth sat like a prisoner waiting for his sentence.

Trish queued in the loo. By this time, the paper had run out and the floor was awash from leaking pipes and taps left running by women too pissed to care.

Gerth was in love with a bloke.

Trish didn't mind gays, well, it's their business, isn't it, but *Gerth*? Mr Whizzkid Normal Yuppie, bursting with hormones and ambition? She tried to picture him kissing a man. Two shaven chins together, lips and tongues – it didn't disgust her or anything, I mean, Michael Cashman was that gay bloke on *EastEnders*, but she'd never thought about it in real life.

She balanced on the broken loo seat. OK, Gerth kissing another man. Holding another man. She thought of Mac and herself in bed – it would be like two of Mac, naked. But what happened next? She'd talked to Christine in her office when Mrs Harding, their boss, had got divorced and was picked up by another woman after work every day. Mrs Harding got her hair cut short and started wearing tailored trousers to work. Christine had gone into hysterics thinking about it, the other woman had short hair too, and Mrs Harding looked younger every day and so happy. Christine said they used appliances and did oral sex, well, you couldn't see Mrs Harding on top. No way. And oral sex with another woman? It was weird enough with Mac, but he did love it. So did she, when he did it. Anyway, that was lesbians. But men? What did they do in bed? She remembered Rixie's series of KY jelly and superglue jokes, he was a filthy bugger, Rixie. Surely Gerth didn't . . .? Or did he? She paddled out of the cubicle to the fag-scorched sink.

Gerth's bloke would be an older man, one of those business men who looked like an Armani advert. That was how they did it, a younger man and an older man a bit like an uncle or a father. Distinguished. Her mind threw her a picture of Danny La Rue. He wouldn't be camp like that, she decided, Gerth would die of embarrassment. You always wanted to mother Gerth, and this man would have taken him under his wing. She painted her lips carefully and wove through the crowd to the bar. Just act normal, she thought, if it was a woman we'd be celebrating and I'd ask them round for dinner. It's only different because it's two men. Unless it was a wind-up? But Gerth's face was too anxious for that.

'Here you are,' she said. 'Champagne cocktails. You can drink champagne with anything. I don't know what to say, really, I'd always found you lot, you know, really taking the piss out of gays, well, I didn't like it, live and let live, but I don't know how Rixie and Dave and Mac'll take it.'

'I know,' Gerth said. 'That's why I wanted to tell you first.'

'I mean,' Trish said, 'is it just a one-off, like, you know the way things blow over? No? Well, I think it's either like it or lump it, your real mates don't care what you do, Gerth, I mean if they drop you, well, they're not real mates, are they? I mean, if you'd killed someone or something, well, fair enough, but you can't help your feelings.'

'That's what I think,' Gerth said. 'It's just how to tell them. Howay, Rixie, man, I'm a poof. Oh, lovely, Gerth, mine's a pint, can you imagine it?'

'What you could do,' Trish said, 'you know, is well, bring him along to meet them, you know, not say anything, then when they know him, I mean, they'll like him, cuz you couldn't be in love with someone horrible, Gerth, could you? And then it'll just sort of happen. You know, if they like him and then they find out he's gay, well, so what. D'you think?'

'No,' Gerth said. 'It wouldn't work, Trish. You couldn't mistake him for anything but gay.'

'Like, how do you mean, ooh, ducky?'

'No,' Gerth said. 'He's just – well, I call him Tinkerbelle. He's blond, like – a hippy, he wears these floaty trousers and scarves and things. He's really pretty, you know, you just know the minute you see him.'

'How old is he?' Trish said, the comforting picture of an older man vanishing and leaving her mind blank.

'Oh, our age,' Gerth said. 'Only he isn't like anyone we know, I can't really think of anyone like him. He – glides, you know, he's just beautiful.'

'Couldn't he wear a suit or something, just for a while?' Trish said, imagining Mac's face over dinner. 'Well, no, why should he? Maybe I'd better meet him, you know, before you come round for dinner.'

'Are we invited?' Gerth said and his voice was so surprised and joyful, Trish nodded immediately.

'Of course you are,' she said. 'Just it'll be a hell of a shock for Mac. If I know what he's like, your bloke I mean, I can make it easier.'

'It won't be easy,' Gerth said; if Callum was here now, there'd be riots. 'Even after you've met him. I hope you do like him, but I don't care, either. I don't mean that to be nasty, but I – well, I love him.'

'I know what you mean,' Trish said. 'Look, leave it with me, Gerth. I'll talk to Mac and make sure he keeps it secret. Then I can ring you if I get any bright ideas. Don't worry.'

'Will it be all right?' Gerth said, 'Will it?'

'Well, I've never seen you look so good,' Trish said. 'Mac said you must be in love, you know, you've got that glow. It's just letting him know who you're in love with. What's his name? Your young man?'

Cassandra, Queen Astarte of the Seven Veils, High Priest?

'Callum,' Gerth said, and the sound was warm on his lips.

'Callum. That's nice. Good luck,' Trish said. 'I'll ring you, Gerth. I want to meet him anyway, but then I'm nebby. Send him my love and tell him to look after you. And thanks in advance for the hangover, it's been lovely. I must get a cab. Night, Gerth. Take care. Do I get my goodnight kiss?'

'Of course you do,' Gerth said, delighted that she still wanted it. 'And Trish? Thanks.'

'No worries, mate,' Trish said, laughing. 'What a dark horse you are, Gerth. I'll ring you tomorrow.'

Easy as that, Gerth thought, she'll sort it, at least she's on my side. On our side. Us. Me and the wife – this is the wife, Mr Bagwig, isn't he wonderful? Cross that one when we get there. He went along the quayside, lights dancing in the river beside him as he walked home to Callum.

15

'Will it just be us?' Callum said, standing beside a pile of discarded clothes, one hand knotted into his hair.

'I don't know,' Gerth lied. 'It'll be Mac and Trish and us anyway. What are you worrying about?'

Callum looked at him.

'Gerth, I know you love me,' he said. 'I just hate meeting new people. One is accustomed to a less than friendly reaction. I know I camp it up and no-one thinks I mind, but these are your friends and I'm very shy. And scared.'

Gerth put on a tape of Mrs Mills Party Time. That usually cheered Callum up, got him strutting and frothy and confident. This time he didn't even seem to hear it. He poured him a glass of wine.

'Drink this, Tink,' he said. 'Dutch courage, eh, I was nearly paralytic when I told Trish.'

'You were so funny when you came back,' Callum said, taking the glass. 'You must have woken me up twenty times to say you loved me, did I know how much. You were so tender and incapable. I'd better sip this, you know how it goes to my head.'

Hands knees and boomps a daisy! plunketty-plunked Mrs Mills.

'Cheers,' Gerth said. 'What is it you call Mrs Mills?'

'The Keyboard Cleopatra,' Callum said. 'The Jezebel of the Joanna. She's such fun.'

'And so are you if you'd just stop frowning and worrying,' Gerth said. 'Come on, that's our cab.'

Mac and Trish were sitting in the garden when the doorbell rang.

'Here we go,' he said, squeezing her shoulder.

Trish's ears strained to hear. Mac's voice. Gerth's voice. Another voice which had to be Callum.

'Trish is slumming it out here,' Mac said. 'We're drinking sherry, but you're welcome to anything.'

Callum's laugh made her turn her head. Whatever image she'd had of him disappeared immediately. This blond youth was Peter Pan, he was Shelley, he was every bit as beautiful as Gerth had told her.

'You must be Callum,' she said. 'Come and sit down.'

'I suppose I must,' he said, twinkling at her. 'Thank you. You're Trish. I don't expect the men of the house – well, mine anyway – to be very good at introductions.'

She smiled.

'It's very nice of you to invite us,' Callum said. 'I gather I'm rather a surprise – even a shock – for you.'

'Well,' she said.

'Believe me, Trish,' Callum said, 'no-one could be more shocked and happily surprised than I. I'd got to the stage of thinking that someone as wonderful as Gerth couldn't exist. In his manifestation as Mr Right. And you're not to worry. I don't hurt people.'

'Good,' Trish said. 'Neither do I.'

'I know,' Callum said. 'Gerth has praised you to the heavens, Trish.'

'You too. I'm glad you came.'

Trish smiled at him, feeling warm and relaxed. Whatever had she been so worried about? No-one could look you straight in the eye the way Callum did and be anything other than lovely. Rixie could get stuffed and she was so glad they hadn't asked him.

'What's this, then?' Gerth said. 'Gone and introduced your-selves, have you?'

Callum reached up and grasped his hand for a second.

'Oh, this is fast becoming a mutual admiration society,' he said. 'I think. I hope. Friends of the Gerth.'

'You're looking very chi chi,' Trish said. 'I love the shirt. Both of you look quite stunning.'

Gerth grinned. Callum giggled.

'You're kinda cute yourself,' he said.

'Where's Mac?'

'Being a bartender,' Gerth sat down and stretched out his legs. 'This garden's coming on.'

'It ought to,' Mac said, appearing with a tray. 'It's had all my sweat for months, sweat and stiff muscles and the wife wielding a bullwhip.'

'You look downtrodden,' Callum said. 'We wives are such tyrants.'

Whoops! The instant intimacy with Trish had relaxed him, but he felt a *frisson* of annoyance – embarrassment? – from Mac. Hush mah mouf, Tallulah, he chided himself, he probably thinks you are the Vile Seducer of innocent heterosexuality. It was not the time to compliment Mac on his brocade waistcoat. It was doggy roll on back and look helpless time. When in doubt, zip the lip.

Mac put the tray down.

'Gerth said cocktails,' he said, his eyes avoiding Callum.

'How lovely,' Trish said. 'You're so clever. What have we got?'

'Well, our guests brought champagne,' Mac said. 'You remember Charlie Chaplin's in Puerto last year? Gerth man, you'd love Tenerife! There was a fella there, George, he was the owner, miserable old sod, wasn't he? He'd retired to the sun and he never even went outdoors. He did this drink called Conquistador and me and Trish lived on it, didn't we? So I've done the best I can.'

'Cheers.'

'That's spectacular,' Callum said. Bugger it, he hadn't taken a monastic vow of silence.

'Thanks,' Mac said, sitting next to Trish. 'It's a bit different, like.'

'I was saying to Trish,' Gerth said, 'the garden's looking good.'

'It needs to with the work I've put in,' Mac said, 'Do you like gardening, Callum?'

'I do,' Callum said. 'I'm restricted to pots and a window box, of course.'

'Where is it you live?' Mac asked.

'Garstone Towers,' Callum said. 'They keep threatening to demolish it, but they never do. I just throw away the letters these days. It's a haven for bag-ladies and unsung war-heroes and widows. I have a dream of a cottage in the countryside with roses round the door, but who doesn't.'

'A vegetable garden,' Gerth said. 'Ducks on a pond and a small sheep or two to keep the grass down.'

'Self-sufficiency,' Callum said, smiling at him.

Mac looked at them, now their eyes were locked on each other. It looked like love, but he felt awkward. Gerth had visited them with two or three girlfriends over the years and he and Trish had sat afterwards, going over every reason why it wouldn't work. Mainly because the lasses were too keen and Gerth was old-fashioned enough to want to be the wooer, the pursuer, the gallant lover on a chase. All that had gone this time; Gerth was softer, even chivalrous, and Callum clearly loved it.

'Would you show me round the garden?' Callum said, interrupting his look.

'Oh aye,' he said. 'There's a lot more to be done, mind.'

'Mac doesn't like him,' Gerth said as soon as they were out of earshot. 'He just doesn't. I know Mac.'

'He does,' Trish said. 'Well, he's just – confused. Think about if it had been him, you know, you'd have been on your guard. It was bad enough for me when we got together. I felt like I was on probation. You and Rixie and Dave watched every move I made. It was awful.'

'Was it? I never meant it to be. I was curious like, about this perfect woman who'd knocked my mate for six, but I liked you straight off.'

'It wasn't you so much, it was them,' she said. 'We were going to ask them today, only you can't have Dave without Rixie and Rixie's gob, well, I wanted a nice time. You know.'

'He's a bugger,' Gerth said. 'I mean, he's a mate but half the time you just want to go, hey Rixie, put a sock in it.'

'He'll be the worst with Callum,' Trish said. 'He'll just see someone pinching his drinking partner and a bloody poof at that. If Dave ever gets anyone, Rixie'll fall to bits.'

'He will, won't he. It's like we go out drinking and it's great for now, but I can see Rixie being one of those lonely old men drinking on his own when he's sixty. Isn't that awful?'

'It'll be his own fault,' Trish said. 'Fill my glass up, Gerth. And cross your fingers about Percy Thrower down there with your Tinkerbelle. I can't be doing with a sulk over dinner.'

'There's a fairy at the bottom of your garden,' Gerth said, laughing.

'Silly sod.'

Mac's whole body bristled as they walked away from the patio. Callum was too pretty for a man. That was bullshit and he knew it. And he didn't look like a hippy, which is what Trish had said. He looked arty farty, like the types who hang around the theatre foyer, types he and Trish whispered and giggled about when they went to a show.

'Yes,' Callum said out of thin air, 'I'd love a garden.'

'Well, this is only a city garden,' Mac said. 'Not enough room for sheep or ducks, like.'

'That's what's so clever,' Callum said. 'It's a rectangle of earth surrounded by walls, but you've made it seem huge. Not all brickwork and squared off. A wild effect.'

'That's what I wanted,' Mac said. 'Arches – well, they'll be covered with climbing things next year and I'm training roses and honeysuckle and clematis on the walls – on these frames, so it's like arches. Trish says it's like landscaping a park.'

'Why not,' Callum said.

'Well, my old fella gave us a book,' Mac said. 'He's got a

yard out the back, whey, it's not twelve foot square. He says it's different levels that do it.'

'*Trompe-l'oeil.*'

'That's the words,' Mac said. 'Planters and raised beds and sunken beds. If there's not much space, get miniature things. Give it a few years and you'll walk in here and think it's Jesmond Dene.'

Callum leaned against an arch and gestured with one hand.

'I can sense water,' he said dreamily. 'There must have been a stream here some time, probably still is. Or a well.'

'So they say. I want a pond and a fountain back here,' Mac pointed to the ground. 'Look back through the arch – see? There's sun here right through to the evening.'

'And the sound of it,' Callum continued his thoughts, 'sparkles on the fountain and that lovely cool splash of running water.'

'That's it,' Mac said; maybe this Callum was all right.

'A man of vision,' Callum said. 'I hope we'll be allowed to see it.'

'Oh, you will,' Mac said at once, 'I hope you'll come here just as often as Gerth – well, before, you know.'

'I think it's awful if you stop seeing your friends just because you've got involved,' Callum said. 'I mean, love is love, but it doesn't make you Siamese twins.'

Don't say more, he ordered himself, do *not* elaborate, we've only just crossed whatever that barrier was.

'That's right enough,' Mac said. 'I think we'd better get back before those two plonkies finish off the Conquistador.'

'Yes,' Callum said, forcing himself not to skip over the grass and land on Gerth's lap. Hands in pockets, one step at a time. He felt triumphant when they sat down and smiled openly at Gerth, giving his anxious face a slight wink in lieu of a kiss. And good heavens, acting played hell with his nerves! It was time for a Sobranie. He offered the shimmering box to Trish who chose pink. Gerth said, no thanks and Mac the same. His fingers hovered for a moment – turquoise? Lilac? No. Callum awarded himself gold.

*

'And so it continued far into the night,' he told Wol next day over the phone.

'Sounds surprisingly divine,' Wol said.

Callum giggled.

'I just wonder what would have happened if I'd mentioned Credsworth,' Callum said, 'not quite the thing to impress one's husband's chums. My dear, I was very Percy Bysshe Shelley. Trish, I guess, would have transmuted mine into an acceptable form of insanity. Mac would have had a private word with Gerth.'

'What about Gerth?'

'He's aware that I had a sort of breakdown,' Callum said lightly. 'Gerthkind cannot bear too much reality. My sort of reality. But then I can't bear too much of his, either.'

Wol thought, no, mate, for ever will be me and you, friends. For ever love is your dream, although it was love that drove you to drugs and close to death. Love makes and breaks you, Callum, be hoped this one is gentle for you.

16

Gerth drove over the bridge from work, Pink Floyd belting out 'Shine On You Crazy Diamond' through the speakers. That was Callum, all right, crazy as a loon and more sparkle in his naked finger than a fistful of Elizabeth Taylor. The driver stuck in the evening jam in the car next to his looked over, hearing the bass thud. Some young idiot in love, he thought, for Gerth's smile blazed through the window as he tapped the steering wheel. Some young fool in love and thinks the world's his oyster and he's got the pearl.

Today Callum had bought a car, and all Gerth's common sense winced at the thought. Getting him through lessons and a driving test had been one of the most bizarre experiences of his life. Who the hell rings every driving school in the northeast to make sure they use lead-free petrol? Callum. And the conversation last night was unreal – Callum and Wol's ideas about cars left him speechless. Gerth looked for speed, safety, reliability, power, aerodynamic chic: everything had to ooze a confident motorway credibility; his car had to cut a dash wherever it went and look good in a car park full of company millions.

None of this meant a thing to Callum, going by last night.

Or to Wol, for that matter. His bull-nosed Morris hybrid was a hand-painted embarrassment, top speed fifty with a good wind behind it.

'Of course, the colour's really important,' Callum said.

'You can always get it sprayed,' Gerth said – for heaven's sake!

'That's a brilliant idea,' Wol said. 'We can airbrush it. We could have your star-sign over the bonnet – and then water spilling down over the wheels.'

'And rainbows,' Callum said, 'sea creatures – mermaids, dolphins . . . make it really beautiful. A truly Aquarian automobile.'

'You're sure to get stopped,' Gerth said, imagining the police clocking him and Callum. 'Don't you get stopped, Wol?'

'Oh, I used to,' Wol said. 'But I quite like policemen – aesthetically, I mean, they're so big. Uniforms do something to me. All that navy blue serge and the baby blue shirts. Cute! I was always getting stopped, but they must have put something on the computer – I'm all taxed and insured and legal, you see, and they leave me alone now.'

'What else?' Callum mused, 'Well, lead-free. And I'd like really comfortable seats – this car's going to take me everywhere. And what about the steering wheel? That car I learned in – the driving school's car – the steering wheel was horrible. Sort of solid, rubbery, like a truncheon. I'd like something more slender, really. What do you think, Gerth?'

'I'm saying nothing!' he'd said.

God knows what they'd come up with.

He parked in front of Garstone Towers. A ferocious looking old woman was coming out of the lift, dragging a trolley and muttering. Gerth let her pass, honestly this place was full of loonies and pensioners. No wonder they kept threatening to knock it down.

Callum met him at the door of the lift and pushed him back inside.

'Come on!' he said. 'And don't say a word! Close your eyes and hold my hand and *trust* me!'

Gerth felt the lift stop and Callum's hand tugging him back outside like a child who's found a secret he's just got to share.

'We're nearly there,' Callum said, 'Open your eyes!'

Only Callum could have found a car like this. Gerth had thought of buying one and tying a huge pink satin ribbon round it, but he felt too silly. And Callum insisted that it had to be bought today. Now he wished he had: at least the daft ribbon could have been removed and stuck on the ceiling with all the cards and wrappings from every gift they'd ever given each other. No-one can see inside a seventh-floor flat, after all, unless they're invited . . .

The main thing that hit Gerth was the paintwork. The background was hot pink and there were circles all over it, coloured like smarties. Surely to God they couldn't have had it sprayed so quickly? And it wasn't hand-painted either, some paint-spray whizz kid had done a perfect job. It had probably cost more than the wheels.

'What do you think?' Callum's voice pirouetted around him.

He stuck his hands in his pockets and tried to be objective. The car was a Volkswagen Polo, which was good enough. It was twelve years old, which was bad enough. It had Wolfrace tyres lifting it clear of the ground – surely it hadn't come like that? The tyres were worth more than the car. Had Wol and Callum gone mad in an accessory shop?

'Wol says the mileage is genuine and the chassis's perfect,' Callum recited. 'Archie, the man in the arches who sold it – isn't that amazing? – he said it turns on a sixpence. I just love it.'

'So who did the paint?' he said.

'You hate it!' Callum said. 'You just hate it!'

'I don't,' Gerth said. 'All I said was who did it?'

'That,' Callum said, 'is part of what's magic. This is the way it was when we saw it. Wol said it would be a gimmick to get people going into the yard, but Archie said no, the last owner had it done at The Bigger Splash, that custom car place in Gateshead. Well, Hockney, I thought, it's an omen! Wol went flying underneath it, and I looked inside – it's got this adorable compass on the dashboard – and I tried to look nonchalant, in case Archie spotted that I was In Love and tried to put the price up.'

Of all the cars in all the garages in the whole of Tyneside . . .

'And,' Callum said, 'Archie said I'd never get it nicked because it's so noticeable. He said it was down on the police computers, like Wol's, so they wouldn't bother me either. Do you love it?'

'You do,' Gerth said. 'I don't know what to say. I'm happy if you're happy.'

'Then be ecstatic,' Callum said. 'Archie said he'd had it for a while, it wasn't to everyone's taste and it was only four hundred and fifty quid as well.'

Gerth's heart sank. Nothing under a thousand was worth driving, everyone knew that – everyone except Callum. And Wol.

'Shall we go for a spin, little Gerthling?' Callum said.

'All right,' Gerth said. 'Are you driving?'

'Oh, the enthusiasm!' Callum said. 'I'm not that bad, am I?'

'No,' Gerth said. 'It's just the way you always slow down to look at things.'

'Well, I don't see the point of speeding past everything,' Callum said. 'I like to enjoy the journey as well as the destination. It's different for you, with all those meetings and deadlines, I know. Let me open the door for you. A spot of role reversal?'

'You're crackers,' Gerth said, sitting in the passenger seat. It was Callum's car all right: the dash was a menagerie of fluffy frogs and snakes and a pink flamingo. A crystal hung from the driving mirror. There was a photo of him and Callum on the sunshade. On the passenger window was a perspex disc and when he looked through it, everything was edged with rainbows.

'Do you like the laser mindbender?' Callum said. 'I wanted to put it in front of me, but Wol said it makes traffic lights awfully confusing.'

Gerth had to admit that Callum's driving was improving. He started the car smoothly and they cleared seven sets of traffic lights and two roundabouts without a hitch.

'It handles well,' he said.

'Doesn't it,' Callum giggled. 'The tyres are wonderful! Archie said you can drive over dunes and up mountain paths with these tyres. All the wild lone places – and Wol's finding out about gas conversion. Apparently it's much quieter and the pollution is virtually zero.'

'Oh, they looked into that,' Gerth said. 'Gas. It's bloody lethal.'

'They did look into it,' Callum said. 'But they realised it would mean an end to petrol revenue and they bought the patent and all the work and have stowed it deep in the vaults of capitalism. Like the eternal lightbulb. It's obscene.'

That was another thing Gerth found with Callum and Wol – according to them, there were dozens of big business plots against ecology and reason. Maybe there were, but what could you do? They told him business was motivated only by profit and if he'd chosen to think about it, maybe he'd have agreed. Life was too short, in Gerth's opinion, you can't beat the system so why waste the time mouthing off about it?

'But we don't fight the system,' Callum said. 'We've opted out of the system as far as possible. Mouthing off, as you call it, is pointing out what's wrong with it; you can't just shrug away a whole green planet because there's something good on the telly, Gerth!'

Put like that, he felt stupid and guilty for a while, but the feeling didn't last. If he sat around all day, maybe he'd have time for the luxury of hippy anarchy, but his job demanded 100 per cent and he wanted to relax after work. Not that Callum sat around all day, Jesus, that sounded awful. Callum didn't even sign on, he eked out the coppers paid him by the wholefood store and the wholefood café, he made meals, he painted, he was never idle. He didn't put Gerth down for having a career, so vice versa was only fair. He told Gerth that different people need different slices from the financial pie, and there was no judgement to be made unless you started trying to grab someone else's slice.

Gerth was surprised as they breezed along the coast road. Callum usually slowed at the empty John Will's building, 'So wonderfully nouveau, let's buy it, it would be such fun!' He drove past without looking and kept on the road where he often turned off purely for the pleasure of seeing an abundant garden and hanging baskets dwarfing one small terraced house on an otherwise barren estate.

Today in the new car he drove with purpose.

'Where are we going?' Gerth said.

'All the way there and back again,' Callum said. 'That's what my grandma used to say to me.'

'Are we there yet?' Gerth whined, and immediately Callum relaxed. He'd been euphoric about the car all day and Gerth's politeness had him on edge. Gerth was playing now – thank the spirits of joy, he couldn't cope with a mood. He reached over and squeezed his knee.

'Love you, big boy,' he said.

'I love you too, Tink,' Gerth said, rubbing his fingers. 'It just takes a bit of time, man, you're full of surprises.'

'You ain't seen nothing yet,' Callum said, taking the turning north along the coast.

17

Callum had agonised for weeks about this – his very own first car trip with Gerth. He decided on a barbecue at the beach, and even bought a T-bone steak for Gerth, apologising in his soul to the animal kingdom, even though the steak was organic from M and S. To counterbalance this act of betrayal, he settled on a three-day a week fast for the next two months to sponsor a horse at the Pegasus Sanctuary. The leaflet came through the door while he was dithering, like the answer to a prayer.

He wanted to perform a ritual with Gerth, but Gerth went very clam-like about magic. A barbecue at night by the sea held the elements of a ritual: fire, moonlight, salt water, a breeze alive with ozone. And he'd made sage-scented candles in deep holders, one for each of the winds. He might just drop that in casually . . .

'One has to treat one's hubby with care,' he said aloud, packing a borrowed bread basket for the picnic.

The smartie-coloured car took them through the dusk. Gerth was thinking of a country pub, but he smiled when Callum drove off the road, the huge tyres taking dunes and grass in their tread.

'See?' Callum said, 'See sea? This is a very special place, Gerth.'

'I've not been here before,' Gerth said, zipping his leather jacket against the wind.

'It makes it even more special to me,' Callum said, 'you being here. We're having a fire and a barbecue. One of those instant ones, they're just marvellous. But you must go and gather wood, while I camp around with this lot.'

Nut rissoles, Gerth thought. Nut rissoles by moonlight. Oh, Callum. His eyes widened when he saw the steak. Oh, Callum!

'I thought you'd never buy meat,' he said.

'I thought you'd be miserable without it,' Callum said. 'Don't run away with the idea that it'll happen again. No dead animals in my larder.'

'Oh, Callum,' Gerth said, 'I'm really touched.'

'You will be,' Callum said. 'That's a promise. Now make a fire like a good boy scout and then you can have some beer.'

'You've gone to a lot of trouble,' Gerth said.

'Nothing's a trouble if you smile at me. Now stop it. Not that sort of smile,' he hugged Gerth and they kissed teasingly. 'I'm hungry for more than just your body. Man make fire! Now! Wife has brought firelighters.'

Gerth combed the dunes, amazed at how cold the sand was at night, as it ran between his fingers, grey with a dash of sparkle in the moonlight. It was ages since he'd been out in the wilds at night. You thought it was quiet, until you stood still and heard the sea and the wind, the wind and the trees, the grasses.

'I was thinking,' he said, as the sticks crackled into flame. 'Doesn't anyone mind fires here?'

'Well, I don't,' Callum said. 'Do you? Is there anyone else? You and your "heavens to Betsy! there might be a by-law!" mentality! What can they do, Gerth? Ask us to move on? This land belongs to no-one. Which means everyone, which includes you and me. Now lie back and drink beer while the wife's slaving over hot charcoal. Lovely, actually, because I'm not. It just does it all for you.'

The moon sailed past clouds into an ocean of navy velvet sparkling like a ballgown. It was a new moon, which was why Callum had chosen today to buy the car. He hadn't said this to Gerth, I mean, if mentioning a pendulum brought a frown!

'Look at that moon, Callum,' Gerth said, surprising him. 'Is it a new one? Or the last bit of the old one?'

Never underestimate telepathy or your own true love!

'New,' he said, 'You'll have to deal with this steak. I haven't a clue.'

Gerth squatted beside the barbecue.

'A new moon, a new car,' he said. 'You always say a new moon is the best time for starting things fresh. I do remember things, you see.'

'That's why I got the car today,' Callum said, scanning his face. Gerth smiled.

'Well, it's just right for you,' he said. 'To be honest, I'd never have bought it, but you know that. Christ, I just got a whiff of that herb you like so much – are these your magic candles?'

'Of course,' Callum said. 'Sage for the sage.'

'Is this a ritual, like?' Gerth said, turning the meat over.

'Of course,' Callum said.

'What do you do?' Gerth said. 'I mean, what's this ritual for?'

'All the better to know you with, my dear,' Callum said. 'You seem to think rituals are all weird and druidic. They're not – at least my sort aren't. Just fire and moonlight and love and well-being. This could be a courtship ritual, only we seem to be married already.'

'Let's make it an anniversary,' Gerth said. 'What is it, a year and seven months? That makes it our eightieth weekaversary. Or our five hundred and sixtieth dayversary.'

'So handsome and mathematically brilliant too!' Callum said, worshipping him. 'I like dayversaries. And diversity.'

Later they snuggled together on the sand in the fireheat, the spent barbecue beside them. Gerth finished his San Miguel.

'You know two of the greatest pleasures in life?' he said, kissing Callum's forehead.

'With you I know all the pleasures,' Callum said. 'Which two?'

'The last drink beforehand,' Gerth said, unbuttoning his shirt, 'and the first cigarette afterwards.'

So much later it was early next day, he flicked a hot ember

from his naked thigh. Callum ran down to the edge of the sea and straight into the icy water for a minute or two.

'You should try that,' he said, shivering like a high speed earthquake by the fire again.

'I will,' Gerth said and sprinted across the sand, roaring as the water chilled him from head to toe.

'That's powerful stuff,' he said, crouching over the fire. 'I could get used to these rituals. Do you do this with Wol?'

'Good heavens,' Callum said. 'We've swum, yes, we've eaten yes, there's always a fire, but a feast of love – that's yours, Gerth.'

'I know,' Gerth said. 'I'm happy. Do you know how happy you make me?'

'I hope so,' Callum said.

It was four in the morning by the time they got home. The ansaphone was flashing and Callum pressed it to play back.

'Hey, Cal, it's Wol. You know our little scheme? It could be happening, there's an interested party. Call me first thing.'

'What's that?' Gerth said, brushing sand from his hair.

'Oh, Wol and I have decided to go into business,' Callum said. 'It's a bit of a secret, in case it doesn't work. I'll tell you if it does.'

'Would I disapprove?' Gerth said, yawning.

'Could, or indeed *would* I do anything for you to disapprove of?' Callum dropped his clothes on a chair.

'Not a thing,' Gerth said. 'Just let me know if you need a business adviser. Hey, did you get an alarm for the car?'

'Don't be silly,' Callum said. 'I've put a spell on it. It's perfectly safe.'

'A spell,' Gerth said. 'The wife's put a spell on the car. That's all right then.'

'My spells work,' Callum said, kissing him. 'Don't they?'

18

Wol was sewing golden fringes on to a taffeta frock when the phone rang.

'There may be a slight hitch for Ms Cogan and the Divine Miss M,' Callum said.

'What? You're not ill, are you?'

'Psittacosis, Wol,' he said. 'The Divine Miss M's husband is threatening to be at home this weekend. Said cute husband actually is not aware that the Divine Miss M exists. Cute husband's wife forgot to mention it.'

'So?' Wol said. 'Do you think Gerth'll have a problem with the act?'

'It's just possible,' Callum said. 'I haven't actually sounded him out on drag, Wol, but I have a gut feeling that this may be a line over which he cannot persuade his twinkly toes to step.'

'I never thought of Gerth as having twinkly toes,' Wol said.

'Exactly,' Callum said. 'Can you see my – nay, our – dilemma? I feel disloyal to a degree. I actually would rather he wasn't here.'

'Now come on,' Wol said. 'Where's your ya-yas, girl?'

'Cowering at the bottom of the closet,' Callum said. 'I'm amazed at myself actually. I've been slapping my wrists into a lather all morning, playing Jimmy Somerville at full volume and slathering my face with slap and then I think of Gerth walking in and I don't know whether to laugh, cry, or dive for the baby oil. Cosmetically speaking.'

'Come out, come out wherever you are!' Wol snorted. 'Callum, you never cease to blow my mind. What does the hubby think you've been doing while he hets around all over the country flogging ski-suits? Hasn't he noticed you've got more money these days?'

'I've been saving it,' Callum said. 'Don't laugh, Wol. I wanted to surprise him with something.'

'Dangerous,' Wol said. 'Callum, you've got to tell him. I mean, sometime we'll be booked for a week night and then what will you do?'

'Cross that bridge when we get there?'

'I think we're there,' Wol said. 'I'm half-way round the hem with a gold fringe. You should be ankle-deep in sequins by now. Is he or is he not going to be here?'

'I'll ring him,' Callum said. 'I can't cope with this.'

'Ring me back straight away whatever,' Wol said. 'Love is not love which alters when it alteration finds, dear.'

'Stop sewing for five minutes,' Callum said. 'Put down your knitting, the book and the broom, and cross all your pinkies for me! Au revoir.'

Wol put the receiver down and wove his fingers and thumbs into a snake's nest of hope. It hadn't occurred to him that Gerth didn't know about their double act. What's to know? But then Callum's new Romance, the Love of His Life, was fraught with surprises. Things that he and Callum and every fairy had lived with for years were a whole new world to Gerth. Who what where when and why all over the place, twenty questions for the most ordinary statement.

Who's this Jools and Sandy then, Wol? Fah gawd's sake!

All the tinsel and twinkle of gay party time – girly names, Hollywood queens from the days when the only screens were big, cult idols, John Waters movies, disco divas, Gay Pride, polari. Even Saint Quentin Crisp! How could Gerth not know about drag – well, he'd know about drag in the straight-pleasing clotheshorse world of Danny La Rue. Wol could just imagine Gerth – pre-Callum – sniggering and sneering with those awful mates of his.

They should be made to stand in front of seven feet of lacquered and lascivious out and proud drag queen – Lily

Savage's polluted lagoon of wit, for example, or the sublimely aristocratic anarchy of her Imperial Highness the Grand Duchess Regina Fong – it would blowtorch their pea-sized brains into oblivion.

Wol was cross. Kerross!

Why should Callum have to give any of this drab fairyless ignorance a first thought, let alone a second? Love love *lerve*, of course, but love shouldn't mean giving up any part of yourself let alone hiding it. I am what I am, even if the world is an ocean of moralistic domestos where your existence is as welcome as household germs.

If Gerth didn't know about something as innocuous as The Divine Miss M and Miss Cogan, then God help him on real issues!

'Mate, oh blood brother of mine,' Wol sighed, watching his knuckles go white and his fingertips redden. 'There's a lot of talking to do.'

19

'You see, the thing is, just listen, Wol and I have a drag act. Drag, Gerth. We put on frocks and wigs and sing. Wol is Ms Alma Cogan, a gay icon with a giggle in her voice, much beloved of our sisters, the giggle, the voice and Ms Cogan herself of course! I am The Divine Miss M, giving a wide-eyed tribute to Bette Midler whose career started in the San Francisco bath houses frequented exclusively by men of our persuasion in a twenty-four-hour celebration of sexual liberation. Very popular until the AIDS epidemic. Which the moneyed straight world of medicine seems unable to cure. I am not *bringing* politics into it, they just happen to raise their homophobic heads whenever you think of anything. Politics is – or should be – people, and we are people too. Gerth. Have you got that?'

On the top deck of a bus, it's easy as pie, it's a piece of cake, thought Callum. I can do it with my eyes closed, one hand tied behind my back, it's all plain sailing along the Fossway, seven stops short of lunchtime reality with Gerth.

Make no bones about it: *Gerth, I've been getting some hand-bag dragging a frock.* The internal monologue camped along without a hitch.

What the hell was he so uptight about, what was wrong with drag? Honestly, you'd think it was the final frontier. If a frock was going to break up him and Gerth, then they were pretty insubstantial anyway. He banished the thought.

It was also how much to say.

When Gerth asked something, he didn't want to know much. What was it, the other day, when he came home?

Hannah was there, she was doing his hair, she had done for years. That was how they'd met. She'd started looking pink-eyed over a wash-basin in Wallsend while he was being shampooed and Callum hated seeing people unhappy. They went out for a drink and he took her to the club and she became a real chum. She liked him being gay, she said it was like having a brother who'd never pull your hair or pinch your arse, just your lipstick.

Gerth was totally confused.

'I thought you didn't like women,' he said once she was gone, 'I mean.'

Gerth meant explain.

'Well, she's like a sister,' Callum said. 'She just likes hanging round with me, and I like it too. I mean, you've got Trish.'

'I suppose,' Gerth said. 'Just – and don't roll your eyes at me, I thought, you know.'

'Gay men hate women?' Callum interpreted. 'Some do. Some straight men hate women. Like Rixie.'

'Rixie loves women,' Gerth said at once. 'He's nuts about them.'

'Does he and is he indeed?' Callum shook his head. 'He has a very strange way of showing it from what you've said. The way he looks at them, the way he talks about them, it's either fear or loathing.'

Gerth frowned.

'Think about it,' Callum said. 'He doesn't have a steady girlfriend. He tells the most awful jokes in front of Trish. All he does with women is drunken one-night stands and degrading conversations with barmaids.'

'All right,' Gerth said. 'Maybe. But what about Hannah?'

'Well, let's see,' Callum said. 'She was having boyfriend trouble when I first knew her and so was I, so we used to be agony aunties for each other. Now she's grown up and got husband troubles. I'm still an agony uncle, of course, and we cheer each other up, just like any friends.'

'Right,' Gerth said. 'Do you want a beer?'

Which was like saying, OK Callum, that's enough, shut up

now. He could have talked about Hannah for ages, she was just wonderful, but Gerth was a working man come home and needing telly screen and lager. Ho hum.

All very well and it was now his stop. He found a quiet table at the back of the café and ordered tea for one.

He smiled, anticipating Gerth. Sometimes he joked about writing the Earthling's Guide to Fairyland. It would be a series of Once Upon A Time stories. Maybe that was the best way to introduce the Divine Miss M.

And then Gerth came in. Callum drank him in as he walked towards the table. The suit said square shoulders, but he knew different. He knew him through and through.

'Hi there,' he said.

'You've had me worried sick,' Gerth said. 'What's up?'

'I said don't worry,' Callum said. 'There's something I have to tell you and I don't want you to get all cross with me.'

'I can't see getting cross with you,' Gerth said. 'Have you spent all the housekeeping on magic beans, like?'

How could he forget this about Gerth? The pixie boy that no-one else ever saw – he loved him for it.

'Hearken unto me,' he said. 'It's a chapter from The Good Fairyland Guide. Pixieville on five dollars a day.'

The waitress hovered.

'Steak and kidney, pet,' Gerth said. 'There's no home cooking these days. Callum?'

'Salad sandwich, please,' Callum said, adoring him.

'Howay then, Tinkerbelle, what's your chapter?'

'Once upon a time,' Callum said, 'there was a fairy who was always flat broke. No-one gave fairies jobs, you see, and this fairy was married and dying to buy presents for his elf. He sat down and thought oh dear oh dear, how can I get some money, what can I do? Well, he could sing and he could dance and he could sew. But how can you make money out of that? Then one day, he got a brilliant idea. If he made some special clothes and asked his friend they could make up a double act and maybe get the fairies' nightclub to pay them.'

'Salad sandwich, steak and kidney,' the waitress said.

'Do go on,' Gerth said, smiling. 'You've lost me, but I'm listening.'

'Well, they did. That is, I did. We did. Me and Wol and that's what we're doing on Saturday.'

'You've lost me totally,' Gerth said, 'Can I have some sauce, pet? Ta. What are you and Wol doing? Just say it plain.'

'We've got an act,' Callum said, honestly, Gerth wasn't making this easy at all. 'Me and Wol.'

'You mean I've got a working wife?' Gerth grinned.

'Don't you mind?' Callum said.

'If you can get paid for singing, pet, I'll stand there and cheer,' Gerth said. 'I'll say, hey, that's the missus up there, I'll kneecap you if you don't clap.'

'It's not just singing,' Callum said.

Gerth looked at him.

'So what else is there? Singing and what?'

'Well, just singing,' Callum said. 'It's just – we dress up.'

'Give it to me straight,' Gerth said. 'You've got me all chewed, your face is as long as Monday morning.'

'We dress up in frocks,' Callum said quietly. 'Wol does Alma Cogan and I do Bette Midler.'

'Well, I don't know Alma – what, Cogan? But I'm getting used to Bette Midler,' Gerth said. 'You sing her stuff a lot already, it should be easy. What did you want to tell me?'

Callum stared at him.

'Like your pie, Gerth?' he said, laughing out loud.

'It's canny,' Gerth said. 'What are you laughing at?'

'You, wonderful man,' Callum said, 'You're telling me you don't mind me dragging up and being the Divine Miss M on stage?'

Gerth laughed.

'Callum,' he said, 'nothing would surprise me with you. You wear make-up already and your trousers are – well, might as well be a skirt, quite honestly. You're more girl than most girls I know, so what's the big deal with a drag act?'

'Nothing,' Callum said. 'If you're here, will you come?'

'Just thinking of you,' Gerth said, 'I've been beating my

brains out what was it you wanted to tell me that was so serious. I thought you'd met someone else. Or you were ill. Or you didn't love me any more. So me wife does a drag act? Put that by what I was thinking, and it's like winning the lottery. I'll be in the front row cheering you on and I'll black the eyes of anyone who looks at you sideways.'

'There isn't anyone else,' Callum said. 'Don't ever think that. I'm in love with you now and always. Just you. Don't ever doubt it.'

20

There wasn't a straight line to be found in The Prohibition Palace. The whole place was modelled on a B movie speakeasy from the thirties, with Rocky Horror overtones. Benny, the insomniac owner, had a penchant for sculpted artex hanging like silver stalactites. He had a passion for gilt rococo, mirrored pillars and the sort of crimson flock wallpaper found in every Chinese restaurant in the seventies. At the bar, the artex stalactites gave way to blunt curves twinkling like Christmas lights. Daylight showed punctured egg-boxes and tarnish, but few of the clientèle ever saw it that way, only Benny, poring over his books, gin and tonic at his elbow, bow tie hanging loose from his neck.

He had ideas, Benny, ideas of louche glamour that he thought were his own, but most of them came from his childhood, when the ABC showed black and white movies on a Sunday afternoon. Women with impossible figures and unlikely lips conceiving passions larger than life for immaculate heroes or gangsters in evening suits; heroines pacing rooms in filmy dresses, vamps tossing fur shawls to the floor in rage. Love grand enough to die for, jilted lovers laughing as they lit cigarettes in long holders and flirting to the popping of champagne corks: broken hearts drowning their sorrow to show a celluloid nightclub world that they didn't *give* a damn.

Benny had owned nightclubs for years, all successful, all a complete disappointment to him. The best he could hope for was 'casually smart, no denim': Saturday night Romeos swilling lager, stiletto-ed floozies tippling rum and black and leaving cigarette burns and yards of soaking tissue with lipstick smears like bloodstains all over the toilets. Glamour? They couldn't even pronounce it.

The only people dressed right were the doormen. Benny insisted on black ties and suits since the doormen set the tone of a club. But the best doormen are equipped with a matching IQ and shoe size. Where was the wit, the sophistication? Benny was a lonely man, his only friend was Stax, head of the north-east mafia. Stax ran the doors, the drugs and the dolls and kept the filth sweet.

'No hard stuff,' Benny told Stax. 'Maryjane, well, she's anybody's. But no gear.'

'Leave it with me,' Stax said deferentially, since Benny was the nightclub king. He paid well and expected the best. Stax carried a fat bankroll in one pocket for those who pleased him, and a gun for those who didn't.

Occasionally over the years, Benny felt the magic of his late-night world, and mid seventies he'd stumbled across the pink pound, the gay boys all dressed up and nowhere to go. He gave them somewhere, for one midweek night at first, then two. Then one entire club, and now three full-time gay places which turned over more business on a Saturday than the rest of his empire put together.

Wol and Callum saw The Prohibition Palace in all its morning-after tawdriness. Benny auditioned acts in the harsh light of day and if they could razzmatazz the empty room they were on. He liked Wol and Callum, they drank tea when the whole bar was at their disposal. He'd been in the business long enough to see many a night star fizzle out like a cigarette butt dropped in the dregs of a wine bottle.

He liked the way they set up in fifteen minutes and changed in less than ten. Enough already with hour-long prima donna shit. Time is money.

And they could both sing, their timing was good, they faked repartee with invisible hecklers and posers. They were clean and didn't think cursing meant comedy. He usually listened to a new act for five minutes, make or break. He let them run through a full half-hour, a solo, a costume change, duet, solo, costume change, duet: they were slick and sassy and Benny took off his glasses and thought of Marilyn and Hedy and Ginger and Judy and Fred and Rock and Errol and Clark.

'OK, boys,' he said, 'Get changed.'

They came and sat at the table, holdalls neatly zipped at their feet.

'I want you,' he said. 'Every Saturday to start with. Can you come up with fresh every week?'

'Yes,' Callum said, 'We will.'

'And money, boys,' Benny said, waving a cigar over his accounts, 'What do you want?'

'Make us an offer,' Wol said, thinking fifty? Seventy-five?

'A hundred,' Benny said, thinking, one-fifty if I'm pushed.

Callum looked at Wol.

'For the first three Saturdays,' Benny said. 'Then maybe fifty on top if it's good going. Cash. And your drinks.'

'One two five,' Callum said, thinking of Gerth and his whizz kid ways.

Benny took their hands.

'It's a deal,' he said. 'A nice little earner for you. You do turn up?'

'Of course,' Wol said, thinking of what he could do with sixty-two pounds fifty.

'Marc'll pay you,' Benny said. 'I deal in cash. Two-fifty in tens on the night. Can I get you anything to drink – to seal the contract?'

'It's a bit early,' Callum said.

'Too early for champagne?' Benny twinkled at them.

'Oh, it's never too early for champagne,' Callum, said, all Lauren Bacall.

'I thought,' Benny said, shambling over to the champagne refrigerator. There was one in every club, just in case the right people ever decided to swan in and make it Dreamland.

'Each,' Wol whispered. 'A hundred and twenty five each!'

'Pinch me,' Callum said.

Benny popped a cork and poured bubbles to the rim of three sparkling glasses. And they toasted and Benny talked. He said:

'Cabaret with a capital C, elegance has got the big E these days, boys, he said I have a whole alphabet for my clubs and most people don't even get to A for allure. You know what I'm saying?'

'I do, my goodness,' Callum said, 'There's no style these days.'

'No chic,' Wol said. 'What's your alphabet, Mr Hartmann?'

'Call me Benny,' he said, he loved them like sons. There was never anyone to talk to, but out of the blue, they were there and so he talked. And talked.

He pulled a folded piece of paper from his jacket and read: 'An Alphabet by Benny Hartmann. Here it is.

'A for allure, you know, a certain look that says it all, not just a low-cut dress and a skirt like a hairband. Or boys with jeans painted on so you don't have to guess. Imagination is sexier than nakedness, every time.

B – beautiful bodies, or so-so bodies in beautiful clothes. C – chic, champagne, cabaret. D – decadence, divine, not sleaze. Diamonds. Diamante. E – elegance. Education too. Smart people out to play. F – frills and frou-frou. G – grandeur. If only I could get upstairs and have split level, the staircase, boys! Made to swish down! Grandeur and good times. H – high spirits. Not hooliganism.

'I – impressive. So you walk in, and with one look, you're impressed. You've seen this place at night. Yes? J – jump for joy. K – Kisses and kings. L – love. Love should be born in my clubs. True love, do you believe in it? I do. I don't know how, but I do. You do? Don't ever stop believing, else it dies, like fairies. M – hey, I'm going on, boys. Enough?'

'Carry on,' Callum said. 'It's fascinating.'

'M,' Benny said, 'The Divine Miss – and you do her so well. But here, I've got M as magnificence, magnificence and mirage. The staircase again, when I can get the next floor. Maybe the whole building, I want glass elevators. You know?'

'How camp,' Wol said. 'Cheers.'

'Camp,' Benny said, writing on to his list. 'Uh huh. Champagne, cabaret, chic and camp. Yes. N is for never never land – you know? You step through the door and the world disappears and your wishes come true. And then O.'

'*Ô, c'est bleu*,' Callum said, dreamily.

'A fairy who knows his Rimbaud!' Benny shook his head in wonder. 'More champagne! You've cheered me up so much, you'll never know. '*Ô, c'est bleu*. Yes. And O, down here I've written orchids and organdie and oasis. P has to be prettiness and poise. Cheers! Q, well, queens and quips and the quaffing of ale. Or champagne. Or good wine. These days they drink out of cans. Oh generation witless and uncouth! as the old man said to the young on and on forever. R is romance. S is sophistication and sparkle, T is tenderness, U is unique, uplifting, V is vavavavoom! W is wit and wisdom. X is more kisses, Y is youthful spirits, even if the flesh is sagging. And Z is zest. There you have it! Benny Hartmann's alphabet!'

'You're a man of vision.' Callum said, fluttering his hands together in applause. Wol nodded.

'And then there's the alphabet of shame,' Benny said. 'You can see it here most nights. Be hoped you can bring a little of the sparkle back.'

'Put us down for A through Z,' Callum said. 'We'll do our best.'

'To Saturday,' Benny said, raising then draining his glass. They did the same and their eyes locked as they flung the glasses over their shoulders.

'To Saturday,' Benny said happily, crunching glass underfoot as he showed them into the bright noonday sun.

'Do you think he's crazy?' Callum said, standing at the bus stop.

'Definitely,' Wol said. 'Completely crazy. I like that in a person.'

'I think it's essential,' Callum said. 'Come over on Friday and we'll rehearse some more. Then your place Saturday.'

'Is Gerth coming?' Wol said.

'No, after all the coming out drama, I'm a sportswear widow this weekend,' Callum said brightly. 'Maybe next time.'

21

Step, kick, shimmy your shoulders, step kick, step kick, waggle your tush, step kick, Egyptian round the stage . . .

The spotlight satellite whirled overhead, beams sweeping the front hem of the crowd. Wol's gold-fringed frock swam in tiny rainbowed lights from the mirrored ball. Callum waited in the shadows. Here he could see all the faces tilted towards the stage, James Dean haircuts, cleft chins and kiss-me smiles; dazzling t-shirts floating in ultra violet, perfect teeth, laughing, pouting, smiling as an arm wrapped itself round shoulders. The boys were out tonight, it was Saturday sleaze and seduction.

He and Wol had lips like luscious bee-stings, courtesy of Mary Quant's Passionate Plum. They dipped their purple mouths into a tub of glitter for the act. Leichner shading gave them Hollywood cheekbones and eyelids and Callum loved the illusion of soft-focus curved flesh and eyes as big as Bambi's floating in pools of silver.

Wol wooed the mike with every movement, it was his dancing partner in a languorous half-waltz, it was a telephone receiver, its lead was the lazy swing of a cartoon lariat.

He started the set with 'Lucky Lips', vamping along the stage like a leaf in the wind, blowing kisses to the whole room. Callum joined him as the crowd clapped and whistled, tossing him a cane. They did 'Walk Down the Avenue', Judy Garland's little tramp in every move.

Wol vanished in the next round of applause and Callum called on the spirit of Bette Midler for inspiration. He called up the Boogie Woogie Bugle Boy From Company B, reminding himself not to rush: act like they love you and you love what you're doing . . . and they will and you will.

They did, they even started miming bugles for the root-a-toot-a-root-toot-toot chorus. Callum high-kicked and laughed aloud. It was crazy, such fun and getting paid for it too!

He dived into the shadows and ripped the velcro from his GI uniform as Wol Charlestoned into the spotlight, his sequinned shift and feathered headband pure Sally Bowles. Under the khaki, Callum had a black body stocking and waistcoat and while Wol warmed up with an orgiastic 'Maybe This Time', he slicked his hair back and blotted his lips to a wicked sliver of vermilion.

'Money Money Money' brought them on stage together: every queen knows *Cabaret* by heart and this was a winner. Everybody loves a winner. All the chat at the back of the room had stopped by now: people balanced on table-tops to see, and if there had been chandeliers, they'd have swung on them.

Add a chiffon flapper skirt and they finished the first set with 'You Gotta Have a Gimmick'. The front row was hypnotised: if Callum and Wol had started doing handsprings there would have been a riot as the audience followed suit. As it was, Callum could see them bumping and grinding, every caress with an edge of sleaze, all the faces turned up towards them just like when he was little and went to the pictures, when movies were big screen, filling your head and heart with dreams.

Back in the dressing room they looked at each other and shared a hug of joy.

'Are we all right?' Wol said.

'We're bloody marvellous,' Callum said. 'After a show like this, I could fly.'

'And you may have every right to, bro,' Wol said. 'I've got a great little lump of red . . .'

'Shush,' Callum said. 'Someone's at the door. Enter!'

'Here's your handbag, girls,' a barman, swaggering in

dressed in a bow tie and lurex shorts. 'Benny thinks you're marvellous, but then he always employs the best people.'

'Larry!' Callum said. 'I didn't know you worked here.'

'Oh, I'm just Lava La Bassinette, dear,' Larry said, sitting down and lighting a joint. 'You're the fucking mega-stars. I thought it was you, then someone said no, you were sure to be on a beach somewhere doing magic.'

'Who said that?'

'Mister Heartbreak, Cassandra, who else? I haven't seen her in centuries. She was barred for ages. Slewed to the tits!'

'Shit,' Callum said, 'I don't need that.'

'Oh, she's on her way out,' Larry said. 'The way she's going, dear! She'll be thrown out and barred again.'

'I hope so,' Callum said.

'I shall see to it personally,' Larry said. 'My pleasure. And I can't sit here on my tush waffing woodbines all night, nice and all. Here's your handbag, as I said, and a bottle of fizz courtesy of Benny. Watch your backs, dears, she's got a mega crush on you.'

He swanned out of the room.

'What was that?' Wol said. 'Callum, what's wrong?'

Callum lit a cigarette and his hand was shaking.

'Mister Heartbreak,' he said. 'Fuck it, Wol, he's the man who gave me my passport to Credsworth. I had hoped never to see him again. Love makes or breaks you – and he's the worst.'

'I'll give them "Eskimo",' Wol said firmly. 'And you give them sheer hell with "Pink Cadillac". Go Millie Jackson on it, she cuts through any crap that comes her way. Don't let the past take now, Cal, get yourself out of it.'

'I will,' Callum said. 'Don't worry. Mister Heartbreak may have caused seismic ripples in his time, but I'm married now and this is *my* time. Furthermore, tonight I am a star.'

'See you in five,' Wol said.

Callum looked in the mirror once he was alone. His eyes were troubled through the cabaret glitz. Cal the knacker. He shook his head, drew deep on the cigarette and looked again.

Better. A gulp of champagne, a cigarette butt ground to shreds by one pink heel – the show and he must go on.

And when he hit the stage, undulating and brash, he knew it was all right. Larry caught his eye and jerked his thumb at the door. Mister Heartbreak was history.

22

'Bumper stickers, Machen?' Hal roared. 'Setting aside the fact that I had to ask my secretary to translate for me, I don't see bumper stickers as befitting the image of The Great Outdoors. Gimmicky fiddle-faddle.'

Gerth smiled and handed a sheaf of photocopies around the table. He cleared his throat.

'This is a market survey on eye-catching devices which fix a product name in the public's mind. For example, even though there are twenty-odd firms producing vacuum cleaners, the general public asks for a Hoover. The survey tested reactions to twelve different visual bites, and I've sorted through the age ranges surveyed, cross-referred with our customer profiles and defined the most popular.'

'Let me look at that,' Hal said suspiciously. 'Jargon! I've always relied on quality. Quality sells.'

'Of course, sir,' Gerth said. 'Without quality, no amount of advertising will bring a consistent market. Our quality is unquestionable. We came in the top three in a *Which?* survey. One of the top three sportswear companies in the UK! But we've never picked that up and used it!'

'Used it,' Hal said. 'What do you mean? Any fool can subscribe to *Which?*. And it's in every public library.'

Richard Norton watched Gerth. The boy was coming on: a year ago he sat tongue-tied and over-awed at these meetings – now, without overtly challenging Hal's authority, he virtually took control. Charm, that's what he'd got, and Richard wondered idly just who Gerth was seeing. A sophisticated

older woman, he decided: Gerth worked and talked with confidence – his raw energy had developed poise and style.

'This is a rough for a flyer,' Gerth said. 'A quote from
Which?, a quote from *Ski Monthly*, a photo of Jurgen Hals,
the Olympic ski winner. That, of course, we'd have to clear.'

'This is the sort of thing that clags up gutters and pavements,' Hal spluttered.

'On recycled paper,' Gerth said. 'The green logo is very
popular these days. It makes people feel they're doing something for the environment. There are also advertisements with
features for local papers, vouchers tied in with new product
lines, badges for free distribution at sports events. I could go
on. But these are just suggestions.'

Hal frowned over the papers in front of him. His blasted
daughter called The Great Outdoors a fifties dinosaur when
she thought he wasn't listening. This could be one in the eye
for her. And Machen was canny enough to have included
projected costs.

'What else have you got up your sleeve, eh, Machen?' he
said, one eyebrow shooting upwards. 'Punch and Judy on ice?
Some talentless long-haired yobbo with a guitar on *Top of the
Pops* wearing our hiking boots?'

He laughed and the table laughed with him.

'Oh that's very good, sir,' Gerth said. 'And, setting humour
aside, all we'd need is a pop star wearing one of our jackets
and we could all retire to the sun. But I feel we must keep
true to the spirit of the firm: everything must be tied in with
sports. A tennis-playing pop-star – yes.'

23

Bagel crumbs littered the white tablecloth and a strip of smoked salmon lay across one plate. A cut-glass dish was smeared with threads of cream cheese and three yellow napkins lay crumpled like faded roses. Mac had left to go fishing and Trish and Gerth sat out the back on the patio, soaking in the Sunday morning sunshine. For all the sleepless hours behind car headlights tunnelling through the dark, Gerth felt good, showered and shaved and comfortable in Mac's burgundy sweatshirt and jogging pants – a freebie from The Great Outdoors. Barefoot in a romper suit.

'What a lovely surprise,' Trish said. 'I'm supposed to be sewing with Mac out of the way but I don't really want to.'

'Lazy Sunday,' Gerth said, blowing smoke into a sunbeam.

Trish wondered what was wrong between him and Callum.

'I'll put on fresh coffee,' she said.

Gerth looked round the garden. The trellis arches were a cloud of sweet peas, pink, lilac, burgundy, cerise. Low-growing plants cushioned the dry stone around a raised flower bed and sherbet-coloured Livingstone daisies tumbled down the wall. A blackbird splashed in the fountain, bees headbutted into curly-lipped mauve bells and one bush was alive with purple cones of flowers and Red Admiral butterflies. He wanted a garden.

Trish was back, with the coffee jug and bone china mugs decorated with playing cards – a gift from him and Callum.

'You were miles away,' she said.

'I'm always miles away,' Gerth said. 'Spend half my life behind the wheel these days.'

'It's going well, though?'

'Brilliant,' he said. 'Brilliant. Hal's talking about the Far East next year. End of next year.'

'Oo, Gerth!'

'Very exciting,' he said flatly.

'What will you do, you know – I mean, I suppose, what does Callum think about that?'

'Laughs and says he's always wanted to be a houseboy.'

'Would he go with you?'

'Well, he couldn't. It's not like we're married.'

Trish put her hand on his arm.

'It must be hard,' she said.

He looked straight at her.

'You've no idea.'

'Try me.'

'What, can I just talk to you, it's just so – I dunno. I don't want advice, Trish, just to talk to someone – and know it won't go further.'

He'd been about to say 'someone normal' and she knew it.

'Of course you can,' she said. 'I'll just get my sewing.'

'Like, it's all over the place,' Gerth said, frowning. 'I mean I am. It's been, what, nearly three years with Callum and it's wonderful. I do love him. He loves me. We've got you two. Rixie was the only real prat when I told him, but that seems light years ago. But then there's life as well. Like, mine is so different from his. Work, I mean. Like I had to borrow you for the Christmas do and then there were eyebrows raised, nothing said, in case I was cheating on Mac. Callum is so different. I loved it at first, it was a kick being with him, Tinkerbelle and Peter Pan and home sweet home. Even if the council keeps threatening to knock it down. And then Mr Machen, sir, executive, for work. I loved being in the office, you know, or at a conference and knowing I was going home to a fairy grotto where Tinkerbelle would walk the aches out of my back and fuss round me. Mr and Mrs. I felt like – you know, thumbing my nose at it all?'

'I know,' Trish said, 'sometimes when Mac and me used to

smoke dope and sit around with nothing on all evening and then I'm back in the office the next day, all navy blue skirt and sensible blouse. It's fun. Makes you feel wicked and exciting.'

'Well, you understand. Only now it's big league: I'm promoted and it's more than just a job.'

'It always was with you.'

'Was it? I suppose. Just I feel so great being there, I mean, Gerth Machen off a council estate in a suit and tie and in an office with my name on the door. This year's company car! None of the lads I went to school with did that. None of my family ever did that. My mum would have been so proud. And then there's Callum and . . .'

'You could lose it all.'

'No,' Gerth said, 'not that. Just – he's from some posh family as far as I know. His dad was a doctor and his mam was a headmistress and he doesn't give a stuff for it. His lot are at the top of the ladder and here's me crowing cuz I'm getting half-way up and he doesn't even want to put his foot on the first rung. Oh shit, that's not it either.'

'Just talk,' Trish said. 'I'm getting the idea.'

'Right,' Gerth said, leaning forwards. 'It sounds daft, but it's like, what's my life about. I love Callum. I love my job. I thought of jacking it in, the job, like, and just odd-jobbing and then there'd be no need to hide. I could wear me earring all the time sort of thing. But then why should I throw away The Great Outdoors?'

'Is it – like – have you changed? And Callum hasn't? I mean, I think he's amazing. He's loosened you up so much.'

'He is amazing. It's when you get loosened up, Trish, you know, like you and Mac getting stoned and naked, well, imagine that was all the time when you weren't working, well, every day when you put on your suit for work; it gets harder and harder to knot your tie. I mean, Callum never has to hide or pretend. He's always relaxed, he's always him wherever he is.'

'And you're not.'

'Well, I am when I'm there,' Gerth said. 'See me at this conference this weekend, I was fucking marvellous. Hal's invited me for a weekend at his family home. "Bring your young lady" – if he knew he'd go apeshit. He wants me to do a language course, he's got big plans for me. I'm the golden boy, Trish. Then when I'm back with Callum, I'm the husband and I love it. But it means like – shedding skins – I take off my suit and I'm his. I put it back on and I belong to Hal. I'm rambling.'

'Is it a bit like,' Trish closed her eyes, 'with the job you know where you're going. You can hack it for dinner dances with me or someone. But where you're going with the job you've either got to be a bachelor married to his work and that means, like, denying Callum? Or you've got to jack it all in and deny it's what you want to do and be with Callum.'

'It is,' Gerth said. 'I mean, I was thinking, even if we got a proper house and Callum wore proper clothes, we can never be a proper couple. And he'd never do it anyway and why should he? So it's give up my job or give up my marriage or carry on being schizo. Or there's another choice.'

Trish looked at him. She'd never heard him say so much since he first told her about Callum.

'Yeah,' he said, 'I could come out at work and watch the shit hit the fan and me freeze on the promotion ladder and get eased towards redundancy and not a thing I could do about it. I've seen the way Hal works. That fella in Cardiff, the one who was fiddling, that's the way he went and afterwards there was rumours about him running off to Rio with a boyfriend. I had to listen to it and put my tuppenny worth about some of my best friends being gay, you know, all objective and watered down. And they took the piss, friendly like. I still have a Jack the Lad reputation.'

'Oh Gerth,' Trish said. 'Oh, Gerth.'

'It's bloody awful,' he said, lighting a cigarette.

'Did you ever think you and Callum would last?' Trish said, pinning ribbon to a peachy satin fabric.

'To be honest, no,' Gerth said. 'Then it was weeks, then

months, then one day he said, well, Gerth, what shall we do for our anniversary? You know that way he has of talking, all severe and his eyes laughing at you.'

'What did you do? I remember the second anniversary party. I was Snow White.'

'And Callum was the Wicked Queen,' Gerth laughed. 'No, for the first one, I booked us into the best hotel I could find, up near the Border. Suits of armour and carpet you could swim through. We had a suite with a four-poster. It was magic.'

'And did anyone raise an eyebrow.'

'No,' Gerth said. 'Callum said they wouldn't, he said the extremely wealthy are allowed their eccentricities. His family's dead posh, so he should know. We acted like it was all natural, we spent a frigging fortune. Callum loved it. So did I.'

'Maybe that's what you need,' Trish said. 'Another honeymoon. There's nothing like it. Me and Mac have them all the time.'

'Mm,' Gerth said.

'You can get too domestic,' Trish said. 'You've got to plan surprises after a while. When you're first together, surprises happen all the time. Just waking up together is a thrill. Then you have to plan treats and different things, otherwise there's no magic.'

'Wor hoose is full of magic, man,' Gerth said, broad Geordie. 'Ah cannot move for pyramids and pendulums, pet. Our lass is worse than them three wifes oot of Macbeth. Ah nivver knaa what she's ganna gie us for me bait, like. Bio energetic salad, she says, and Ah say, aye pet, gan canny wi' they mung beans, Ah've a meetin' at work the day.'

Trish giggled.

'You're quite a shock for Callum too,' she said.

'Me?'

'You. Mr Normal. Nine to five and weekends too. Suits! It's a culture shock for him.'

'I'd never thought of that,' Gerth said. 'Where do you and Mac go for these honeymoons? The nicest place.'

'I've got some brochures,' Trish said. 'Hang on, I'll get them.'

Gerth flicked through country cottages and cut-price breakaway weekends. Give Callum a choice and he'd head for hills or the sea or a forest.

'Oh, these pearls are fiddly,' Trish said. 'I wish you could use glue.'

'What are you making? Callum's been doing cabaret frocks for the last few weeks. You sit down in our house and your arse gets covered with sequins these days.'

'These are bridesmaids' dresses for my sister,' Trish said. 'She's getting married next month and I was daft enough to volunteer.'

A shadow of melancholy drifted over Gerth's eyes. Proper married. He'd like that. Ah well.

'Can I use your phone?' he said.

'Course you can. And you'd better find the offie if you want any more wine before tonight.'

Gerth jammed the phone between his ear and shoulder and spread out the brochure and his diary and his credit card and dialled himself an instant honeymoon. Just like that.

24

Callum was quite relieved when Gerth mentioned the month's language crash course. This, their third year together, had been more hectic than he liked. There had been little time for dreaming and wandering, what with domesticity – and the surprising success of Ms Cogan and the Divine Miss M.

A month without Gerth sounded quite pleasant. Time to get grounded again, get a balance, re-establish his inner calm.

Oh dear. He could tell that Gerth was less than pleased by his reaction.

'I can be away for longer, if you like!'

'It isn't that,' he said. 'Silly Gerthling. I've got used to you going away every other weekend, right from the start I've handled that. It's show biz, my darling. I never thought we'd get anywhere much with it and now we have – well, it's a pressure. You are superb under pressure, you thrive on it. I do not.'

Gerth scowled. He'd got a thousand things to say to soothe Callum and Callum didn't need soothing and he was cross.

Callum did need soothing, as it happened. He needed Gerth to say, hey, you're doing fine, he needed Gerth to indicate that he would rather stay with him than go on the course, not Gerth's eyes begging only to be allowed to go without a drama.

For a moment he wondered about sulking, which would make Gerth reassure him. But he didn't want to sulk, he wanted peace. He didn't want to be bombarded with details of Gerth's career and how necessary this course was. Neither did he want to rush through yet another Saturday leading up to a glitzy night with Benny Hartmann: he was sick of the regularity of it. And Gerth might decide to row, not comfort, and he simply couldn't be bothered with it.

Good God, he was feeling very Garbo today, very much wanting to be alone. No Gerth. No Wol, even.

'It couldn't have come at a better time,' he said. 'I think I need my own company for a while, Gerth. You're not to worry.'

Gerth was infuriated, robbed of the chance to be masterful and reassuring, he was going away for a month for chrissakes and Callum looked almost pleased. He wondered about starting a jealous inquisition, but then thought, why bother?

'Anyway,' he said, 'it's not till next week, Cal. And I've got a surprise for you.'

'Mm?'

'I've booked us a honeymoon,' Gerth said, his voice pleading that Callum should be pleased, delighted even.

Shit, Callum thought, another hotel where I have to act . . .

'Where?' he said.

'We don't have to go,' Gerth said, stung by his indifference.

Callum sighed.

'Oh to be a woman,' he said. 'I could then be pre-menstrual or post-menstrual or inter-menstrual. Oh for the seasons of dodgy hormones racing through my blood and dictating my moods! I don't know why, Gerth, I just feel incredibly flat. And now I feel like a bitch because you want me to be all thrilled and I'm just thinking, help, packing, help, acting in front of strangers. I think I'm tired.'

'Oh, it's an off day,' Gerth said, back-pedalling from fury to care. 'I get them too, you know, usually when I come home on days like that; you're all bouncy and I could clag you.'

'Are those the match of the day video and lager evenings?'

'Yes,' Gerth said. 'I feel like – piss off, world. Piss off job, piss off Callum, piss off everything.'

'I heard a song once,' Callum said. 'Fuck off Friday. I'm having a fuck off Wednesday, Gerth, can you bear me?'

Gerth smiled at him.

'Course I can,' he said. 'You bear with me, as well. I'll see you later.'

He kissed Callum and went off to work, wanting to snap his fingers – done it! – he was free to go on the language course, they were off on a honeymoon and the break would do them both good. He drove to work, feeling masterful.

'Extraordinary,' Callum said to Wol over the phone. 'Neither one of us said "I'll miss you", or "I don't want you to go", or "I don't want to go, but . . ." Should I be contacting Relate?'

Wol tried to keep the elation from his voice.

'No,' he said. 'But you have been Siamese twins for three years, Callum, and you are so very different. Sometimes people need a space to grow. They come back together again and it's wonderful – both have got new things to share.'

'Do you think?'

'Yes,' Wol said, delighted that Callum would be Callum again for a whole month, like he had been before Gerth, like he was only when Gerth wasn't there these days.

'Where's your honeymoon?' he asked, feeling disloyal.

'It's a surprise,' Callum said. 'I hope I don't have to fake that it's marvellous, but I just don't think I could handle a hotel again. It would be like after the show with Benny's bunch for a whole weekend and no you there to dilute it. But I expect I'll love it when I get there. Gerth's even said he'll pack, all I have to do is be ready by five-thirty on Friday. And it can't be far, because we're whizzing back for Saturday night, I didn't even have to remind him about the show. He is good.'

'Yeah,' Wol said. 'He is. See you Saturday.'

25

Purple hills and clouds that ran together, soft autumn greens broken with blazes of bronze and scarlet; they were driving due west. The road curved through fields of sheep and cows lurching home for the night. Callum felt good for the first time in days the minute the road cleared the last red-brick streets and tatty video shops; the raggy skirts of the city clung to the ground and then vanished in the rear-view mirror.

They had only been driving half an hour when Gerth said: 'This is it.'

He turned the car on to a wide track and the tyres crunched stone chippings. They went under an arch of tree branches and all the trunks were grey-green; birds twittered; the track was pitted with sloshy puddles. It was just the sort of place Callum would have chosen on his random drives, but he waited for the inevitable vista of beautiful country home turned grand hotel. There would be lawns hoovered like a golf course. A row of expensive cars parked out front. A drawing room full of cricket trophies and men in expensive suits with women in designer clothes, talking and listening more intently than husbands and wives ever bother to. He and Gerth would raise eyebrows and he'd act nonchalant, *café au lait* camp. He braced himself.

'Seventeen,' Gerth said, turning at a wooden sign carved with the number and an arrow.

The track narrowed and bushes brushed the car's metal flanks. Gerth flicked on the sidelights and Callum saw a rabbit dart off the path.

'This is it,' Gerth said. He pushed a button and windows vanished, admitting only the sounds of the night now that the engine was silent.

They were parked outside a wooden cabin in a clearing. It could have been hundreds of years ago in Merrie Englande, or on the new continent of America. Callum opened the car door and stepped outside. Overhead a half-moon rode in the darkening sky and the stars were just beginning to be clear. Underfoot, leaves and bark. He raised his head, eyes closed and breathed in the smell of it all. Leaves, berries, leaf mould, running water.

Magic.

And Gerth was standing, awkward as when they'd first kissed, shy as a child with his first egg-box creation from the nursery, needing to know that his mum thinks he's simply the best.

Callum raised his arms to the sky and thanked all of nature.

'I love it,' he said softly.

And he loved the way Gerth unlocked the door with a flourish and swept him up in his arms to cross the threshold. The cabin was stripped pine inside, stripped pine and chequered curtains, a vase of wild ferns and flowers on the table, a pyramid of logs beside the fireplace.

'Man make fire,' Gerth said, setting him down on the floor and kissing him.

Callum went into the bedroom. A four-poster bed, a lavish bedcover and tie-back floor-length curtains in rosy paisley. The window gave a view of the valley at the edge of the woods. He smiled dreamily. And then there was the bathroom, with a bath big enough for two sunk into the floor. Better still, this bath had a dozen jets: he imagined them sitting in the foam, hot water massaging every pore. Over the bath were three chrome showerheads as big as soup plates: they could create their own tropical waterfall pool here.

'Oh, Gerth,' he said, leaning on the doorpost, 'it's magic.'

'You like it?' Gerth grinned as the fire took hold. 'You really like it?'

'You know I do,' Callum said. 'Do you?'

'I could handle living wild, like,' Gerth said. 'Especially when you've got all this.'

'Grizzly Adams meets The Hilton,' Callum said. 'This is the sort of place I want when I grow up. I've always wanted it, even a cave would do, I don't want to grow old in a city.'

Gerth had a clear picture of his old age. A stone-built mansion with a sweep of a drive, a magnificent Rolls Royce parked by stables . . . he couldn't quite see Callum there, but the firelight drew them together in a golden glow and his mind wheeled to the back of the house, where Callum would sit in a rose garden, looking up at him and smiling.

'I could never see you in a cave,' Callum said. 'But something like this, not too big, I could go for that! How clever of you to find it.'

'We've got Trish to thank,' Gerth said. 'She gave me all these brochures, you know, romantic weekends all over the place. I knew this would suit you.'

'It suits you too,' Callum said, and once again Gerth saw and heard that intangible quality in Callum that took his breath away. He was someone who had more – height? strength? – when he was naked, and when he was out in the wilds, he drew a dignity into his very being that vanished in the concrete and brick of a city. His voice was lower, slower; he relaxed and the fluttering camp was stilled.

'You're a chameleon,' Gerth said, watching him.

'Yes? Yes.'

'Well, you look like you belong here,' Gerth said. 'As if you've invited me into your home, like. You look like you've been here for ever. And then you look the part at The Prohib-ition Palace. Two minutes in there and you'd think the place was built for you. How d'you do it?'

Callum squatted on the floor beside him.

'I take myself with me wherever I go,' he sang softly. 'But I couldn't live in the PP, that's acting. Here I could live. Only I bet it costs the earth. Amazing how getting back to nature costs so much these days. Self-sufficiency if you can buy your own acres . . . but I'm not getting into that. I want to enjoy this lovely bit of Now you've found for us.'

26

Callum decided to use the month of Gerth's absence for all the things that had been put on ice since they'd been together. On ice, or relegated to widow's weekends.

Mainly he felt out of touch with nature, the earth, the seasons and the stars. Nature calls, nay screams, he mocked, driving out of town. Pre-Gerth, his rosy-tinted Mr and Mrs Scenario hadn't involved giving up any of himself, but it had happened. Never consciously, more an erosion as subtle as the way the tides alter a shoreline. One year there's a headland spiked with sea-grass, and someone builds a chalet there. Next year, the chalet is bonfire debris, the grasses are drowned and the sand has slipped away. And the tides roll on, heaping stolen sand up somewhere else, miles away.

Their honeymoon in the woods had been magic, through and through. There was a sexual intensity like when they'd first been together. Callum found himself cursing like a whore, howling like a she-wolf, absurdly beating his chest, Tarzan on acid. There was an edge of danger in power and submission, and Gerth loved it, he loved it. Gerth reached into the utterly vulnerable soft guts of him, and with a twist could disembowel him, or with complete tenderness, fly him to the seven rings of Saturn, so his head held all of the sky.

Whether locked in passion, or linked like a Chinese puzzle in sleep, or waking before consciousness crept in, their bodies had no qualms or quarrels.

On a desert island together, Callum thought, we are fine.

But then comes the day-to-day business of what we've chosen to do in our lives.

With Gerth away, he let himself think deeper.

'I want a baby,' he said out loud at a traffic light, 'a baby to show this lovely world. A baby to bring up with love, a baby whose being will simply delight me – and Gerth. No expectations, no pressures. Just love.'

He drove to a river and sat on the pebbled shore one afternoon. A baby. The last jigsaw piece in his dream.

'I wonder,' he said to the flowing water, 'are my choices so hard for him to live with, share, enjoy? What do *I* do which tells me I am me? I eat – and we do that together. I make magic – and we could do that together as well. I need to spend a lot of time out of doors, out of the city. He's welcome. I am one half of a surprisingly successful drag act and Gerth gives every sign of being pleased and proud of me. I live where I am, I love this part of the world, I'm happy to travel, but this feels like home. But wherever he is, I'll roll up my tent and be there with him, for he is home. I want our baby and I'll do all the shitty nappies and night-time feeds; all he has to do is be a daddy. As much or as little as he pleases. I have my friends and their lives cross mine and he's more than welcome, for my friends are moondust and marvellous. But what about him?'

He fell silent as his busy mind listed all he knew of Gerth's life.

He wants to be successful and rich and he says he wants to share it with me.

He works in a totally heterosexual environment where *we* have no place.

He wants the approval of people who can never approve of our love. He's got it, while the shutters are closed on me, but *we* will never have that sort of approval, never in a month of Sundays.

He's never said much about babies.

'I am a ball and chain to him,' Callum said out loud. 'And I love him and he loves me.'

The last three words hung in a web of mist on the shifting surface of the autumn river.

'Should I start looking for a daisy to shred?' he asked the rippling water. 'Are those words you can't – won't – take? Isn't it true?'

Not true enough . . . he heard the phrase inside his head and shivered.

'I would like it to be true,' he said, feeling very small against the tree roots weaving at his back, above his head.

Since Gerth was not there, he found he could be a creature of the night again. He had seldom been out past midnight in the last three years, where before, there were few nights spent sleeping, and fewer spent indoors. Moonlight bathed him and fed him and taught him. It always happened at night, revelation, sights that spoke to his spirit.

Sure, in the daytime, he could see – oh look at that field of poppies, those buttercups, the scarlet pimpernel on the rusty earth track, the speedwell blue as the heavens above.

Moonlight and silver-etched grasses, shadows as solid as great drops of black water. Moonlight allows only black, silver and grey. When he left the river it was well past moonrise, and as he drove – nowhere in particular, he wished for magic. Magic always, under moonlight, every day, magic to wrap him close to Gerth. Sitting by the river had brought him tears, the terror that Gerth might one day go and never come back, and would a baby make that better? And if it would, was it fair? Or was a baby just another crazy dream?

The road was silver as a river in bright sunlight. There is no word to rhyme with silver, Callum thought. Grass verges were glass in the moonlight, hedges blocks of tar topped with diamonds. Then suddenly – a hare leapt from the glass and stood on her indescribably elegant back legs, looking at the car headlights. Callum thought it was daft when people said animals were curious or hypnotised; putting human reactions on to animals is silly: my cat loves me, she's so affectionate. I got news for you, presh, Callum had said it often, your cat is simply unable to use a can opener, and miaowing cutely at you is easier than running round all night chasing mice.

The hare stood there, probably thinking, 'What's that? It wasn't there before.'

No matter what she was thinking, she was simply beautiful.

Then she leapt in slow motion across the road, back again, in elastic zigzag flight.

He killed the headlights and idled behind her, out of gear. She flew along the silver river road and there was no fear in her flight; she was delighted with herself and sure of every move. Then she stopped, one paw raised, her ears decoding the darkness. He depressed the footbrake and watched her.

He wanted to be out there with her, not sitting in this bubble of glass and metal. Switching off the engine would startle her: he and his car were a big creature she'd come across moving, growling; and growl they must while she was there, to keep her there. And opening the door was certain to send her back to the tarry hedgerow. He opened the car window slow as a cat stalking. Chill scents of night fingered his face, the hedgerow rustled, he sensed the lean heartbeat of the hare.

> *when the hare dances*
> *it enchances*
> *all your life and dreams*
> *if by moonlight*
> *and it's bright*
> *then nothing is as it seems*

She turned as he watched her, and stared towards the car, her eyes a hologram of rainbows in the moonlight. She paused, dropped her front paw and zigzagged straight at him then took off. He saw her pale fawn belly stretched taut above the windscreen and jerked his head round. She landed behind the car then danced away down the road, back towards the river.

He got out of the car and sat on the grass.

All your life and dreams . . .?

'Life and a lover?' he mocked himself gently. 'Mummy and daddy and baby makes three – that'll do for me!'

Part three

....

Dazeland

27

Later that week, Callum took Wol to see the hideaway chalet in the woods, but the owners descended on Callum's smartie-coloured car and ordered them to leave. It was Private Property, couldn't they read. In mandarin Chinese, Wol told them that their great-grandmothers must have copulated with bullfrogs, and their great-great-grandfathers had navels filled with the shit of diseased yaks.

'Clear orff!' the owners brandished a mobile phone.

'May the heavens rain woodworm on your endeavours,' Wol added, bowing, 'and may the rivers of the world rise below your property.'

They then both cleared orff, as requested, bloody foreign hippies.

'So much for back to nature,' Callum said. 'Did I tell you about the hare?'

'It enchances all your life and dreams,' Wol said. 'Hold that next to your heart. And where now, maestro?'

They drove in the dusk to a wild wood on the banks of the Coquet. As they padded through the bracken, both stopped. A tawny owl sat on the ground ahead of them, preening. When every feather lay combed and sleek, she looked at them and took off over the river. Her wings spread wide and beat slowly.

'We're wise to be here,' Callum said. 'And just as she – or he – is seeking food, so are we. My spirit is ravenous and restless. I crave wisdom and peace.'

Wol hugged him. A shadow of the old Callum was in his voice and growing stronger by the minute.

They sat by a rocky ledge, dreaming into the river. Callum slept after a while and Wol swam, then sat silent until he was dry. He dressed and woke Callum.

Just like always – before Gerth – they wondered about tomorrow on the way home. The hills? The sea? A market, a boat-trip? Where to go and what to do: the day was newly born and full of promise. Callum felt wonderfully tired when he finally went to bed, ignoring the flashing light on the ansaphone, turning the ringing tone off, taking the batteries from the doorbell. He got up again and hauled the television into an alcove, unplugged it and covered it with a shawl.

In the morning, the room looked wonderful and he shifted things round the way they'd been before the TV demanded its fixed two cubic feet. Sorry, Gerth, he thought to himself, but I married you, not a cathode ray tube.

The ansaphone told him that Gerth loved and missed him and he smiled. He toyed with the idea of ringing Gerth's hotel and leaving a loving message from his wife. What would Gerth do if he got the message while surrounded by his business peers? Pass it off as a joke? Probably. But he was a bad actor and if Big Daddy Hal was there, he'd read his face with those shrewd eyes, blue and bloodshot under tufty silver eyebrows – *you make him sound like a dyspeptic giant hamster, Gerth!*

The phone rang.

'Hello?'

'Callum? It's Bastian. Mum's been hinting that I should ring, since we haven't heard from you for a hundred years. Waited till she was safely shopping, you know how she talks and I have to repeat it to you, most irritating.'

'Bastian,' Callum said. 'Is everything all right?'

'Yes. That's what I'm supposed to ask you.'

'Yes, then. Very.' Callum twisted the phone wire round his hand.

'Hum,' said his brother. 'You'll have to give me a bit more than that; mum's been fretting about how she never sees you.'

'I only upset things if I visit,' Callum said. 'I never mean to, but – well, you know.'

'I do,' his brother said. 'I'm the one who got married and I still get fretted over. You can talk to me, you know.'

'Oh, brother! Right,' Callum said. 'I'm touched that you called. My big brother! My hero! Um. I'm working now – it's a drag act, but you can tell mum it's theatre. She won't approve, but at least she won't worry that I'm starving.'

'Oh, enjoy your youth,' his brother said surprisingly. 'You're bloody lucky to still have one at your age. But then so am I. It must be genetic.'

'A youth?' Callum giggled. 'I've got a youth as well, Bastian. Gerth. I'm in love, but Mother won't want to know about that.'

'Is he nice? Solvent? Sober?'

'Yes to all three. He's a rising executive, Bastian, very un-me. But it's been just over three years now.'

'Must be good,' Bastian said. 'You were never one to compromise.'

'If there were a church to bless us,' Callum said, 'we would be married.'

'Hum,' his brother said. 'Anything else I can say to mum? Filtered through elder-brotherly discretion?'

'Job,' Callum said. 'Say something like I'm happy in my personal life. Fulfilled. A happy chappy. You know. How's dad?'

'Wedded to the garden as usual. He's developing roses with a built-in resistance to greenfly. Had you heard?'

'Last time it was crossing honeysuckle with Russian vine,' Callum said dryly. 'Sweet scent and rocketing growth. How did that go?'

'I missed that one,' Bastian laughed. 'I was hill sculpting in Brazil for a while and then there was Expo, so maybe that was then.'

'How's Rosemay? And the children?'

'Marvellous,' Bastian said, his first hint of unguarded warmth in the conversation. 'I look at them with complete astonishment. They're so self-assured. They know what they want to do. Gemma's going on the stage; I'm her chauffeur to every dance and drama class in Surrey. Tristan's going to be a racing driver. Little bugger wrote off the mini last year.'

'How old are they now, Bastian – I thought they were babies.' Callum wrapped the phone wire tighter.

'Gemma's fourteen and Tris is twelve,' his brother said. 'Rosemay went mad about the mini, I said, sod it, at least he's alive. She wanted to ban him from driving, but you see, on private land – anyway, he's rebuilding it. I reckon that'll teach him to know a car, respect it – do you think?'

'My man is a car fanatic,' Callum said.

'Well, you're always welcome here,' Bastian said. 'That'd cheer up mum and I could be the buffer, the older brother buffer. Rosemay often asks about you.'

Callum knew he meant and didn't mean it. He wondered about taking Gerth to stay there.

'Thank you,' he said. 'We'll see. I mean it.'

'Well,' Bastian said briskly, 'I can say something to mum anyway. I think she thinks she'll see you dead in the papers one day and feel guilty.'

'Oh, I won't die for a long time yet,' Callum said. 'And I doubt that I'll ever be newsworthy.'

'Well, keep in touch,' Bastian said. 'And if you need anything, for heaven's sake say so. Midas is doing very well, you know.'

Do I need to be told, thought Callum waspishly.

Midas was Bastian's brain child, a landscape gardening empire which guaranteed gardens to fit your dreams and pretensions. He was seriously expensive and phenomenally successful. He listened to grandiose plans and wishes and translated them into vistas of incredible elegance and subtlety. Princes, rajahs, film-stars, royalty, recluses: the Midas touch brought Eden to their feet.

'Midas!' Callum said. 'I remember you naming it, Bastian,

just laughing and saying why not? That's our dad in both of us. I must come and see them. And you and your lot.'

'He's all right, the old man,' Bastian said. 'And mum just worries. I can understand that better, with Tris and Gemma. But you could do a weekend here, you know, you and your chap and mum and dad. Dilute it, God knows there's room enough here for no-one to bump into anyone else unless they want to.'

'Maybe,' Callum said, plans forming in his mind. 'What about yes? Would you be horrified if I said yes? Say – the weekend after next? Me and my friend Wol and maybe my chap Gerth? If he's not working?'

'Why not?' Bastian said. 'I needn't say you're coming, just in case . . .'

'I'm awful at turning up, aren't I?' Callum said. 'But I think I just might. I've got a car these days.'

'A car? You? Right,' Bastian said. 'Let's do it.'

'Why not?'

They hung up. Callum felt twitchy. He always needed a heavy dose of his own kind when his family had been in touch.

'Rosemay,' Bastian said, 'would you mind if . . .?'

'Menus,' Rosemay said, 'and Callum and his friends can camp out in the cottage. Most suitable. And that's your fraternal duty done.'

Bastian smiled and kissed her and wondered why the gods smiled on him.

28

Another benefit of Gerth's absence was that Callum's friends called round more. He decided to celebrate with a tea-party, sandwiches and cakes and doilies and party hats. A very merry un-birthday! That would wash Bastian right away, as well. Hannah came first, brushing at her latest hairstyle, a crimson mop with indigo lines shining through from her scalp.

'The Picasso of the shears!' Callum said.

'I frigging wish,' Hannah said. 'I'll get arthritis in me fingers from wrapping curlers in Wallsend, but all them salons in town, well, I've been there and asked, and me voice doesn't fit. Ye knaa, reet geordie an' all. "Aow, naow, thenk you, we don't have any vacancies at present." Southerners, man, I hate them!'

'Whoops,' Callum said. 'I do apologise.'

'Not you, you daft queen,' she said. 'You're not from this frigging planet, Callum, let alone the south of bastard England.'

'Actually,' Callum said, 'I had proof of my roots the other day. My big brother did the checking-on-me phone call. He rings every year or so to make sure I'm not dead. I'm going down to see him in a couple of weeks. Why don't you come too? Bastian's the perfect host.'

'Bastian?' Hannah groaned. 'I suppose you got off light with Callum. That's Sebastian, I suppose?'

'I suppose. He's fifteen years older than me. My parents must have had a mad moment; I was always a surprise to them. My mother is convinced that my "condition" is due to being a mid-life baby. I couldn't say Sebastian, and he hates Seb. I was a bit of a let-down – still am, in their world!'

'Well, you're looking good enough to me, Houston,' Hannah drawled, mid-Atlantic. 'The hubby's away – how long for?'

'A month,' Callum said. 'Initially.'

Hannah raised her eyebrows. She couldn't stand Gerth, but with her record, what could she say?

'Meaning?'

'I have a feeling that his promotion is going to take him abroad,' Callum said. 'I did a tarot when he left – for him, you know. Definitely travel, lots of it and no sure sign of me.'

'What's his card?'

'That's another thing. He was always the Prince of Cups. Only he seems to be moving towards the lofty loneliness of The Emperor.'

'And you're The Fool?' Too bloody wise for mini-Hitler Gerth, thought Hannah.

'Always, Hannah. Me and my little dog and my spotty hanky, skippetty hop around the world with butterflies at my heels.'

'Do you think everything's all right?' Callum asked her. 'Wol's coming, and Trish. She's a friend of Gerth's, really. She was the first person he told about me. We hit it off straight away – she's nice. And pregnant.'

'Don't give me that hippy dippy shite about welcoming every child that's born,' Hannah said, lighting a cigarette.

She looked at the table and snorted.

'Could you not have fitted in a few more doilies?'

'Women!' Callum said. 'They have no idea!'

'And there's the doorbell,' Hannah said. 'You can do my cards later; I'll be staying for the cocktails after tea bit. Mark's picking the bairns up and I said I'd be late.'

'He is useful,' Callum called over his shoulder. 'A very handy man!'

'Aye,' Hannah said. 'But he's gotten ower fond of football and sleeping for my liking.'

'Trish!' Callum said. 'Meet Hannah, the hairdresser from Hell. Or heaven, depending on her mood. Now, how would you like to sit?'

'Hello,' Trish said. 'Oh, cushions, Callum. Lots of them.'

She arranged herself carefully.

'The bump,' she said. 'Requires t.l.c.'

'Aye,' Hannah said, smiling at the memory. 'You think, oh, I'll just go upstairs. I'll just get on the escalator. I'll just catch a bus. And then you have to think, how? Do these people know I'm walking and sitting for two? It's like having a permanent low-slung rucksack on backwards.'

'You've got a baby?' Trish said.

'Three of the buggers,' Hannah said. 'Eight, seven and three and a half. And that's me lot.'

'Don't listen to her,' Callum said. 'She's enough to drive Victoria Gillick to the nearest branch of Marie Stopes.'

'Am I shite! I'm just not a rosy-tinted poof, man. I wouldn't swap me bairns for the world, I just know what it's like, man.'

'Are you all rosy tinted, Callum?' Trish asked.

'Ever so,' he said. 'Life in general, babies in particular.'

'It's womb envy,' Hannah snorted. 'What you can never have you want.'

'Do you really like babies?' Trish said, amazed.

'Don't sound so horrified!' Callum said. 'I love babies. Just me and my hubby have certain biological malfunctions standing in our way.'

'No,' Trish said. 'Sorry. I never thought, that's all.'

'Oh yes,' he said seriously. 'I now have almost everything I wanted. A husband, a flat, and a job that pays me for doing something I enjoy. A baby would be wonderful. I think whatever sex you are or aren't, there are those of us who would like to be mothers. Fathers. Parents. Whatever.'

'What about Gerth?' Trish said.

'Yeah,' Hannah said. 'What does your other 'alf reckon to breeding, moi dear? Can't see him with his Armani cuffs dipped in Milton.'

'Oh, Hannah!' Callum said. 'You can't stand him, can you?'

'As long as he's good to you,' Hannah said. 'You've borne with me through Dopey Davy, Handy Harry and Robert the plonkie. To name but a few.'

'Hannah is a true romantic,' Callum said to Trish. 'Romance has to be true or they're out on their arses.'

'That's only since Davy,' Hannah said. 'I tried six years with that bastard. Six years of his nervous stomach, his traumatised spine, weak chest, inflamed ears, sensitive throat: I was a walking pigging medical dictionary with Davy. You know what finished me, Trish?'

'Tell me,' Trish laughed.

'Well, idiot chops, me, I sort out all his defective parts. I'm cooking vegan and sleeping on planks to suit him. There's ionisers in every room. I don't smoke in the house. We shop at the rip-off Body Shop. I'm just sitting back one day on the balcony with me fag, thinking, ah, he's all better now. Now I can start living and concentrating on the bairns. My lass thinks all visitors have a stethoscope and a little black bag. And Dopey Davy the bugger – walks in wreathed in smiles because he's found a bastard dentist who's told him his roots are very unusual. He'll have to have his jaw broken to put them right. I says to him, right, Davy, I'll break your frigging jaw here and now, if you're not packed and out in ten minutes. I called him a taxi to take him home to his mam. After that, I thought, never again. Six years with happy face! I'll never put up with shite for more than six minutes now.'

Trish laughed helplessly.

'Tea?' Callum offered. 'And that'll be Wol.'

'Hannah! Trish!' Wol said, 'Isn't this nice? Have you heard about our visit to the ancestral home?'

'I think we should get a chara,' Callum said. 'All of us and your bairns as well, Hannah. I'd love to see my mum's face! And my brother's!'

'That's bairns for you,' Hannah said. 'Vicious!'

29

The weekend at Bastian's estate filled Gerth with incoherent longings and stuttering frustration.

Bastian was to-the-manor-born suave, delighting in his family, delighting in his work like a brilliant child who's just discovered how to whizz through the secret levels of an electronic race 'n rescue game. He owned a Porsche Carrera, a real De Lorean and two Rolls-Royces – a Corniche and a Silver Shadow. His other cars, he said lightly, were scattered all over the world: it was so handy. He gave Gerth what he jestingly called a guided tour, and they lingered in his huge offices, Bastian flipping up business programmes on the computer screens, amused at Gerth's genuine enthusiasm. He splashed malt whisky into crystal glasses and smoked slim grey cigarettes from a pirate's chest on his desk. Gerth was hypnotised. Midas was a hi-tech monorail of an operation, flying high on inspiration: it made The Great Outdoors feel as old-fashioned as wax tapers and ancient clerks dipping quills into ink-pots in fusty Dickensian chambers.

'The fax machine,' Bastian roared with laughter. 'Magic! Internet – I helped design it. And this 3D videophone, Gerth. It's all toys! Look – let's take a look at Rio . . .'

Gerth's mind went into overdrive.

He would work late at the office, he'd turn his flat into a powerhouse, devising a package that would knock Hal's socks off and blow TGO – and himself – into the twenty-first century.

Bastian had everything Gerth wanted. Before this day his

ambitions had been huge, but unfocused. Money, good suits, fast cars. This year, next year, sometime: now Bastian had given him a blueprint.

And he was amazed by it all.

But mostly by Callum. How could he live as he did when his family lived as they did? How could he say he was happy in Garstone Towers when his brother had a manor house, a lake, acres of gardens, a garage any oil sheik would be proud of?

'Wouldn't you fancy a place like this?' he asked lightly: Callum mustn't know how important the question was.

'God, no!' Callum giggled. 'I'd never find anything. I'd have to change bedrooms every week at least. Most disturbing. Would you?'

'Oh, aye,' Gerth said, keeping his voice casual. 'I wish!'

Bastian had two grand pianos, and Callum and Wol played and sang duets – 'Ten Green Bottles' with Liberace frills and swirls, Hollywood medleys. Playing at playing, Gerth thought, overawed, you don't play honky tonk on a Bechstein.

'He's such a talented boy,' Callum's mother said, walking round the garden holding Gerth's arm. 'But he's always needed looking after. So flighty! He could have done anything. Maybe he will now.'

It was a question and her fingers pressed Gerth's arm.

'Maybe,' he said.

'She likes you!' Callum told him when they were alone. 'My mother is not a tactile person. She kisses the air by one's cheek. She has really taken to you, Gerth, I'm so pleased.'

Callum's father, Hubert; well, Gerth thought, he's the absent-minded professor. He'd shown Wol his greenhouse as soon as they arrived, and Callum giggled and said he probably thought Wol was his son.

That had Gerth puzzling, too. Wol was – well, Wol, and that meant scruffy, eccentric, weird; and there was Callum's father – a doctor! – chatting away as if they were old friends. But then Wol was like Callum, at ease anywhere.

He knotted his tie for dinner.

As he walked down the staircase, he worked out how he'd tell Hal Bagwig about this weekend. He'd take photos in the next day, make sure Callum and Wol didn't appear in them. He would have to drop Midas into the next conversation he had with Hal. He stood in the lounge drinking sherry and taking in every detail of the room.

30

'It's good to be home,' Callum said, dumping his Afghani shoulder bag on the floor and flinging the windows wide open. '*Love* the tidy green air of Surrey, but it has a stifling comfort after a while. Don't you think?'

'Mm,' Gerth said, half-listening; his mind had been racing around Bastian and Midas all the way home. 'I'll make martinis.'

'Wonderful!'

'It's your family, Tink,' Gerth called from the kitchen. 'They're – well, not what I was expecting. Except I don't know what I was expecting.'

Callum shrugged and took the glass.

'They're very nice,' he said carefully. 'And so is this! Lovely. Cheers! So handsome and so talented! Did you like them? I don't mind if you didn't.'

Like? If you can be overawed and envious and mind-blown by people, and like them as well, then yes, Gerth liked them.

'Of course I liked them,' he said. 'Especially your brother – he's just – well, he's a genius.'

'Dear Bastian,' Callum drawled. 'He's very impressive, isn't he? Now, I must get on with this headdress. Benny's got a sort of Mardi Gras in mind. Do you like it so far?'

Gerth looked at the polystyrene head with its silver wire cage and turquoise satin skull cap. Callum was setting a fan of peacock feathers in place, his deft fingers selecting buttons and beads and strings of sequins.

'It's very you,' Gerth said. 'It'll be amazing. It always is.

Just – your family, Cal, I – just wonder why you've never talked about them. I mean, my lot, well, they're all right. But they've lived in the same few streets for the past hundred years – they think you need a passport to go into Newcastle. I go there and I feel like I'm in a time-warp.'

'Are you ashamed of them?' Callum said. He'd often wondered if that was why he never met them, or if Gerth was ashamed of him.

'No,' Gerth said. 'Well, not really. Just we've not got a lot to say. I mean, they'd die if they knew about you. When my mam was alive, she'd get the neighbours in to see me like I was a prize pigeon. *When are ye ganna treat we to a wedding, like, Gerth?* My dad doesn't say much now she's gone. Get him down on his allotment and you cannot shut the old bugger up. But it's all the past, him when he was a boy, when he was in the army, you know, like he's never been alive since.'

Callum strung a web of sea-green love beads and said, mm. Gerth talked most when you didn't look at him.

'But that's my family,' Gerth said. 'You can see how I found yours so strange.'

'Strange?' Callum laughed. 'I'm so pleased you said that. They've always thought that I'm the strange one. The family queer.'

He spread glue on a flame-shaped piece of velvet and started to push rainbowed sequins into place.

'You see,' he said, 'Bastian was nearly grown-up when I was born. He was everything they'd ever wanted in a son. He'd done everything they ever wanted. Choirboy, captain of cricket, rugby supremo, academic whizz, an all-rounder and so nice with it. No-one on this earth has anything nasty to say about Bastian, because he's such a wonderfully decent chap. You see – I'm trying to talk about my childhood and it's Bastian, Bastian, Bastian. My mum showed you the photos – he was handsome, athletic, brilliant – everything. I'm the soppy little blonde in the background. And then Bastian turned into this international business dynamo. Even his business is green and clean. And he found Rosemay, the dream wife, and they had the two dream kids – did you like Gemma and Tris?'

'Well, you know,' Gerth said. 'Yes. I'm not much of a one for kids, but they were – well, really polite.'

'Seen and not heard?' Callum watched his face. The children hadn't made any impression on Gerth. From the word go, they'd monopolised him and Wol. Gemma had taken him on a bike ride down to the lake and they'd danced together and she'd shown him her ballet steps. He'd tap-danced on the stepping stones for her. She had him sussed all right, a great big girly. He'd thrilled at her bright eyes and dreamed of the day when he could dance with his own child. Tris had dragged Wol under a car in the first hour and Wol split his time between oily spanners and Callum's father's garden and greenhouses.

And Gerth – well, Bastian seemed to have adopted Gerth and Callum assumed they were busy being businessmen.

'Anyway,' Callum said, 'when I was born, you see, there wasn't much left for me to do. They'd assumed Bastian would be an only child. I think they felt guilty for having me so late and they thought I was delicate.'

'You? Delicate?' Gerth snorted. 'You look delicate, I suppose, but you're the healthiest human being I've ever met, and you're strong. As I know and appreciate.'

'That's Bastian too,' Callum said, sighing. 'He said he wanted a brother not a doll. He got me swimming and running and even boxing – can you imagine? He toughened me up. I was his creation and I simply worshipped him. We went pot-holing and rock-climbing and skiing and sailing. My mother used to flutter round me when we were leaving as if I was made of china.'

He sighed again.

'It was a very privileged childhood, Gerth, but you never know that at the time. I didn't have to decide anything, you see, my mother fed me and clothed me, my father trained my mind and my brother rounded me out.'

He stood back from the headdress and nodded.

'Strings of pearls,' he said. 'This is becoming quite a marine extravaganza. Maybe a mermaid?'

He dug in a drawer until he found the pearls and sat cross-legged threading them.

'Anyway,' he said, 'that's how it was until I was about fourteen, and Bastian got married and started going abroad a lot. It left a big gap, but also, so much open space. I'd always been walking in his – very amiable – shadow and suddenly, well, who was I without him to guide me?'

Gerth watched his face, while the sunny reels of childhood played through his mind. Callum looked older all of a sudden.

'Very predictable, I suppose,' he said. 'I was at this boarding school and they threw me out for smoking dope. And buggery, but they were good enough not to mention that to my ever-loving parents. Buggery! My very first lover, David. They threw him out too. The head master said I was a blot on their – and Bastian's – good name. I feel he enjoyed caning me. I felt sullied. I ran away from home after that and joined a sort of hippy convoy – again – so predictable! But I loved being stoned, Gerth. It was a relief to smoke something or snort something and sit paralysed, nodding, giggling because I just couldn't get my words together. Call it freedom.'

'You still smoke a lot of dope,' Gerth said, uneasy with this tone from Callum. He hadn't heard it before, self-mockery with an edge of bitterness.

Callum gazed at him.

'Less since I've known you,' he said. 'Dope stops one feeling what one is feeling. I like what I'm feeling these days.'

'Go on,' Gerth said. 'The hippy convoy.'

'Well,' Callum said, 'the hippy convoy wasn't entirely happy with me being gay; it threatened the beardy brown rice macho types. I drifted off and wound up in London and became a sort of pretty houseboy to a businessman I'd met at a club. He was very rich and I was fond of him and he took care of me. Then I was trolling down the King's Road one day, and bumped into Bastian. He'd hired detectives to find me, and had come to talk sense to me and take me home.'

Callum pursed his lips.

'I didn't want to go. But Bastian said my mother was ill. Then my businessman came home and wouldn't believe he was my brother and all hell broke loose. He threw me out. Could I have another martini?'

He draped the pearls on the silver frame and wound silver thread to hold them in place. Gerth made more martinis and lit a cigarette, trying to imagine Callum as a rich man's plaything – he couldn't see his free spirit enduring that now.

'Thank you,' Callum said. 'To us. To now.'

'Cheers,' Gerth said. 'Go on with your story.'

'It sounds like a story, doesn't it?' Callum said lightly. 'A pilgrim's regress. Well. I was out on my tush, dear, down to the last fiver but I was not going to go home. Bastian kerb-crawled me in his Rolls – of course – and all the queens were agog so I got in eventually, out of sheer embarrassment. He took me back – home. Well, my parents' home.'

He cut into a length of aquamarine silk and started to chalk scales onto it.

'I'm not over-fond of being discussed,' he said wryly. 'Particularly in the third person when I'm sitting in the room. But I sat there, and listened to their plans for me. Bastian knew a lawyer who could destroy my businessman. I murmured something about consensual sex but Bastian said I was a seventeen-year-old fool and just to jolly well sit down and listen. Bastian knew a marvellous drugs rehab man. A client of his, a solid chap. After I'd passed through his hands, Bastian would find me something in Midas. A creative post, he said, you're my brother and we should stick together. I had a week to think it over and meanwhile no drugs in the house and I was grounded.'

'What did you do?' Gerth said. 'Christ, my father would have knocked seven colours of shite out of me.'

'That would have been easier in a way,' Callum said. 'Guilt tripping is a *specialité de la maison* with the oh-so-civilised classes.'

He held the tail behind him and swished along the floor.

'I worked out the time when I'd be unwatched for longest,' he said. 'I left just after Bastian had gone to bed. By four o'clock I was in Soho, drinking lousy champagne in an all-night dive, and by eight o'clock I was stoned out of my brains in some rather sweet queen's flat in Camden Town.'

He spread glue and carefully scattered glitter along the chalky scale marks.

'You see,' he said, 'I could have gone clean, and worked for Bastian. But what about *me*? Working for Midas would have been a breeze, but there, I'd have been in his shadow again. I had to be with people who didn't even know who Bastian was. I was afraid of him swamping me, carrying me along in his wonderful wake. Do you understand?'

'I'm beginning to,' Gerth said. He'd have liked an older brother like Bastian – how easy his life would have been!

'Well,' Callum said, 'I'm glad. I was sick of having to be grateful. And, for the next little while, I did dope and a bit of drag and more dope. I came up North at one point when I felt Bastian getting closer – *some very handsome omie in a Roller asking for you, dear!* I stayed because I feel safe and none of my family have anything to do with here. I wrote to Bastian *sans* address and told him not to worry and promised to send a postcard every so often. Which I did until I hit the needle.'

He looked at Gerth's astonished face.

'Yes, my dear,' he said. 'Since this appears to be confession time. You are married to an ex-junkie. Very ex. You will perhaps understand my obsession with health and safe sex if I tell you that I've seen how people live and how they die when they contract AIDS. Two very dear sweet friends of mine, and I was there until the last. It could have been me, so easily. I had a sort of total breakdown and landed in Credsworth. I've mentioned it to you in passing. And there I met Wol. Someone utterly like *me* – for the first time, Gerth. The brother I wish I'd had. That's when I started to live, really. Dear Wol.'

'Did you and Wol ever . . .?' Gerth had wanted to ask him this for ages.

'Never,' Callum's eyes twinkled. 'We are too fragile to be together that way. We need husbands – well, I do more than Wol. Wol's too scared for romance, he's in love with his garden and his van. I want everything, but then, I was a spoilt brat from the word go.'

'So why go to Surrey now? I mean, why did we?' Gerth said.

'I went,' Callum said, dropping a kiss on his nose, 'because we were invited and because I'm happy as me now. *I am what I am!* I don't need handouts from Bastian, and no-one can draw comparisons between us any more. I find I can even like him now. He can't take me over any more. And of course, the main reason I felt strong enough to go is because I'm married. I have the most handsome and wonderful husband in the world. Baby, it's you, you make everything possible. I'm so proud of you. Of us.'

Gerth hugged his dear slender body close and kissed him. But he was still puzzled. If I was Callum, he thought, I'd forget the past and cash in, with a family like that. And not just for the money, although I earn in a year what Bastian picks up in a day! God, the elegance and the luxury and the sense of belonging – I'd be there in a flash, it would be so easy.

But then, he wasn't Callum, and he knew that Callum never took the easy way.

31

Gerth's dissatisfactions and ambitions piled up like dominoes. Callum's complete indifference to all his family's wealth and his brother's fabulous success. What would he do when Gerth started to rocket along the Midas path? What would he do when Gerth went abroad – and to implement his plans he must go – for as long as it took? Acting at business functions was second nature to him, he could stand that. In fact, the idea of Callum at his side made him blush. He started feeling irritated by Wol, too, and the drag scene and the rainbow chaos of Garstone Heights and its misfit inhabitants.

All these dominoes balanced against Love. And when he looked at Callum, often, they simply vanished and only Love was there.

But then there was daylight and work, and long evenings while the spreadsheets piled up in his flat. Soon he'd be ready to stay all night at the office, stretching the DTP system to its limits. And then, hello world!

He felt like a tightrope walker; every time he was home with Callum, he was itchy to be away. He tried to tell Callum about it, but Callum laughed and said he'd never understand, he was just thrilled that Gerth was so involved with the job.

The only person Gerth could have talked to was Mac, but Mac was full of his new family. There was little room for friends.

Mac and Trish were so close all the time she was pregnant, walking along the street, leaning on each other. When they sat together, Mac would put his arm round her and his other hand on her bump and their eyes met like lasers. After little Stuart and Amy were born, they had everything, they deserved it: a boy and a girl all at the same time, an instant family. Their house was full of cards and toys and the bright chaos of a new generation.

Gerth was Stuart's godfather and that touched him deep inside, somewhere he'd never felt before. It was a link to normality, a causeway from the paradise island where he lived with Callum to the mainland and the rest of the human race. Holding ten and a half pounds of little boy struggling in Mac's family christening gown made him almost cry. He bought teddies and trains and bells and a mobile for Stuart, he called in at lunchtime and talked to him; Trish said it was a blessing to get a free babysitter. He even felt protective when Callum came with him, Callum who would spend an hour chasing a fly out of the flat rather than swat it.

'I think he's seeing another boy,' Callum joked to Wol, but Gerth didn't laugh. Had he even heard? A sort of silence came between them even while they made love.

'What are you thinking, my Gerthling?'

Oh nothing.

Oh this and that.

Oh you know.

They even found themselves talking like people they'd laughed about before. Along the lines of: had a good day at the office? and the washing machine's gone wrong. The world of work, the world of domesticity: talk to fill silence.

After the christening, Gerth's dreams started.

Dreams of babies crawling out of the room, babies toddling round the corner, babies that vanished just as he reached them, babies in his arms and suddenly just empty clothes, still warm.

Sometimes it was a baby in his arms, crying, and him trying to feed it with an empty bottle. He went to the fridge and filled the bottle, only it was empty before he got back to the baby, or it was full and the baby was gone.

Babies, babies.

He always woke up feeling relieved – no babies in real life, except Stuart and Amy and he could simply hand them back.

The thought of being a father! It suited some people – as if they were born to it. Gerth watched Mac and it seemed that Mac was simply more himself than he'd ever been before. All at once he was a dad twice over, and his arms were made for rocking Amy or Stuart to sleep. His fingers pegged out tiny vests and t-shirts, they folded nappies and tested the temperature of milk as easily as they'd pinned wires and tightened nuts in his beloved classic Rover, as deftly as he'd weeded and clipped and planted the long-walled wilderness at the back of the house. Mac was a daddy, he'd play football and bandage knees and buy bikes and ice-cream and give pocket money. One day he'd be a granddad with the privilege of spoiling his grandchildren rotten, telling them tall stories, making coins appear from mid-air, walking down the street like a god with a smooth new hand in his old paw and two bright new eyes adoring him.

Gerth wished sometimes he'd got married and been a dad before he met Callum, got it out of the way before he found his true love. Like old Tony down at Strings, four children and a divorce before he knew he was gay. Now he had Cleo, his lover; an amiable ex-wife who swore she'd known all along; four tolerant children who loved him to bits and took the piss out of him. And three grandchildren who knew nothing about why Granddad lived with a man, just that Granddad and Cleo loved them all and would take on the world for them.

And Bastian was a dad – with a wife and nanny.

But he lived with Callum and he loved Callum.

And, anyway, with his career rising like the sun, right now there was no time to even think about things like babies.

32

'I feel I'm losing him,' Callum said lightly, patting his hair. 'He's gone all silent and sad. Then sometimes our eyes meet and he goes all sparkly and tender. It's very confusing.'

Wol heard the needle-sharp glitter of lies.

Once, Callum thought, once in the last three months he's gone all sparkly and I've felt so good and the next day we might as well be in Alaska.

'Do you know why?' Wol said.

'I'm not sure,' Callum lied, then brittle as an icicle. 'Gerth and I seem to have reached a conversational cul-de-sac. Do you know why? Have you been plumbing the depths of my husband's psyche on the sly?'

He started sobbing as soon as the words were finished, sobbing from the gut, crumpled like a puppet whose strings are cut. Wol cradled him and rocked and sh-sh-ed.

'Don't be like that, Callum,' he said. 'This is your blood brother in his home which is your home, not some dilly-dally queen in a bar.'

'He's changed,' Callum said, 'with a vengeance. Lovely little Stuart and Amy have arrived on the planet and Gerth's been practically living at Mac and Trish's – which I definitely don't mind. I've positively encouraged him! Everyone should welcome a new life with joy.'

'You go as well,' Wol said, 'don't you?'

'Sometimes,' Callum said. 'Only I – maybe a bit oversensitive? – I feel that he'd rather be there without me.'

'Really?' Wol was amazed. Outside of work, Callum and Gerth were seldom apart and both seemed ecstatic about it.

I breathe in, he exhales . . .

'Yes,' Callum said. 'Nothing he's said, but when did Gerth ever say what he means? I have to guess. I think he's broody. It's getting to me. I may have picked it up wrong, but he's never tried to persuade me to go with him just lately.'

He sniffed back tears and Wol made tea.

'You said broody,' Wol said. 'Isn't it enough for him, being godfather?'

'No,' Callum said. 'It's set him wondering about everything; he's so bad at talking about things that matter and we've scrubbed around most things quite successfully. But this is different. I think – and tell me what you think – it's being a dad that's got to him. Rather, not being a dad. He knows he won't be while he's with me, and he does love me, that I don't doubt. Just that we can't have babies. Without a lot of planning and red tape.'

'He could be married to a woman and still not have babies,' Wol said. 'You're not depriving him.'

'Gerth doesn't think like that,' Callum said. 'He likes – needs? – to say it's X's fault, therefore eliminate X. X could be me, X could be being gay. X could be us, X could be him. I'm worried sick.'

'It shows,' Wol said. 'Hasn't he thought of it before?'

'He's twenty-seven,' Callum said. 'And so am I and so are you. But where you and I have been of the other persuasion since the cradle and it's our life, he is about as gay-aware as you or I were at fourteen. I cry about babies from time to time – I'm sure you do too. But it's just not on the agenda. I wish it was! Our bright sparks will rocket and dance and whirl and then – phht! Into the stars. We are not eligible for the genetic pool. There are ways, but Gerth just won't talk, so I don't even know for sure that that's what's on his mind.'

'Can I tell you something,' Wol said, 'something no-one knows but me and one other person?'

'A secret?' Callum said. 'I thought we had no secrets?'

'After today we won't,' Wol said. 'I suppose I'm ashamed. No, not that, just can't work it out in my own head, so why trouble you.'

'Speak,' Callum said. 'It's safe.'

Wol closed his eyes.

'It was years ago, I was a teenager, camp as Christmas on the Eastwood estate, mummy and daddy hinting that there'd be no tears shed if I moved out? I had blue hair, which my dad said was all right, your hair grows out, it was the earring and the nose ring and the clothes. I was in my I-Am-The-Monster phase, love me or loathe me, at least you'll know me. They did throw me out when I started wearing make-up but I'm getting ahead of myself, as they say.'

'I know all this,' Callum said. 'Tell me the bit I don't know.'

'It was a woman who lived a few streets away,' Wol said. 'Her old man was in Durham – he'd held up a building society or something – and I used to go round there and smoke dope and hang out and she liked it because no-one would talk about me – the local bender – being there. My first fag-hag. She used to talk to me about her old man and how she'd leave him only he'd come and find her anywhere. I was a sort of silent agony aunt, you know, I rolled the joints and made the tea and mixed the drinks and went out for chips between agonies.'

Callum looked at him.

'Anyway, one night we got drunk, really drunk. She liked martini and she wanted to feel happy, so we just kept drinking. After a while she was going on about how maybe I wasn't really a poof, I was so young, too young to be sure, had I ever done it with a woman. You know. Well, I hadn't done it with anyone but my own sweet self at that stage. Anyway, she got me into bed and it was really nice, I was too pissed to do anything, but it was nice sleeping with her.'

'My aunty tried that on me once,' Callum said. 'I let her get falling-over drunk and put her to bed and went home.'

'That's what I should have done probably,' Wol said. 'But I didn't. I started sleeping there just as a friend. Then one night, we were cuddling in and it sort of happened, we did it and it was – well, all right, I suppose. She said you couldn't judge by your first time and we did it again in the morning. It was nicer then and we went on doing it; I got into it. We did it all the time, it was weird. It didn't feel quite right, but it was nice. She said I was gentle and we could laugh. Then I went round one day and she said she was going away for a while, down to her sister's. She said she'd ring me and write, but she didn't. She was away for ages – almost a year – and when she came back, she engineered this real row with me. Her old man was due to come out a few months later. She said she'd had a kid, my kid – our kid, I suppose – and had him adopted. That's why she'd gone away.'

'Jesus,' Callum said. 'What did you do?'

'What could I do?' Wol said. 'She hadn't even put my name on his birth certificate. I don't exist in my only child's life, he'll never know who I am. She wouldn't even tell me where she'd been, there was nothing to go on. I rang an adoption agency and they said it was a common problem – can you believe that! – but was I sure I was the father, with a woman like that, you couldn't really tell. A woman like that! Like she was shit. And she wasn't.'

'Oh, Wol,' Callum said. 'Oh, Wol.'

'Anyway,' Wol said, 'her old man came out and went back to beating her up and she wouldn't speak to me and I kept crying and I looked so awful I started using a bit of slap and my loving Dad threw me out. It was three weeks before my eighteenth birthday.'

'Nothing you could do?' Callum said.

'No,' Wol said. 'What was worse, I managed to see her the day I was going – that was the last time I saw her and she said it wasn't true about the baby, she'd just wanted to get rid of me before he came back. I said, you could have just told me to go; is it true, or isn't it? She just laughed and said it was probably best I didn't know, seeing as I was gay what would I want with a kid? She was out of her box.'

'What happened to her?' Callum said.

'She died,' Wol said. 'Smack. I wanted to go the same way until I met you in Credsworth. The knacker house.'

'So you'll never know,' Callum said.

'No,' Wol said. 'Never no way no how. So I may or may not have leapt into the genetic pool. If I did, I hope the kid's happy. I look at kids, though – ten-year-olds now – used to be toddlers, then five-year-olds – and I wonder. I don't even know his birthday.'

'Poor woman. She must have hated men,' Callum said. 'With reason.'

'She did,' Wol said. 'I thought she liked me, but I think maybe she'd been so fucked over she couldn't treat a man like a person. She couldn't take it out on the bastard she was married to, so I got it all. But this doesn't help you with Gerth, does it?'

'More than you know,' Callum said. 'It's stopped me thinking about him for a while. It's getting that I'm all nervous when he comes home. I was even glad when he went away this weekend.'

'Oh dear,' Wol said.

'Very oh dear,' Callum echoed. 'I'm scared.'

33

Hal Bagwig had booked the conference room in the Manchester Metropole, Victorian municipal splendour, red brick smoked black from industries long forgotten. Gerth checked into his room, showered and shaved and changed. He'd blown a lot of money on this outfit: his Thomas Pink glazed sea-island cotton shirt, his first handmade suit, a striped silk tie suggesting an education he'd never had, a small diamond tie-pin the double of Bastian's. He'd been at the solarium for a half-hour every day; what had Bastian said, quoting Aristotle Onassis: *get a suntan, it makes you look prosperous.*

He looked at himself in the full-length mirror and grinned. Bloody fantastic! He hadn't even shown this lot to Callum, an acid burn in his stomach as he realised why. Callum would have laughed – then recognised how he had copied Bastian. But that wasn't it. No, Callum would have read his soul's ambition and seen the inevitable ending between every line. He gulped Glenfiddich from the mini-bar and scrubbed his teeth. Finally he slipped on his brand new antique gold ring, its tiny diamond glittering pure rainbows.

There was a nameplate in front of every one of the thirty-six chairs ringing the table. Gerth joined his colleagues by the coffee machine, noting that none of them sported a Windsor knot. He couldn't be sure, but he sensed glances of envy and admiration coming his way.

'What's all this about, Gerth?' Edward, manager of the Manchester operation, edged him away from the group.

'How do you mean, like?'

'This meeting,' Edward said. 'Did you not get a memo?'

'Hal called me,' Gerth said.

'Aren't you the blue-eyed boy! Imperative that you attend to discuss some interesting ideas from Gerth Machen, Newcastle Branch.'

'Wait and see,' Gerth said, grinning.

There was a bronze mirrored wall in front of him, and he still looked more tanned than anyone else in the room. Praise from Edward! Everyone knew the Manchester operation was the flagship of The Great Outdoors.

Hal came in, flanked by two secretaries. He made straight for Gerth, hand extended.

'Smashing to see you, young Machen,' he said. 'By, it was a good day we found you, lad. I've had the girls run off copies of your – paper. More like *War and Peace*, lad, you must have put in some overtime. I feel that dinner this evening would be in order. Yourself, Edward and of course, Richard.'

'Lovely,' Gerth said, his heart racing like the engine of a powerboat.

At the meeting Hal wrung the English language of platitudes and fulsome phrases. Gerth was a colossus and Gerth's document was a map for the future. They should study it as carefully as Elizabethan mariners lucky enough to get hold of the charts drawn by Sir Francis Drake. It was the key to the new world.

Gerth listened, smoking Turkish cigarettes rolled in dove-grey paper. When he got to his feet, they all applauded, none more warmly than Hal himself. He wanted to leap on the table and whoop! It was really happening. He had done it.

34

Gerth pushed a disc into the grafixcope and dimmed the lights.

The screen was filled with the words THE GREAT OUT-DOORS, followed by footage of hang-gliding over patchwork fields, water-skiing on a vast blue lake, the last thirty seconds of the World Cup final, dazzling ski-slopes, Wimbledon, Silverstone, an Olympic hurdler in slow motion.

'Winners all,' Gerth said, borrowing Bastian's rich confident voice, 'and I hope to show you how we, The Great Outdoors, can lead the field.'

The giant screen lit up with the words TOTAL ENVIRON-MENT. The letters ski-ed off the screen to be replaced by the image of The Great Outdoors store in Newcastle.

'Let's start with what we've got,' Gerth said. 'We design, manufacture and retail all our products. All this, as you will see, can be streamlined. Let me concentrate on where we meet the public: our retail stores where we already have a wide range of sportswear, excellent assistants, a maximising of space. And there's nothing wrong with it.'

Three customers gave their enthusiastic opinions of the shopping experience in The Great Outdoors.

'So,' said Gerth, 'why change?'

The screen filled with the names of all their rivals and the number of retail outlets they had.

'Change,' Gerth said, 'can be thrust upon us and believe me, it will be. My business contacts in Midas and other inter-national concerns have made me all too aware of this. I see this as the time for us to initiate change. Where better to start than the point where we meet the public?'

He heard the ripple of whispers at the name Midas, and noticed Hal Bagwig making notes. That was his ace and he'd dropped it in, smooth as Diamond Jim Brady playing poker.

A computer graphic 3D image of an empty store appeared.

'This is our drawing board,' Gerth said, 'and this is what I call Total Environment.'

The screen panned in on one area of the store and images appeared bright as holograms.

'Behind this rack of ski-clothes,' Gerth said, 'you can see a wall video of the Winter Olympics. Immediately, the customer is inspired by the best the world has to offer. He dreams of new feats, new heights, new achievements, and in his mind, The Great Outdoors will fulfil his dreams.'

The images built up behind him.

'I would propose that we divide our stores by sports categories,' he said. 'For canoeing and yachting, we run the white water races and round the world races as background, so that the customer can experience the thrill of his chosen sport *in situ* – we have given him more than a set of garments, we have transformed him into a man worthy of The Great Outdoors. A total experience.'

Behind him, a skier flew like an eagle.

'We introduce a brasserie: coffee and snacks with suitable names, somewhere for people to mull over their potential purchases. Again, you see the use of video. Imagine it: everywhere the dynamic image of winning, of excellence, and our customer feeling that we can make him a part of it.'

The screen panned away to show a whole city.

'We research every local event, fair and festival and we are there,' Gerth said. 'We are on billboards, on posters, on handbills, in papers, we are everywhere and when the customer comes in, we offer him everything he's dreamed of. And more.'

A hot air balloon rose behind him and drifted serenely over a stately home into the rolling English countryside.

'This is a blueprint for every store in the UK,' Gerth said. 'In the UK, in Europe, in the – as yet – untapped markets of the Far East and the United States. This is the way forward: a total product, from drawing board to purchase point. The Great Outdoors – a total environment.'

Hal stood up and started to clap and everyone else followed. The applause gave Gerth's feet wings of flame as he went back to his seat.

Late that night, Hal walked him to the bay window of his penthouse suite. Below them, the city of Manchester glittered and hummed. Hal put a paternal arm round Gerth's shoulders.

'It's all yours, young Machen,' he said, waving his cigar across the skyline.

What! Was he getting Edward's job – just like that? How could Hal say that when Edward was sitting there? How could Edward sit there, smiling? Richard was smiling, too.

'Yes,' Hal said, 'your loyalty is beyond question and your talent – by God, you remind me of myself when I was young. I'm giving you a free hand. How's about a spot of bubbly to celebrate?'

The four of them chinked glasses.

'Yes,' Hal said, 'we've discussed this at length, me and Edward and Richard. There's no holding you back, lad, or we'll lose you. Us old hands have been stumbling about in the dark on this one. But you're our beacon, Gerth. Young, free, single and talented! Here's to all our futures! I'm giving you Hong Kong.'

Gerth swayed slightly, dizzy with the words.

'Nothing to say?' Hal was twinkling.

Gerth threw his head back and roared.

'Here's to the future! Hong Kong!' he said, hurling the champagne to the back of his throat. Edward refilled.

'You fly tomorrow week,' Hal said, slapping a plane ticket onto the table. 'That is, if you're free?'

Gerth picked up the plane ticket and kissed it.

'Free as a bird,' he said, raising his glass. 'Here's to Hong Kong!'

35

When he reached Newcastle, Gerth made a zigzag detour to take him back to his own flat. The High Level bridge, the Redheugh bridge, the swing bridge – Callum's favourite, with its daft blue and white wrought-iron towers, floating like a Lego model in the shadow of the Tyne bridge. He drove along the quayside, past the waterfront restaurants and bars, memories at every window.

He was going to see his dad the next day to tell him he was leaving. He'd have dinner with Mac and Trish, load Stuart and Amy with gifts and sweets. Richard had invited him to a farewell celebratory dinner. There would be an evening party from work to send him off in style.

What else?

Oh yes.

He would put the flat in the hands of an estate agent. Callum, of course, would have half a dozen friends who'd like to rent it, but he didn't want that. It wasn't just the way they trailed things around and dropped them, dead flowers left for months in a vase because they looked 'amazing with the sun coming through them . . .' They just weren't his sort of people. And he wasn't coming back.

Packing, he thought, shopping, saying goodbyes.

What else?

Oh yes.

Callum.

He squirmed at the thought of telling Callum goodbye. He played with the idea of pretending it was a few months, and it might be simply *au revoir*. He could suggest they try a trial separation, but the idea curled up and died when he let the reality of Callum into his mind.

Callum knew him too well for lies.

That angered him: Manchester had been a grand performance – good enough to earn him a golden key and a free hand half-way round the world. They believed in him. Who the hell did Callum think he was with his laser sharp blue-eyed honesty?

It was just like the first night they'd been together and he'd woken in a panic, wanting out: just like then, he could only think of a row to end it. Maybe he should have barged out of the mad hippy eyrie that night – but then he'd never have met Bastian.

The part of Gerth which loved Callum was speechless at this callousness. It's my career! he snarled aloud. It's my life.

They'd had fun, lots of it, him and Callum. He'd never deny that. It just happened that it was over. Why the hell didn't Callum want to end it, why did he have to be the baddie? He wasn't, he told himself, but the one who leaves is always the baddie. It just wasn't fair, it took guts to finish something. He parked, full of indignation at the script he'd wished on Callum, streams of accusations that Callum would never utter.

It was easy to pack up his flat: he hadn't lived there properly for over three years and he wasn't a hoarder. He looked at the suits in his wardrobe with amused contempt. He'd never wear them again, now that he had a taste for Mr Bundy's Bespoke Tailoring. Maybe they'd go to his dad. Or Oxfam. They'd be appreciated there.

He made a coffee and sat by the phone, making a list of people to call. Callum's name was last and it was hard to put it down on paper, underneath 'flat agency', 'utility companies', Trish and Mac. He flicked through the directory, and as he spoke, his hands embellished the capital C with leaves and flowers; he made a spider's web holding the other five letters. Added dewdrops. Sketched a sunrise over the sea. Drew a crude robin. Scored an arrow through a heart holding the initials G. l. C. and made blood drop all the way to the bottom of the page.

His hands were cold and shaky as he lit a cigarette.

The ticket for Hong Kong sat on the mantelpiece with his passport and driving licence and birth certificate.

I was born. I can drive. I can cross international borders with the sovereign protection of Her Britannic Majesty.

I'm leaving next week.

Maybe he'd write to Callum.

He rang Trish.

'I need a bit of a heart to heart,' he said. 'Can I come over?'

'Of course,' Trish said. 'I'll put the kettle on. I've got some news for you.'

Gerth was touched that she sounded so genuinely pleased.

'Girls' talk,' Trish told Mac. 'You take the babies out to the park or something, and bring in something nice to drink.'

'Yes,' Mac said. 'How do you think he'll take it?'

'Shock, alarm and then pleasure,' Trish said. 'Like Callum said, it's the only way.'

Gerth didn't know that Callum had also had a heart to heart with Trish and Mac. He hadn't a clue that Callum had rung every adoption agency in the country until he found one which was happy to consider single-sex couples. Callum had put his finger on what he thought was the root of their awkwardness and, after mulling it over with Wol and Hannah, and checking with Trish and Mac, he'd come up with adoption as Plan A. Hannah had even offered to be a surrogate mother: if Gerth blenched at the idea of a stranger's baby, that was Plan B.

'Maybe it'll be twins,' Callum said. 'One blonde and one dark . . .'

'This is Plan B, ye daft geet poof,' Hannah said. 'Not a word of it unless Plan A doesn't meet with his lordship's approval.'

Mac pushed his twins on the candy-coloured swings and told them they might be having a sort of cousin soon, Uncle Gerth and Cal might have a baby, what did they think? Their eyes told him that anything he said was wonderful; their smiles turned him into a genial god. He could see why Gerth had got a bit broody, looking at his lovely children, and though the idea of gay adoption had stopped him in his tracks at first, now he couldn't imagine why. It was the only way.

As Lord of the Universe, Mac conjured up ice-cream cones, then turned their buggy and behold! He had created a pond with ducks on it. Amy and Stuart stretched out their sticky hands and shrieked.

'And we'll get some pink champagne for Mummy and Uncle Gerth and Cal and me, and you can have cherry pop,' he told them, his heart bursting as they sang out dadadada – *that's me* he thought.

Daddy Mac.

He couldn't wait to see Gerth's face.

36

'So what was your news?' Gerth said, lighting his fifth cigarette.

Trish was stunned. Thank God she hadn't burst out with Callum's news first; her heart bled now she'd heard that Gerth was through with him. There wasn't an inch of room for negotiation in Gerth's plans. He was just asking her how to say it was over without upsetting Callum more than necessary. And she had the distinct feeling that it wasn't even to save Callum's feelings or pride: it was simply to make Gerth himself feel less of a shit.

'Doesn't matter,' she said. 'I can't remember. It's gone.'

Mac would be back soon and Callum was coming over – just to surprise Gerth, to celebrate his news with them all. She'd offered to put the idea to Gerth and been amazed that Callum leapt at her offer. Callum even knew that Gerth would call on her and Mac before he came home. It was that bad between them.

And here was Gerth saying it would never be better between them, he had decided. His voice sounded dead when he was talking, but it came alive as soon as he switched to his brilliant career, to Hong Kong. Every word sparkled: he used to talk this way about Callum.

'What do you think, Trish?'

She looked at Gerth. *I think you're a bloody fool.*

'I think you – should be really careful,' she said. 'True love is hard to find. Make sure you're not being hasty.'

If there had been a flicker of doubt from Gerth, she'd be telling him about the baby – *come hell or high water, Trish, if my husband is intent on being a daddy, a daddy he will be!* – bless you, Callum, she'd said, you're just so good. *Not good, Trish, that's Mother Teresa and you and your angelic babies. Not good, just that I worship him, all I want is his happiness. Which is my happiness, so you see, not entirely good. Just a tad selfish.*

Gerth stood up and walked over to the window.

'No,' he said. 'I just can't see any future for us.'

'I've just got to ring a friend,' Trish said.

In the bedroom, she punched out Callum's number. She had to stop him bouncing through the door with that crazy smile, she couldn't bear to see him knocked cold, it was too cruel. Damn, damn, damn, it was the ansaphone.

She knew he'd left, he was probably filling a taxi with flowers and champagne right this minute. Could she get rid of Gerth? Or was it just meant to happen this way?

She went back to Gerth.

'He doesn't know I'm back yet,' Gerth said. 'Maybe I should just go over right now. No time like the present. What do you think?'

'Don't keep asking me what I think,' Trish said. 'This is just so awful.'

'I know,' Gerth said. 'Can I call you later? Cry on your shoulder?'

Trish could have punched his suntanned nose. She froze as the front doorbell rang.

37

'We met on the doorstep,' Callum said, kissing Trish. 'Shift the prunes and custard and puréed spinach over and make room for this!'

He was radiant in black and white silk, a turquoise cravat fluttering at his neck. He handed her a bottle wrapped in tissue then turned to help Mac lift the buggy over the front step. Trish stood as if turned to stone while they unstrapped the babies, laughing.

Help, she thought, someone's got to do something and I just don't know what.

'I've got one of those as well,' Mac said, nudging Callum and holding out a carrier bag to Trish. 'I hope yours is pink and fizzy too, we can't go mixing our drinks, can we? Hey, what's up, Trish?'

'Trish?' Callum said, looking concerned. 'You look terrible. Here's me bursting in full of the joys and never noticed. I am sorry. What on earth's happened?'

'Ask Gerth,' she said, her eyes flashing. 'He's in there. Ask him.'

She took the buggy handles and shot into the kitchen and shut the door. The radio came on immediately. Mac looked at Callum. He was ashen.

'Look to the lady,' he said quietly and walked into the living room.

'You must know I'm here,' Callum said to Gerth's back, after a moment. 'What's all this about? Trish looks like she's seen a ghost. What is it, Gerthling?'

Gerth turned and looked at Callum's feet.

'What's happened?' Callum said. 'Has someone died? God, I don't mean that, how tasteless of me. What is it?'

'I'm going to Hong Kong,' Gerth said.

'But, baby, that's marvellous! Recognition at last!' Callum said, his cheeks flushing pink. 'Stuffy old TGO is finally appreciating you. Wait till you hear my news!'

Gerth wouldn't look at him. Callum began to feel scared.

'Oh, come on, strong man,' he said, keeping his voice calm. 'I know you've been wanting this for months! And I do know you can't take me with you. I've been prepared for this. We managed a month apart and henny penny, the sky is still blue and sunny up there. How long is it for? It's not the end of the world. Anyway, Benny's got some seedy Far Eastern connections, he can fix me and Wol up with some cabaret, he's said so, so at least I can visit.'

Gerth inspected every stitch in the toes of his shoes.

'I don't know how long,' he said. 'It could be permanent.'

'Is this the bum's rush?' Callum laughed. 'You just wait and see how busy I've been on our behalf.'

'Stop it, Callum,' Gerth said. 'I'm leaving next week. Listen to me.'

'Love to,' Callum said, perching on the sofa. 'Every syllable you utter is imprinted on my heart.'

Gerth turned away and looked out at the garden, feeling suddenly sick to his guts.

'It's over, Cal,' he said.

He could feel his heart banging against his ribs.

'Over?' Callum repeated.

'Over,' he said.

The room was utterly silent.

'Has something been going on that I should be aware of?' Callum said, his jaw shaking. 'Lipstick other than mine on your collar? Who is it?'

'It isn't anyone, Cal,' Gerth said. 'It's just I can't see how we'd work with me away indefinitely. And that. Everything. I won't be back here.'

'No-one,' Callum said. 'You're leaving me for no-one.'

'It's my career,' Gerth said angrily. 'You've never been interested in my career, you've always laughed at it and it matters to me. I want to get on.'

Callum flared his nostrils.

'I have done nothing but support you in your career,' he said flatly. 'I've never complained about weekends away, business dinners, Christmas parties without me, I have never made an issue of my invisibility. I've always been proud of you. Or maybe you don't think I was.'

'It's not that,' Gerth said. 'But you don't – well, understand what I want.'

'Wash your mouth out,' Callum said sharply. 'Remember who you're talking to. This is the wife who's typed your reports and pressed your collars and hankies. This is the three a.m. listener to your office worries. This is the voice which has constantly said, shush, Gerth, it'll be all right, whatever bastard things have happened at your office. When we came together, I knew you were in a different world. I thought I'd done everything I could to – accommodate that. Clearly I didn't.'

'It's just that . . .'

'What I find difficult,' Callum cut in, '*most* difficult, is that this doesn't seem to be a discussion. If we were going to make a go of it, then there'd be some point in talking. I said, you said, I did, you did, I didn't, you didn't. There seems little point discussing the past when you've decided there's not going to be a future. That is what you've decided, isn't it? I want to be clear.'

'Look, I love you, Cal,' Gerth said, 'but it's changed. It doesn't feel like in love any more. We've grown apart.'

'Goodbye,' Callum said, crossing his legs and taking a cigarette from Mac's sandalwood box.

'I don't want to hurt you . . .'

Callum lit the cigarette and blew the match out with a puff of smoke.

'I really don't want to hurt you, Cal,' Gerth said, kneeling in front of him.

'The dead feel nothing,' Callum said, his eyes glittering with tears.

'But have *you* been happy? Have you?' Gerth implored him.

Callum gazed into Gerth's eyes, longing for it all to be not true, not happening. But there was nothing left for him in the brown depths. It was over.

'Try not to be cheap,' he drawled. 'As far as I was concerned and I have said this from the start, I want marriage. Which, I will remind you, means for better or for worse. Companionship. Sharing. Love. Something rare, precious and beautiful. If things go askew, a working together to right them.'

Gerth stood up.

'I was not aware,' Callum said, 'of a unilateral opt-out clause. I would have thought that three and a bit years deserved fair warning before dissolution. But there you are. And here am I, still trying to talk to you, for God's sake! You've made your decision – so goodbye.'

Gerth walked over to the window.

'Will you be all right?' he said.

'Who frigging cares, dear!' Callum exploded. 'No, I will not be all right. What do you expect? A firm manly handshake, a clap on the shoulder? Want a cliché, Gerth? Something like it was fun while it lasted? All good things come to an end? Better luck next time? Or would you prefer tears? Don't leave me this way? Couldn't we just give it one more try? I swear I'll change? Give me the script, Gerth and I'll do my best to deliver it with feeling.'

'I'm so sorry. I'd like to keep in touch,' Gerth said. 'Maybe we can be friends?'

'Not bad,' Callum said. 'Rather Australian soap opera.'

'Cal . . .'

'Try this,' Callum said. 'Goodbye. Gerth exits and gets into his beloved car and sniffs back a few tears in which sorrow is mingled with relief. He will roar off down the street and meet some old friends and get drunk and wonder if he's done the right thing. He will never see Callum again for the rest of his life. Occasionally, nostalgic after too much to drink, he'll wonder what would have happened if they'd worked it out and stayed together. But he will never know. That's what's going to happen.'

'It's so – final.'

'Dumping one's partner generally is,' Callum said. 'I take it I have been dumped? Or do you want to try and work it out? Think carefully, Gerth. I don't give second chances.'

'No,' Gerth said. 'Like I said, it's over and I'm sorry.'

'Goodbye then,' Callum said.

'Goodbye,' Gerth repeated.

In his car he was angry, he wanted to go back – not to sort it out though, and that's the only way Callum would let him back. He drove round the corner and parked, rubbing away the beginning of tears. He was free just like he'd wanted to be, his whole life ahead of him . . .

Part four

....

Driftland

38

Trish came into the living room. Callum was standing looking out of the window, and she put her arms round his slender back, her heart longing to wrap him close and tell him everything was OK. He patted her clasped hands and she felt him shudder with tears.

'There, there,' she said shakily. 'There, there.'

'Where?' he whimpered. 'Oh God, where?'

They stood for a long time together and it seemed to Trish that his body was shrinking, all firmness falling away. His hands went icy.

When he turned, his face had lost all colour and his lips were grey. His eyes were dull and he looked past her.

'Have to sit down,' he said, and his cheeks went taut with the effort of taking the few steps to a chair. He collapsed like a silk scarf sliding from a table to the floor. His body had no substance and his arms sprawled, fingers plucking at his hair, one hand cupping itself round his chin and mouth, the base of his thumb rammed between his teeth.

Trish didn't know what to do. She glanced out of the window – they'd put balloons in the trees and hidden shiny parcels all over the garden for the babies and the new baby to be. Oh Jesus.

When she looked at Callum again, he was staring at her, his teeth working at his hand. His eyes were like shattered mirrors. He let his hand drop and she saw a bright bead of blood welling from his skin.

'Would you mind terribly,' he said, his voice hoarse and

bright, 'would you mind – I think I'm going to be sick, Trish, I want Wol.'

He staggered to the door and she heard him stumble upstairs to the bathroom. Mac came in then, with Amy and Stuart clutching at his jeans.

'What's happened?' Mac said.

Trish flicked the radio on. They never let the children in on adult dramas. She took Mac's hand and led him into the hall.

'Gerth's going to Hong Kong,' she said. 'He's finished with Callum.'

'Did you tell him about the baby?' Mac said.

'He told me about Hong Kong first,' Trish said. 'He's full of it, his brilliant career, he was crowing about it. Callum is just one of those things. Yesterday's news.'

'Oh shit,' Mac said. 'Poor Callum.'

'I mean I couldn't tell him then,' Trish said, tears dropping down her face. 'Maybe I should have, but he was different, Mac, you know the way he used to be, years ago, all me me me and I'm top of the world? I felt paralysed.'

'You're right,' Callum said from the stairs. 'Do forgive me for eavesdropping. Oh dear sweet Jesus, you're right. That's the bit of Gerth I've always been afraid of, the career man, you know . . .'

He sat on the bottom step, his arms round his knees, his head resting on one side.

'I had a king in a tenement castle,' he said. 'No, dear Trish, you're right. If he'd chosen me and the baby over Hong Kong, then he'd have ditched us both sooner or later.'

'Did you tell him?' Trish said.

'Moi?' Callum laughed and the sound jarred around them. 'No, I didn't. I accepted his abdication and cut short the speeches. I mean, goodbye is goodbye. One might have appreciated an opportunity to plead one's case, but he obviously had packing to do and I didn't want to keep him.'

Tears flooded in after his brave speech, and he mopped his cheeks with his hands.

'And I won't keep you lovely people,' he said, tossing his

head back. 'Did you ring Wol? Never mind. May I? I must leave you to your afternoon. Don't worry about me, Trish, Mac, I'm quite a survivor.'

He sighed and looked at his feet.

'Shit,' he said, 'my legs won't move. Oh shit.'

Mac dialled Wol's number from the kitchen.

'Just come over,' he said. 'Callum needs you.'

'Ten minutes,' Wol said, grabbing his car keys.

39

Wol flew in to see Callum sitting at the bottom of the stairs. He was smoking and Trish had put an ashtray beside him.

'How kind of you to come,' he said to Wol, extending one icy hand.

'What's up?' Wol clasped his hand, rubbed it, drew it against his face and blew warm breath on to its lifeless fingers.

Callum waved his cigarette and puffed like Bette Davis on Mogadon.

'I think I'm dying,' he said. 'I don't seem able to feel anything.'

He started humming and his hand went limp. Wol put it carefully back on his knees. It flopped on to the step and Callum turned his head and looked at it, blank. Trish took Wol into the kitchen.

'It's Gerth,' she said, 'he's going to Hong Kong and he's ditched Callum – just like that.'

'What about the baby?' Wol said. 'What about everything – oh, hey now, this can't be happening.'

'It is,' Trish said, sniffing back tears. 'I didn't get a chance to tell him. Gerth. He came bursting in, full of himself and the new job and Callum was – oh, just something to deal with. He talked about getting rid of his suits in the same breath. I couldn't say anything.'

'Fuck!' Wol exploded. 'What a bastard! Jesus, it's all so sudden.'

'I said that,' Trish said. 'And Gerth just said things hadn't been right for ages. You know, like he'd rehearsed it.'

'Things haven't been right for ages? What does he expect?' Wol said. 'He's been living at his fucking work for weeks – months now, and Callum's just been getting on with it, wondering what's wrong and respecting bloody Gerth and his career. You know, he's been chatted up and wooed every night at the club, he's even been teased about where's this mysterious boyfriend and he's managed to laugh it all off. Oh shit.'

He went into the hall and sat next to Callum.

'I gather Trish has updated you on the latest episode of this soap opera I call life?' Callum giggled and picked up another cigarette. 'He *laaarves* me, he *laaarves* me not! Just like that. I think I should be feeling heartbroken, Wol, but I just don't feel anything. Could you light this cigarette? I've spilt the matches – and the babies – could you . . .?'

Wol lit his cigarette and packed the scattered matches back into the box.

'I'm so sorry, bro,' he said. 'I'm right here, love, and I'll stay with you, if you like.'

Callum blew smoke and twisted his fingers through it.

'It was going to be so lovely,' he said. 'Me and Gerth and a baby and a beautiful house and a garden. Everything.'

Wol put an arm round his shoulders. All he could feel was bone and muscles tight as bowstrings. Callum clasped his hand.

'Was it a bad dream?' Callum said. 'I mean, was I playing God with some poor little baby? Have a baby and put it all right? I didn't mean it badly, it just seemed so – perfect.'

He sighed and closed his eyes, leaning back against Wol.

'It wasn't a bad dream,' Wol said. 'It was a beautiful dream. But only beautiful people can have beautiful dreams, and I think Gerth – well, I think he's a shit.'

'Don't say that,' Callum murmured. 'There is no Gerth any more, Wol. Just imagine. Three and a bit years of my life with someone who doesn't exist any more. It's like when Maddy and Chris died, you know, Wol. Just bodies lying there, full of drugs, and you know you'll never see them smile again.

Never have a conversation with them again. And now Gerth. Smack and AIDS and ambition knocking three people I love out of my life.'

He snuggled against Wol.

'I'll have to think of Gerth as dead, Wol, is that wrong? Just if I let myself picture him, somewhere, everything about him going on without me, because he doesn't want me, no, I can't handle that. Just let him be dead. That's all.'

Wol ruffled his hair and rocked him close.

'But we must let the babies have their party,' Callum said, opening his eyes. 'They'll be so disappointed. I can manage it, Wol. Just help me into the garden and we'll have the party. For the babies.'

'If that's what you want,' Wol said. 'I can take you home any time, you know.'

'I know,' Callum said. 'And thank you. I think I need to go on living. Do you know what I mean?'

'Yes,' Wol said, helping him up. 'I'm here.'

'For this I want an Oscar,' Callum said. 'But first, darling, a glass or three of champagne, I think.'

'You're my brother,' Wol said, and they walked into the sunlit garden.

40

Wol noticed Callum's eyes dart to the ansa-phone the minute they got back to Gar-stone Towers. He seemed taller as he sashayed across the room and pressed play. He gazed into the mirror and started dabbing his face with colour.

Beep.

'What ho! It's Bastian here. Just to see how you are. I'll be in – um – Java for the next little while. Rosemay's got the number. Talk to you soon. And best wishes to you and that chap of yours – from all of us. Bye.'

Beep.

'Just for once,' Callum said, his eyes glittering above a painted smile, 'big Brother has got it wrong. This calls for a joint, Wol, don't you think? And would you book a cab for The Prohibition Palace? I must keep busy.'

'Now?' Wol said, amazed at Callum's composure. He'd kept the babies shrieking all afternoon, tap-dancing round the fountain, turning cartwheels along the lawn, a sheave of Trish's borrowed scarves turned him into the Pied Piper. Wol was expecting him to collapse, now he was back home, but he seemed vibrant, driven by some supernatural energy.

'No time like the present,' Callum said. 'We have a show in three hours, Wol, and it must go on. *Dear*. Let's run it through.'

As they worked, Wol felt Callum metamorphose into pure camp. His wrists were languid putty, each hip-swing was Busby Berkeley and his eyelashes fluttered like butterflies gorging nectar.

By the time they got to the dressing room in The Prohibition Palace, he had charmed the cab-driver, blown kisses to the bar-staff and winked at the hungover clientele.

'A real dish on table three,' he cooed, silvering his eyelids. 'Fresh and hot and hunky, Wol, I might disgrace myself.'

If that was his way of dealing with it – well, thought Wol, it beats tears and emotional self-mutilation. Then Callum turned to him and the pain in his eyes stabbed straight into Wol's heart.

'I might be a total bitch tonight,' Callum said. 'If I take the piss out of you, don't take it personally. I need to queen it – nay – Catherine of Russia it – tonight.'

'Feel free,' Wol said. 'Whatever gets you through.'

'Bless you,' Callum said. 'And – Wol. I'm in the shit market again. A regular little lumpette for moi, chéri! I don't think I can do this bit straight.'

In the bar after the show, Callum swooned his way through a cluster of queens buying them drinks. Benny motioned them over to his table. Important guests, meet my stars!

Callum flirted shamelessly with Stax, the mafia man, someone whose way of life he despised. He turned the charm on to Benny's blonde toygirl and screeched about foundation garments and uplift brassières.

'You're different tonight.' Benny refilled Callum's glass over and over. 'I think you must be in love!'

'Oh must I, Mister Hartmann?' Callum's voice drawled bathos. 'Surely not! I've done that, and I would like to think that I never do anything twice.'

'Whatever it is, enjoy,' Benny said.

'I plan to,' Callum said. 'Have you seen the bona gams on that! Lovely lallies, and I am a leg queen.'

Benny looked over to a clone in a white leather jacket.

'What about the husband, Callum?' he said, chuckling. 'Away on business again?'

'Husband?' Callum trilled, flourishing the naked third finger of his left hand. 'I don't recall a wedding, and I surely would have remembered the frock!'

Benny laughed and ordered more champagne.

Callum fished for and hooked, the blond white-jacketed clone, then cast him back into the waters of long past midnight. The taxi took him and Wol back to Garstone Towers, and he sent Wol home.

'I have to be alone, dear Wol,' he said. 'Whether for Garbo or emotional garbage, I don't know, but no, I won't do anything desperate. If the urge comes, I shall ring you. But it won't.'

Wol wasn't happy about this at all.

'Listen, oh wise one,' Callum said, lurching with champagne. 'I'll go to bed and sleep and tomorrow I'll go to the sea. And when I come back, I'll organise my kind of dinner-party, with my kind of people. A sort of last supper. You. Hannah. Tony. Cleo. I won't do myself in, Wol. No. I think I shall not hang myself today – or any other.'

Death, he added in his mind, would merely bring me to the land of the dead and that was where Gerth had chosen to be.

There was no flashing light on the ansaphone and his head reeled with the silence. He rewound his Noël Coward tape and went into the bathroom to splash his face with icy water. He gazed into his own eyes in the mirror and whispered *congratulations*. He pushed his teased hair back from his face.

'Well,' he said softly, 'Miss Helpless Girly, six foot two, eyes of blue, thanks for this evening. You little heartbreaker, darling, come and stay with me any time. You have my full permission to screech your tits off. I shall call you Maria, flibbertigibbet, will o' the wisp and clown.'

He rolled a joint and pushed play so that Noël Coward would sing him through sleep, or whatever happened next. Only when he heard 'I'll Be Seeing You' did he start to cry.

41

Rain splotched on to Callum's windscreen as he parked up behind the dunes. It was dry as he got out of the car. He jumped over the stile and ran along the winding sandy paths until he saw the ocean. He paused and let his gaze sweep the length of the sands.

Nobody.

He slung his shoes into his magic bag and rolled up his jeans. The water felt good on his legs, salty slaps chilling him to the bone. He ducked his head into the foam and his ears rang. On this bit of the beach there was a charred piece of corrugated iron and he constructed a windbreak for his fire. The flames ripped sideways across the sand and smoke stung his eyes.

He crumbled bitter herbs into the embers and snuffed deep as they burned. He'd been here so many times . . . my God, even for his first trip in the smartie mobile with Gerth. He chanted a song of ending and rubbed bars of ash on to his cheekbones. Once more to the sea to wash it all away, to cast the hot ashes to the tides. He scrubbed the gritty water into his face until he was gasping with the chill of it.

Then the clouds rumbled and he sat cross-legged only yards from the waves. A flight of sandpipers skimmed the waves and vanished towards a distant dark tree. Rain fell once more, a torrent, each drop huge and hard, soaking through his t-shirt, running down his face and neck like a waterfall.

He sat as lightning cracked and thunder shook the earth itself. Fierce-fanged lightning speared the horizon, ripping the deep purple clouds apart. The air was electric, dangerous and thrilling. With some difficulty he made a joint and lit it, cupping the hot ember against his palm to keep it dry.

'I am Callum,' he shouted, leaping to his feet, his body an elongated X, arms stretching to the heavens.

He stood until the rain stopped and only then did he let his arms drop. His body folded back on to the sand and he waited for the rainbow. Here it came, ushering away the bruised thunderclouds, holding in its arc a softer grey, a dove grey – peace, the rain has stopped and will not drown you.

He trudged back up the sodden sand, his clothes heavy with water, his plimsolls squelching streams from every lace-hole. He turned and raised his arms again.

'I am Callum,' he called again, and the sea-gulls screamed his name back at him, 'I am your priest and servant.'

At a garage, the cashier looked at him strangely and he caught his reflection, distorted in the plate-glass window. No shoes, a face smeared with dirt, his hair a saturated hank of seaweed. He smiled at the cashier deliberately, remembering how loonies and hoboes get a wide berth. That would come in handy.

Back in Garstone Towers, he stripped and towelled himself dry. Wol had left two messages and was coming over soon. Well, that was nice, but he felt a part of himself draw away from even that human contact. Mr Coward was about all he could handle hearing, and he forced himself to comb his hair and put on some clothes through 'I'll Be Seeing You'.

My anthem of loss, he thought, and life goes on, and I have a last supper to arrange and phone calls to make. Sure enough, Cleo and Tony were thrilled to be asked and that older man voice, been it and done it and still here, felt like a comfortable chair and slippers. Hannah asked him, didn't he want a lodger – the bairns were driving her up the wall and for tuppence she'd dump them with social services. But, yes, a night off would be a blessing. She'd bring a gallon of Walker's finest rotgut.

By the time Wol arrived, Callum had set a tea-tray with a cloth and cups and saucers.

'A nice cup of tea and some sinful biscuits,' he said, his words tinkling like a teaspoon stirring sugar. 'You must help me with this menu, Wol, I feel Dame Fanny Crackpot sweeping over me.'

Wol sipped his tea and looked at his broken-hearted friend. If he could keep this up, maybe he wouldn't fall to pieces. It was like dancing on a bed of nails: do it fast enough and you feel no pain.

'You see,' Callum added brightly, 'there's a lot of me that has been in the closet since my – entanglement. Bits that have brought me through most things. My early warning system is on red alert. My many selves have a lot invested in avoiding a return to Credsworth. Non, non, chéri! Love may drive us crazy and its absence even crazier, but there's no need to go to the nuthouse to prove it. And now for my last supper menu?'

'Red dragon pie,' Wol said. 'Salad and couscous and lychees and cream.'

'Yes,' Callum said, 'and champagne for Ninotchka, the divine Mr Coward for nostalgia and a tray of joints by way of anaesthetic. All to be enjoyed among our own kind.'

Their palms met in affirmation.

42

For the first year after Gerth left, when Callum felt anything at all, he felt like half a person. Sometimes less, for there was a raw wound right through him. It felt like it would never heal. At the edge of his pain there was a fizzing numbness like scar tissue. His eyes were a mirror where a stone has hit: the image is fragmented, the angles never quite right. He started wearing shades when he went out.

'I am Kay,' he thought, 'and the Snow Queen has driven me to her ice palace and I am so cold I don't even know what cold means any more.'

With Gerth he had felt complete. He flowed effortlessly from camp to cordon bleu, painting pictures and painting walls, making shelves, carving wild creatures from wood, creating carnival costumes. Love in every deed, his whole body electric with tenderness and passion. He was always a queen whether on the stage, the dance-floor or whirling around the ceramic hob – even bent over the Workmate, every gesture was regal.

This first year alone again, he wore his many selves like costumes: each self had its own way of talking, its own gestures, its own music. He grew very thin for none of him wanted to eat. Only Wol's pink-cross parcels kept him going.

Wol noticed, Wol fretted, but like a true friend, he said nothing, just shrugged as Callum summoned one façade after another. He was still on his feet, after all.

In the club after a show, he was Maria, the helpless girly.

Sometimes, when he wasn't performing, he'd join Cleo and Tony at their table and spectate in safety.

'*Mon Dieu!*' he'd say, patting his hair, 'why are all the boys so *jeune* these days, chéri, so terribly jeune and pretty?'

'Who says vaudeville is dead?' Cleo declaimed. 'You're very Jules and Sandy tonight, Cal. You want to be careful. You might just turn into a PAP. You have been warned.'

He'd roll his eyes at the lone figures at the bar, older men with careful hairdos and immaculate clothes, too eager to offer drinks when anyone came near them.

'Pathetic Ageing Poofs!' Cleo shuddered. 'There but for the grace of God, dearie! And the love of a good man!'

Callum tossed his head.

'I cherish my own company, Cleo,' he said.

Cleo laughed and patted his knee.

'So do we, bonny lad,' he said. 'So do we.'

'And I must freshen my lippy,' Callum said, making his way to the gents, with an exaggerated hip-swing.

'Is he all right?' Tony asked Wol.

'He's making the best of a bad situation,' Wol said. 'Takin' any kindness that he can, to quote the great Ms Jackson. He seems to want to be alone, and he knows I'd move in and baby-sit if he wanted me to.'

'Sometimes it's the best way,' Cleo said. 'I was a very alone queen before young Antoinette swept me off my feet, wasn't I honey?'

Tony smiled at him.

'Oh, yes,' he said. 'Alone – not lonely. But Callum's very young – and fragile. He's getting too thin, and no-one will say anything these days. It's lonely you have to watch out for.'

'Right,' Wol said. 'I will.'

'Oh dear,' Tony said. 'Here comes my son. Will it be nagging or a straight request for cash?'

Tony's son liked to be the parent, and Wol watched hungrily while he sniffed Tony's glass and scolded him. There was something about family that made him wistful and he sighed. Callum was his family and now they both felt adopted by Tony and Cleo, with Benny Hartmann as godfather. He'd got so excited by the idea of Callum and bloody Gerth having a baby and him being a sort of uncle . . . He wondered about his own child. If he had one. These days, with Callum so distant and brittle, he'd even thought of going to look for his child. When Callum was really on his feet, maybe he would.

'Who's the hunk?' Callum breathed into his ear.

'Tony's son,' Wol said. 'Performing his filial duty. Married.'

'Shame,' Callum said. 'I shall have to cast my beady little eyes elsewhere. I feel a flirt coming on. Do you mind?'

'Bro,' Wol said, 'I shall watch and enjoy.'

He heard Callum laugh when someone called him the tart with the broken heart. He saw him lure a boy in black denim on to the dance floor, and he watched him whirl, Queen Astarte of the Seven Veils again, while the denim queen shuffled around him, out of time.

'Home,' Callum said. 'I must get my beauty sleep. Do distract that boy while I escape! *Au revoir!*'

43

Wol had no idea of how Callum spent his days now. They were together for their shows, but Callum had started rushing home afterwards, and he came to the bar less and less. His last supper had been just that. When they did meet, Callum didn't seem unhappy, more to have slipped into a distant reverie. Often he didn't seem to hear what Wol said, or he just smiled politely, as if words were too much of an effort.

Callum had absented himself by degrees from all the things they used to do. If he went to the sea, he went alone. He made no response to Wol's plans for Solstice, although he certainly wasn't home that night.

He was very thin, but that had happened gradually, and he scolded himself – in his role as Nurse Florence Nightshade – into taking vitamins when he simply couldn't chew or swallow. He was very stoned most of the time, and Wol couldn't penetrate that self-contained haze.

Wol thought that maybe now was the time to go searching for his child. Now or soon. His only ties were Callum and their act, and he mentioned going away to Callum several times, but he couldn't be sure that Callum had taken it in.

And Callum found that he wasn't sleeping at all and it didn't bother him. He floated in his living room some evenings, never bothering to answer the phone or even switch on the ansaphone. He felt as if he was in an isolation tank, and happy with it – well, not happy. Just it seemed completely right to him. One day he bumped into an angry little woman on the balcony, dragging a trolley packed with plastic sacks.

'Growmore,' she hissed at him.

'Yes,' he said, 'I must. Thank you.'

He wished Wol would stop throwing threads of worry through the haze and just leave him be. Living and partly living.

And while he was immaculate on stage and on his rare appearances in the club, the rest of the time he didn't bother to shave or dress. He wore the same clothes until they were filthy and he didn't mend anything; he looked at the holes in his shoes and shrugged. Let it be.

He found that people avoided him when he went out, walking round him as if he was a burst carton of milk. In the shops they seemed surprised when he had the money and served him quickly. He tried going into the local pub and they refused to serve him and he laughed like a madman as they bundled him out of the door.

'I am the Ragga-Vagabond,' he muttered in the park, and sifted through a bin. He colonised a bench and fielded scandalised glares from passers-by.

'I am the Geek,' he hissed at his gaping shoes.

One week he forgot to go to The Prohibition Palace and Wol carried the show by himself. Benny was sympathetic, but he lined up another act immediately. He'd seen the manic degeneration of Callum and dozens like him over the years, and business was business.

'Give it a while,' Benny said to Wol. 'Call it a vacation. Get back to me when Callum's got his head together again. Really got it together again. It's the way with artistes, you're all so temperamental.'

Wol nodded. Fair enough – and now there was only Callum to hold him here while his head reeled with unanswered questions about his child. One way or another he had to know.

On one of his park days, one indifferent January morning, Callum the Hobo, the Ragga-Vagabond, became mother to a golden-grey Christmas puppy cowering in the bushes. He heard whimpers and crouched in the snow, making soothing noises. The puppy came crawling towards him, wagging its poor little tail, its sad eyes cringing. Its thick fur was spiked with mud and its paws were cut and stiff.

Callum picked it up and it licked his face. He could have smothered it with a pent-up hug, for that hesitant tongue was the first warmth he'd felt for an eternity.

He cradled it all the way home, and named it Wolf.

'You have to be fearless,' he told it, 'like your ancestors. And then of course, you'll love the divine Wolfgang Amadeus. Now, let me do something nice for your feet.'

The vaudeville crew who carried Callum's broken spirit through the days took Wolf to their hearts. Florence Nightshade bathed and bandaged his paws, Dame Fanny Crackpot fed him, the High Priest of Natural Wisdom took him for long walks once his paws were healed, Maria fussed him, the Ageing Poof sighed over his youth and beauty, Queen Astarte danced him into a frenzy.

Most of all, the Ragga-Vagabond loved him and guarded his life with his own.

And the Ragga-Vagabond was Wolf's hero.

44

Wolf made Callum get up in the mornings, his tongue laughing, all bright-eyed and eager for fresh air and a run on the overgrown green seven floors below. Wolf wagged his gold-plumed tail and told Callum he was God, he was the great dinner lady in the sky, as he cocked his head to one side and flirted with his beautiful brown eyes, knocking one deep brown paw against his dish. Wolf ate in great happy gulps and so Callum started eating again, sitting on the floor next to him.

Wolf got fleas in the summer and scratched all night. Next day Callum bought shampoo and a comb for him and washed and groomed him until his thick coat lay silky and magnificent. His drying coat smelt clean and Callum noticed the staleness of his own body, the filth ingrained in every fibre of his clothes. He bathed and shaved and looked into his tired eyes in the bathroom mirror. His hair was broken ended and long.

Hannah, he thought, Hannah will cut my hair.

He made a pile of all his clothes and split it into three. One was to be junked, either too filthy or bought to please Gerth. One could be washed. One could be worn straight away if he ironed it. He made the unfamiliar trip to the launderette and left everything there to be service-washed. Then he walked the four miles to where Hannah worked.

'She's not here any more, pet,' said a woman with 'Eileen' embroidered on her overall. 'She works from home. Has been for about two years now.'

'I've been away, you see,' Callum said, backing out into the street. He wasn't good with people at all these days. Thank God for the certainty of Wolf's lead tugging at his hand.

His feet took him to Hannah's door.

'Well, who's been understudying the bloody Scarlet Pimpernel,' Hannah said. 'Come in. You and the dingo.'

'I'm sorry,' Callum said, 'I haven't been too well lately. This is Wolf.'

'I've knocked on your door more times than I can remember,' Hannah said. 'I thought you'd moved. And I've phoned, but I just get some pre-recording saying that this number is no longer recognised.'

'I'm sorry,' Callum said. 'I changed the number. Then I was just out of touch with everything. Everyone. Except Wol, he's got a key. Only I haven't seen him for a while. I expect he just got fed up with me.'

'He's gone away,' Hannah said. 'Surely he told you?'

'I seem to remember something,' Callum said, frowning and closing his eyes. 'No, it's gone.'

'Hopeless Harry, you,' Hannah said, making tea, forcing her voice to be abrasive and cheerful.

'I think he said something about going south,' Callum said. 'Something about family. I don't know.'

Hannah sighed. She knew Wol had said Callum wasn't too good these days, but she was shocked by the change in him. His face had a curious blank pallor. He looked like her dad when he knew he was dying of cancer. Waxen like a death-mask, chalky in the sunlight, bloodless. She had learned to be brisk and sarcastic as she took care of him and he said he'd rather have her than her sister moping round like a nun.

'I suppose you want a free haircut,' she said.

'Yes, I do,' Callum said, his hands warming round the mug of tea. 'I'm sorry I've been so – pathetic.'

'So am I, bonny lad, believe me,' Hannah said. 'That's your last apology by the way. Heavenly Hannah forgives you for being an inadequate wimp. And let's have no more of it.'

'How are the children?' Callum said.

Hannah laughed.

'Much better now I've given sod features the order of the boot,' she said. 'Moody Mark – you remember him? Last time we spoke you said he should start dusting down his suitcases. It took me two years then I thought, Hannah, this fella's killing you. No violence, not even a cross word. Just night after night of slippers and telly, I thought I'd lost me sex appeal.'

'Who is it now, darling?' Callum said, the icicle glitter of The Ageing Poof sparkling into his voice.

'Well, *darling*,' Hannah mimicked, 'me, myself, I. And a toyboy who I keep on a long leash. Young Derek from Glasgow. He's allowed to stay a couple of nights a week. He keeps proposing to me. He's company.'

'But you're not in love?' Callum said.

'Nah,' Hannah pursed her lips. 'It's just not there with him. Or maybe it's me. I dunno. It does. Anyways, let's get this hair cut, Callum, you look awful.'

Wolf beat his tail against the floor as she started. He liked Hannah, she was good to Callum and that was how it should be.

Back at home, Callum hung his clean clothes up and started to spring clean. It was exhausting, and the dust dried his throat, but it was good to feel alive again. For years all he'd played was a song with the lyric '*most of the time I feel half way all right*'. That just wasn't good enough any more.

He filled the flat with *South Pacific*, ignoring the automatic tears and forcing himself to sing along. His voice was weary, the high notes cracked, the low notes growled, but it was his voice again, at long last.

45

Some time after he got his voice back, Callum was astonished to hear the letterbox rattle on a Tuesday morning. Thursday was giro day, the only post he ever expected. There had been one airmail letter in Gerth's handwriting, but he'd written RETURN TO SENDER on the back of it, and crossed out his address, adding NO LONGER HERE to the front of it. There had been some postcards from Wol, trees at Virginia Water, Virginia Woolf's house, a packet of Golden Virginia. Wol was OK. Wol was fine. He'd be back soon. He sent his love. Callum couldn't remember when he'd gone, or why. He stuck these to the wall, and wrote 'WOL'S CORNER' above them. No-one else wrote to him.

So he was fully expecting another cryptic postcard – maybe a house covered with Virginia Creeper, since that appeared to be Wol's theme.

But this was a brown envelope, and he stood sipping tea and looking at it. Maybe it was a work rehabilitation interview. They usually lasted about two minutes. Anyone looking at him could see it was hopeless.

Wolf batted the envelope along the passage.

Callum picked it up and went into the living room. He put on Mary Coughlan, planning a melancholy ride along the boulevards of smoky broken dreams, rolled a joint, lit it and turned the envelope over and over.

Postmark: Newcastle.

Mr C. Cassel. That was him. Cassel in the air.

He jerked his thumb along under the flap and took out a piece of folded paper.

DO NOT IGNORE THIS LETTER.

None of it made much sense to him. He skimmed through to the last sentence.

'We, the council, will do everything we can to assist you with relocation.'

But he had no plans to move – had he?

No.

He shuffled outside and leaned on the balcony, blowing smoke. A man appeared from next door, which was rare. He was an old man, a widower, slightly deaf. Mr Eliot, the perfect neighbour. He was holding a letter out towards Callum, the same as the one he'd just read, except for the name.

'Can ye make sense of this, lad?'

Callum forced himself to focus.

Another neighbour appeared, Mrs Rose, an old lady, the white paper shaking in her hand. And another. They grouped around Callum as if he could help. Someone made a tray of tea, someone brought plain biscuits on a plate.

'They're going to demolish Garstone Towers,' Callum said, the words sinking into his brain. 'They're knocking it all down. This time they mean it. There's even a date. We've all got to move.'

'By,' Mr Eliot said, 'ye knaa! It's like a high falutin' eviction. Get oot wi a lot of long words wrapping it up. Where are they ganna place all of we?'

'That's the last thing they care aboot!' Mrs Rose said, her hearing aid whistling.

'It's not for six months,' Callum said.

'Six months is nowt,' Mr Eliot said. 'I nivver thowt I'd see this day! It's just like thirty years back when they put this place up. We'll have nae choice. Like it or lump it, ye're oot.'

'I'm too old for this,' Mrs Rose said.

They stood in silence, as the truth of it hit them. Most of them had been born in Garstone and thought they'd end their days here, high above the ground, but at least it was ground they knew. And now they wouldn't. Just like that. One by one they went back behind their front doors and sat looking at their homes, stunned.

Two months before the demolition, the council rehoused some fourteen thousand people all over the city; people who'd lived next door and round the corner or up the balcony all their lives now lived a bus or a train ride apart and most of them never saw each other again. For a few years a spider-written Christmas card. Bumping into each other once in a while brought a grateful flock of *d'ye remember* and *it seems like yesterday*.

Maybe another thousand emigrated. Canada, New Zealand, Australia, anywhere a relative could be found stuck in new and foreign soil like a grappling hook, the blood tie a rope smooth with red tape, a rope you could haul yourself up on if you stuck to it.

A few hundred found a room with family, some welcoming, others dutiful and resigned.

A hundred or so took up residence in hospitals for the aged and infirm.

And the rest?

A lot just went no-one knows where, leaving rent arrears and flats stripped bare, might as well if they're knocking the buggers down.

Some bright spark sold a hundred or so empty flats to a foreign business concern, had a face lift, stole a passport and fled to the sunshine.

The council trawled the flats the weeks before demolition was due and dumped their catch in bed and breakfasts, half-way houses, hostels.

The police did a further trawl and upped the overcrowded prison statistics. We shall not be moved, the locked vans sang and thumped all down the High Road.

The day the crane moved in with its whirling ball and chain, you'd have thought a miracle was about to be performed, for people lined the site, pushed back by barriers and truncheons and uniforms. A miracle or a funeral cortège for someone local and dearly loved. By night, fifty flats lay like smashed crates, their walls broken tablets of concrete and brick. Beside the debris, above the huge metal feet of the crane, stood the next day's work. A lofty wall that was the inner husk of six flats. Like a noughts and crosses grid, it was scored with broad parallel lines of iron and concrete that had been floors. Floors framing the walls of rooms where people had lived. One wall had rose-patterned wallpaper and a real-log effect fire hanging like a half-pinned brooch. There was a torn poster of Che Guevara on the top wall and the word REVOLUTION spray-painted in red. Students. Twice, the symmetrical sadness of a staircase zigzagged like a shadow. Once it crossed age-yellow paint where ovals and squares of white were all that was left of pictures, maybe a mirror. No-one would ever climb these stairs again.

That night there was a storm. Oh, the heavens were clear enough, the stars were bright, the moon was one of God's fingernails curved white and clean. Only the gentlest of breezes fluttered through the ribbons of wallpaper.

This was a storm that had been brewing in computer files and papers and in-trays and words half-said and hints and secrets rolling around the council chambers like fluff under the furniture in a house gone to seed. Months and years the council had been a well-made bed, with hospital corners no matron could fault. This storm whipped back the sheets and there wasn't even a mattress, let alone a pillow.

Can of worms, people said on the radio and television, hornet's nest, Pandora's box, dirty washing, skeleton in the closet. Corruption in high places and low.

All council work was suspended at midnight. The council was bankrupt – so was the government, so was the world, but that didn't come out.

The contractors took the crane away in the morning.

And, by the way, the day the crane came, in spite of searches high and low, Garstone Towers wasn't empty.

Callum was still there, Callum and Wolf on the seventh floor. They'd hidden in the water tank cupboard when the searches were made. The searchers had assumed that Callum's chaos was abandoned rubbish and moved on.

Up on the eighth floor, right over his head, in the highest and hardest to let flat in all Tyneside, was Eleanor Crumsty, the fierce little woman with the trolley.

And nobody knew they were there.

46

Eleanor had been given the flat after a long run-in with the caring community's red tape: the police, a spell in Credsworth, sleeping in the same bed Callum had used, years before; social services, social workers, six months on a locked ward; doctors and psychiatric outreach workers. A middle-aged amnesiac tested their systems to the limit. Nothing could be done without a date of birth and a national insurance number, and what either was – if there had been either in the first place, well, Eleanor Crumsty hadn't the foggiest idea. Eventually, they'd awarded her an emergency number.

YX531499Z was her passport to society.

When they told her, she laughed – got your number, she thought.

They examined her teeth and decided she was between forty and fifty.

'1953,' she said, surprisingly, one day.

The outreach worker was thrilled. Eleanor snorted: it was the date of the coronation, glazed on to the mug she was holding. But it seemed to make all the difference to them. What fools they were!

No matter. She took the date of the coronation as her birthday, easy to remember. When they asked her about it, she said, 'I was a coronation baby.'

It had a ring to it.

The number on her very own front door was 898. No-one saw it really, apart from her. No-one bothered her, squirrelled away on the top floor, mind your own business, who else should be minding it. Once she was settled, and fairly sure no one would move her on, gid aht of it!, she decided on a garden, something she'd dreamed of for years. Live your dreams – hadn't Rangoon said that to her? Ah, Rangoon, that and so many other words! A prince among men, but oh so long ago. From time to time, Eleanor's mind would throw her clear images like stills from a movie, although she had no idea when or where they came from. One of them was a garden and it made her sad and furious when it disappeared as fast as it had come.

She hauled bags of fertiliser and soil up the stairs in her old trolley – a lady needs a trolley – and hardly ever said two words to anyone.

When she read the eviction letter, she laughed and laughed. As if they thought demolition could shift her! You are where you will be, that was Rangoon again. She crawled out on to her balcony roof and lay there spread-eagled when the searchers came, and climbed carefully back down when they left. Later she watched the first day's work of destruction and cast curses on the crane.

And the curses worked – just like that! The crane never crushed another brick. Awed by her own power, she went wild with her window boxes and filled her stairs with trays of earth and peat and seeds. She never saw Callum, never associated the faint music through the floor with a real person.

Home.

It was home.

One day she looked at her sitting room floor, wondering.

Her memory threw up the words 'carrot seed', and there was a sweetness in the sound. Carrot seed and joy. She half-closed her eyes and she could see feathery green fronds at her feet in a dark room. Her room? As she watched, the room glittered with broken shards of mirror, and her head filled with the scent of earth and flowers . . .

''Twas brillig,' she said. 'Even in the depths of night, Rangoon. ''Twas brillig and the . . . something? What?'

She rolled up the rug and stuffed it in a cupboard.

'Rangoon,' she chanted over and over, heaping up soil.

47

For a few weeks after the demolition stopped, Callum took a different route back to his flat every day. In case . . . well, who is interested in a middle-aged poof, dear, he jeered at himself, *nulle personne, chéri, Callum Cassel, nul point!*

'I beg your pardon,' he murmured, falsetto. 'But there may still be a tall dark handsome stranger searching for a girl named Maria!'

His body shrugged into his hobo self and shambled along, muttering nonsense. Callum had found that untouchable is best for out of doors.

One day, he found the lift was no longer working. On the third flight of stairs, he paused, then pushed the doors on to the balcony of floor three: he had never been here before. He knew at once that it was deserted, and anyway, he had Wolf walking two steps ahead of him.

The door of the first flat hung half-open. 327. He went in: it was a mirror-image of his own. The tiled passage was tufted with black foam. In the bathroom, there were four holes on one wall: these people had even taken the mirror. The tiles were smashed where they'd tried to prise them off and the bath had a hole in it.

He could picture them leaving, kicking the plastic side of the bath to uselessness – if we can't use it, no bastard else is going to! The very words were still in the air. On the sink a bar of soap, pink gone dry and streaked with grey. More puddles of foam carpet backing like fungus. At the tiny window a frill of lacy net hanging from a nail.

The grey fossil of a dishcloth lay hunched in the kitchen sink, and a copper wire pan-scrubber was stuck to the draining board like a sea-urchin. Here, the lino tiles were cracked and curling. One of the cupboards held two chipped cups. The living room was bare except for a moss-green carpet with bright islands where there had been chairs and a sofa.

Callum felt like an archaeologist, making his own sense and nonsense of the odd objects left by a dying race who'd had to move on.

The bedroom was the saddest place in this flat. It was sunset pink, a shadow of dust where there had been a movie star canopy, probably lace. He stood under this pyramid and looked out of the window: all he could see was tree-tops and the wide blue sky. Mr and Mrs 327 had lain in this bed night after night, woken morning after morning and smiled at each other, sat up and had cups of tea and looked at the view. On one wall, clear as a stencil, a lacy framed mirror had hung. Mr 327 would have checked his tie in here, Mrs 327 her earrings and lipstick.

He tiptoed out of the husk of their lives.

328 and 329 were locked, but 330 didn't even have a door. He went into a corridor painted buttercup yellow, walking on a purple carpet. Mould was creeping along from the empty doorframe. The living room was sky blue with a streaky navy skirting board. He saw a coronation saucer on the windowsill, the young queen moustached with cigarette ash, her consort's eyes rimmed with twin monocles of nicotine. Caterpillars of ash and troughs of brown lay between upright dog-ends. In the bedroom a dead mattress lay, contour-lined with piss and passion, the carpet burned through all around it. The top of the toilet cistern bubbled with cigarette burns and a cork-effect filter floated in the bowl.

'Here lived the Soddit family,' Callum told Wolf. 'We can't be bothered to reach the ashtray, so sod it! Can't be bothered to get up and piss, so sod it! Oh – we've got to get out – well, sod it all!'

It was dark by the time he'd explored all the flats on the

third floor. Maybe tomorrow he'd try level four. It fascinated him. Most of the time these days he was stoned – it was better to take the edge off reality than eat, he'd found. And begging didn't pay well enough for both. Hunger made him dizzy, dope made him high, the strain of his taut nerves brought vivid flashes of hallucination. Seeing Hannah had exhausted him, to speak to someone who spoke back had been a novelty, and the words echoed round his mind, like a promise that he was really there. He'd liked it, and he would go back . . . sometime. But only Wolf was solid and alive these days and he didn't need words to know how Callum was feeling.

In his wanderings, he felt that the shell of Garstone Towers was peopled by reluctant ghosts clinging to years of memory. He could have been in Pompeii, where petrified corpses lay clutching jewellery and bags of coins. A few minutes wasted to grab their worldly treasures and the lava was on them, killing them as surely as sea-water flooding the lungs of a deep-sea diver whose breathing pipe is snagged and slashed by coral. It was the underbelly of Pompeii – all that was left in these rectangular caves had been abandoned as worthless.

After a while, he knew many flats in his block from the inside. Daylight and his dog woke him, and dope sent him dreaming on a quest for a particular view. He often returned to the bedroom tree-tops of 327, sometimes with a thermos of tea and a heel of bread for a lonely picnic.

He became aware that someone was still living above him. There had been noises which he'd vaguely thought of as pigeons or sea-gulls. One day he decided to wander along his balcony and go upstairs to the roof, but he drew back into a doorway when he saw two black boots at eye level on the staircase. The boots went upwards and he peered slowly after them. Two boots and the black hem of a long coat. And the wheels of a trolley.

He noticed a plastic crate on one step, filled with earth and small green shoots.

He hung a red cloth over his balcony and a yellow rag at his window. From the ground he squinted upwards and got his bearings. There was another flat directly above his and a blur of pink and green along its window-ledge. Anyone who grew flowers couldn't pose a threat and so he relaxed. Wolf never flickered at the sound of their footsteps, so they must be all right. If they'd wanted to be known, they'd have come down long ago. At night he sometimes looked up at his glo-starred ceiling and bid whoever it was good-night. Sweet dreams.

Part five

....

Crazeland

48

Wol drove past dreaming spires without seeing them. Bicycle lanes and leafy avenues gave way to blue steel industrial units and barren concrete sites, 'Patrolled By Guard Dogs 24 Hours'. Darwin Newtown sprawled off the ringroad, a half-boarded estate where mini-roundabouts and sleeping policemen had been laid in the road at hundred-yard intervals in lieu of the real thing.

It was weeks since he'd started this quest, prodding his mum and dad and old neighbours without raising too much curiosity; phone books; days down in London in Catherine House going through the registers of births and marriages. Finally, the electoral roll had given him an address.

A blue-tagged sapling with broken branches tilted at the paving stones. Cranmer Close was a cul-de-sac and Wol parked his van opposite number 12, rolling a cigarette. He was shaking from non-stop driving and nights of sleeping in the van.

'I'll find out one way or the other,' he said out loud.

The cigarette was half-smoked when he spoke again.

'Maybe.'

He wished Callum was beside him right now. The old Callum, the real one. Only the last few years, with Callum so fragile and needy, Wol had driven himself ragged. This quest was for himself, and Callum just couldn't focus anywhere away from his own broken heart. At least he now had the dog, Wolf, and Wol had absolute faith in dogs.

As he crossed the road, he shoved his hair back and wondered if he should have combed it. Too late, and a comb didn't make much difference anyway. He knocked at number 12.

The door opened a few inches on a chain and a snarling muzzle poked out towards his knees. A Rab C. Nesbitt clone glared at him.

'Get in, you bugger!' he told the dog and jerked it inside. 'He'll have your leg off. What are you after?'

'Is Mrs Martin in?' Wol said. 'Gloria Martin?'

'Who's asking?'

'Wol,' he said. 'I knew her sister.'

The door closed and the man shouted into the house.

'Gloria, it's for you. Some lad who knew your Chrissy. Geordie lad. For chrissakes, Gloria, can you hear me? This bloody dog's driving me demented!'

'Shut the dog in the back,' this was a woman's voice. 'I'm not opening the door till you do. One of these days there'll be a court case. You and your bloody animals!'

The door opened wide this time and Gloria Martin stood there in a jade and lilac track suit, bleach-blonde just like Chrissy had been, the same hard mouth and fuck-you-fella laughing eyes . . . Wol wanted to cry.

'Well?' she demanded.

'I used to know Chrissy,' he said. 'I wanted to talk to you, if you don't mind.'

'You're not Himself, are you?' Gloria said. 'No. If you were Him, I'd set the bloody dog on you and bugger the police. Are you a friend of his? That bastard husband of hers?'

'No,' Wol said, 'I was Chrissy's friend.'

'You'd best come in,' she said.

She shifted a pile of clothes from a broken-backed sofa in the living-room.

'Bit messy,' she said, 'but if you knew Chrissy you'd be used to that.'

'I don't care,' Wol said, taking in the ripped wallpaper, a gaping hole in the ceiling, plaster ground into the carpet directly underneath. Rows of upright dog-ends lined the fireplace, the windowsill and the table. Gloria lit a cigarette, coughing. Wol could hear the dog snarling through the wall behind him.

'Cuppa tea?' Gloria said. 'I've only just fell out of my pit.'

'I'd love a cup of tea,' Wol said. 'Milk, two sugars if you don't mind.'

Gloria opened the living room door.

'Can you get that bloody kettle on, Ricky!' she shouted. 'You know mine and he'll have two sugars.'

She closed the door again and slid a heavy iron bolt home.

'That effing dog,' she said. 'I won't have him in here. Ricky only took him to stop him getting put to sleep. I'll do it myself one of these days.'

'I don't mind dogs,' Wol said.

'You would this one,' she said grimly. 'It's supposed to be a pit bull, ugly bastard it is. Ricky says it's temperamental. I said, yes, half temper, half mental. You can't even be nice to it else it wets itself. I'm sick of it.'

'Oh, it must be awful,' Wol said.

'It's been brutalised,' Gloria said. 'The bloke Ricky got it off, well, he wanted it to fight. Say no more! The fighting ring he was in got busted and he's banned from keeping dogs for five years. So you can tell how bad it was. Of course Ricky had to bring it here, he's too soft. But it's got to go.'

'Gloria! Open this door! The dog's out the back.'

She let Ricky into the room.

'I'm off out,' he said. 'Here's your tea.'

'I hope you're taking that thing with you,' she said. 'And don't start. The only way we can keep it is chained up and then it howls non-stop.'

'I'll take him,' Ricky said. 'I'll see what Maz says.'

'I'd be a lot happier if you got shot of it,' Gloria said. 'I'm not having a go, Ricky, but them next door have got kids and I'd never forgive myself.'

'I'll see what Maz says,' Ricky said. 'He could be a good dog, you know. With the right handling.'

'Well I'm not bloody Barbara whatsername,' Gloria said. 'Got enough bother house-training you.'

'I love you too,' Ricky said heavily. 'I'll sort it, Gloria. See you later.'

Wol heard the scrabble of heavy paws on lino and the front door slammed.

'He won't be back for a while,' Gloria said. 'What's this about – Wol?'

'Yeah, I'm Wol,' he said, and gulped his tea.

He started to roll a cigarette, shaking his head when she held out her packet.

'I don't know how to start, really,' he said.

'Well, *you* came here,' she said, sitting back. 'I never asked you.'

'Right,' Wol said. 'It's about Chrissy. She came and stayed with you, didn't she – a few years before she died? While he was in Durham.'

'Yes,' Gloria said, her eyes careful. 'What about it?'

'Well, just before then,' he said, 'that's when I knew her really well. We were just friends – at first.'

'I didn't have you down as a ladies' man if you know what I'm saying,' Gloria said. 'I don't have nothing against your sort, either, lots of them are better than normal blokes. Not normal, wossname, you know what I mean. No, it sticks out a mile. Even Ricky spotted it, else he'd never have left me alone with a man. He's too jealous.'

'Yeah,' Wol said, grinning. 'You are what you are. Only, you see, for a while I wasn't. I mean, with Chrissy.'

'And?' Gloria stared at him.

Wol closed his eyes.

'Right, Gloria, this is what it is. When Chrissy came back, she said she'd had a baby. I would have been the father. She said she'd had it adopted. Only later she said she was just winding me up. Then she said I'd never know; that was when her husband was due to come out. Then I didn't really see her again.'

'That sounds like Chrissy.' Gloria started to laugh. 'This is bloody priceless. Chrissy and her bloody messes. Oh I'm not laughing at you, Wol. No. Just let me think a minute. Cold, isn't it? I don't know what I can tell you.'

She lit another cigarette and lit the gas fire. She doesn't believe me, Wol thought. He pulled a chain from under his sweatshirt.

'Look,' he said. 'Not that it'll mean much, but this is half a heart Chrissy gave me. She wore the other half.'

Gloria rubbed the thin gold between her fingers.

'So it was *you*,' she said. 'Well, I'll tell you what I know. When Chrissy came down here that last time, tell the truth, I wasn't too pleased to see her. Chrissy always meant trouble, I know you shouldn't speak ill of the dead, but she did. She couldn't walk a straight line without getting bored, Chrissy. I'm a bit like that, mind. What she told me was she'd got herself this toyboy while sod-features was in the nick. That must have been you. Ever see yourself as a toyboy? Well, that's what Chrissy said you were. Unless that was another bloke.'

'I don't think so,' Wol said. 'I was just about living there.'

'No, she always had them one at a time,' Gloria said. 'Anyway, she said this toyboy had started off dead romantic, and she showed me the heart, just like you've done now. Only she said the toyboy didn't realise what her old man was like, and she was scared. I said to her, do you love him – the toyboy? She said she couldn't answer that. Well, what happened, after a month or so down here, she was really sick one morning. Then the next. Up the duff and Himself due out in fourteen months with good behaviour.'

'I wish I'd known,' Wol said. 'I'd have been here.'

'Me and all,' Gloria said. 'Wish you'd known, I mean. It's a horrible thing being pregnant when you don't want to be. On your own. And with someone like him hanging over you like a court case. What do you want to know, anyway, Wol? It was all years ago.'

'I just want to know,' Wol said, 'what happened.'

'I can't see what good it'll do,' Gloria said. 'But I can't see the harm either, not after all this time. I'll make another cuppa, eh, it's a bit early for me, all this chat.'

Wol picked up a photograph in a brass frame while she was out of the room. Ricky dressed up as Fred Flintstone and Gloria as a French maid. Both holding up pint glasses and laughing. He wondered if she had any photos of Chrissy. He sat down and puffed stale smoke.

Gloria came back in, her hair brushed and pink lipstick softening her mouth.

'Anyway,' she said, giving him tea, 'Chrissy asked me could she stay here and have the baby. She knew she was pregnant all the time. I didn't like it, but she was my big sister, it's blood you see. That's what I was thinking in the kitchen. That baby would have been your blood, and you're one of those blokes who feels it. Believe me, there's not many. That's why I put up with Ricky. He's dead good with kids. Soft as shit on the inside, Ricky. You're just soft.'

Wol shrugged.

'No, you are,' she said. 'Shame Chrissy didn't hang on to you. She got all soppy when she was about six months gone, crying all the time, said she wanted to ring the toyboy – you – and run away with him. You. I said do it, girl, you've got nothing to look forward to with the bastard you married. Only she wouldn't. Well, you know she didn't ring. She said you probably wouldn't want to know now she was pregnant. Silly bloody cow!'

Wol started to cry.

'Sorry,' he said. 'I wish I had known.'

'You can't help it,' Gloria said. 'You've got to see her side. You were seventeen and bent. My hippy toyboy, she called you. You were a pothead, that's what she said, lovely, but you were always stoned. Her old man was thirty-eight and a psycho. He'd have tracked her down no matter what. And Chrissy, well, she was nearly thirty. She was thinking, well, now's all right for having a toyboy, but what about when I'm fifty and he's only thirty-something. You wouldn't want to know.'

'I would,' Wol said.

'Well, yes,' Gloria said. 'You can say that now and it's

probably true, but how the hell could Chrissy know? Even if she thought it, she couldn't be sure? Could she? You tell me.'

'I know,' Wol said. 'It's all too late. What about the baby?'

Gloria looked him in the eye.

For one dazzling moment, he thought she was going to say that Chrissy had left the baby with her and she'd brought it up, and in a few hour's time, his thirteen-year-old baby would bounce through the front door from school and he could be a friend, an uncle, anything . . .

'Chrissy had it adopted,' she said flatly.

'Oh,' Wol said, his stomach knotting. 'What was it? A boy? A girl? Please tell me, Gloria.'

'It was a little boy,' she said. 'Ever so sweet. It had little curls all over its head, nearly white, and lovely blue eyes. I only saw it a few times, but it was yours all right, Wol. But Chrissy signed the papers a week after it was born and that was the end of it.'

'What was his name? Did he have one?' Wol said.

'Oh yes,' Gloria said. 'Mind, they'd have changed it once he was adopted. They usually do. She called him Wayne Tyrone. Or was it Tyrone Wayne? I know she'd thought of Clark or Errol, but I said to her, for God's sake, Chrissy, give the poor little bugger a chance! You know what she was like for old films.'

Wol smiled. Yes, Chrissy loved her old films; they'd stay up all night watching them. But the name on his birth certificate was Wayne and Chrissy knew that.

'Wayne Tyrone,' he said.

'That's it,' Gloria said, 'Wayne Tyrone Boone. She went back to her maiden name, our mum and dad's name for his surname. But like I say, that'll have been changed once he got his new parents. They put pressure on her, mind, people like to adopt tiny babies, you know, and she had to decide before she could really think straight. It's not right. I even thought of taking him myself, only the bloke I was with then put his foot down. I shouldn't have listened, but there you are. If it had been Ricky, we'd have had him like a shot. It's open house with Ricky. But we can all know what's right when it's too late.'

'You don't know what date it was, do you?' Wol said, a vague and wild hope flickering at the back of his mind.

'It was autumn,' Gloria said slowly, 'because he was due out in the late spring. September time – no, later than that. October? I can't be sure.'

'It doesn't matter,' Wol said. 'You've told me more than I ever hoped for already, Gloria.'

'No,' she said. 'It's got me thinking. Mind, I wouldn't have told you nothing without that heart. You showed me that and I knew it had to be you. It's nice Chrissy had someone nice even if it didn't last long. But that date – it'll nag at me now till I get it right. Do you do that? Drives you mental. October I could just about swear to. I'll put the kettle on. Me brain works better with tea swilling round it.'

Wol sat back and stretched.

Wayne Tyrone Boone, October the something, thirteen years ago.

It was enough.

49

Lying and staring at the ceiling, playing Sade, one hand ruffling Wolf's warm fur, drawing deep breaths of sweet smoke: Callum most evenings. It was lonesome, familiar, relaxing. He never put on the lights after dark, in case someone noticed and started asking questions and coming up with tidy answers, like making him live somewhere else, or parcelling him off to Credsworth.

Right now, it seemed as if there were cracks in the ceiling, but he wasn't worried; there were a hundred other flats he could live in if this fell around his ears. It was probably just a trick of the darkness.

In the morning he looked again – the cracks were spiders' webs, that was all, and he was glad. Spiders make a place safe and lucky. He was pleased when the webs grew every day, but although he looked all over for the spider, he never found her.

'We have company,' he told Wolf.

Wolf wagged his tail.

Later he found a film of plaster flakes on the floor below the webs. Later? It could have been a day, a week, months, he hadn't a clue. He giggled at the thought of a steel-fanged spider chomping through concrete, spitting out paint.

Since Gerth left, time was a runaway train with no brakes and no driver; a train which might be careering along full pelt or standing in a forgotten siding. Everything was so dark, how could he tell?

He had, for example, gone to bed one night in spring and woken when the leaves were falling from the trees.

Another morning he was queuing outside a supermarket,

and then the manager was hustling him out into the dark street because they were closing.

He rang Wol once and was still talking into the receiver when Wol came through the front door.

It had been a hell of a year when Gerth left: grief makes nonsense of time and space. It was even worse when every calendar and newspaper told him three, four, five years had passed.

Now it was only minutes that escaped him usually. Maybe that was the smoke, but if he went straight for too long, like a whole hour, the skin started to peel from his body and his heart exploded like an overloaded balloon. His eyes dissolved in tears and his mouth fell agape with all sorts of sounds dribbling into the air, cries from depths he couldn't get out of. Mewling. Puking. Oh, babe, I miss you, Callum wept.

Wol had made sure there was always a lump of shit and a packet of sage and giant Rizlas for him to smoke.

He'd made pots of rice and pasta for Callum to eat, and coaxed him into the bath, where he washed him like a mother bathes her new-born child.

And now Wol was away and Callum had the floaty dreary feeling he simply wouldn't be back.

Lying on the floor, staring at the ceiling, listening to Sade, he started to laugh.

'Christ,' he said to Wolf. 'Do you see what I see?'

Wolf looked up and growled.

'Carrots,' Callum said, standing up and staring. 'Real live bright orange carrots. Oh dear.'

It wasn't the carrots themselves that bothered him: he could check if they were real by climbing up and touching, pulling, tasting. But if they were a hallucination, then that threw everything back into the shifting parameters of Driftland. Driftland was filled with the sort of questions that blew his mind, had him gasping for reality like a fish suffocating suddenly in dry air. In Driftland, he shot from one shock to the next like a pinball desperate not to trickle off the flashing board. Driftland had tipped him over the edge and into Credsworth the first time; it was a land where insanity is the only conclusion.

He didn't want to go back to Credsworth, indeed he and Wol had as a life-pact that neither would ever return to the shadows of days that never ended and crazy vigils of nights too dangerous for sleeping. In Credsworth, days were made safe only when your back was against two walls where they met at a corner. Nights were never safe.

And how could he keep the pact when Wol had disappeared: no-one else understood just how bad a bad day could be. Wol knew the nights when it felt like swimming against a black current in an icy river; Wol knew the relief of dawn after a night like that. All he had to say was – Wol, it's one of those times, and Wol would help him through.

Who else was there?

He'd seen Hannah's face when he turned up on her doorstep; he had a sixth sense about what went on behind people's chosen expressions and words. If he went to her now, crying *help, it's starting again*, she would probably think that Credsworth was the best place for him.

He could ring Bastian, good solid happy Bastian, and if he asked, Bastian would come and get him and take him away down south to his fairytale estate. It was too far away.

Faces and names tripped through his mind. Larry and Bella and Cleo and Tony: all the amiable queens who lived in clubland and would welcome him there. None of them would simply come to Garstone Towers and be where he was.

Wol would have come to where he was and stayed with him through the mists and mazes.

Healing had to be on his ground to be real or not at all. It would be easy to close the door of his flat and go to any number of nice places with good people. But they weren't his places and they weren't his blood, not his true blood; there was only Wol who was his blood and Wol was away and he couldn't remember why or where he had gone.

He forced himself not to look upwards. His fingers were cold as he rolled a joint. The smoke would warm him, the drug would curl around his fractured mind. Anxious reality would shuffle to a safe distance and sanity or insanity would simply not matter quite so much any more. Please, he thought, please.

He ruffled Wolf's lovely head and rifled through his albums for Stevie Wonder's 'Secret Life of Plants', Vangelis's 'Soil Festivities'. If there were carrots above him, growing as if his ceiling was the surface of the earth, not some arbitrary layer of concrete and plaster hundreds of feet high in the air, then so be it. And the music would be a welcome. His speakers fed the air with synthesised explosions of roots and leaves and he sprawled on the floor, glancing upwards through the smoke.

Yes, there were carrots.

Whoever lived upstairs must know about them. And if they didn't, then they should be told, before the floor collapsed and they hurtled downwards into his room.

50

Callum finished the joint and stood up, clutching the wall until the floor stopped rocking. He dropped his turquoise bead round his neck for protection and clarity.

'I'm going visiting, dear,' he told Wolf, climbing along the wall to the door. 'I don't know if my neighbour likes dogs so I'm going to have to leave you as a châtelaine. Indeed, I suspect that my neighbour is wise enough not to like people, so I shouldn't be long.'

Wolf sat in the passage, looking injured and abandoned as only a dog can.

Callum dithered at the mirror. What sort of impression should he try for? Miss Girly? Queen Astarte? Florence Nightshade? The ageing poof with his cod French? None of them seemed appropriate. His face shifted until the Ragga-Vagabond surfaced in his eyes and he borrowed a little of Miss Girly's blue-eyed charm, giggling as he whisked along the balcony and through the double doors to the staircase. He passed plastic troughs of flowers on every step and that cheered him. It was like Wol's fragrant back yard.

'Stop thinking,' he told himself. 'We are out to pay a visit. Present tense leads to future perfect.'

He hesitated on the top step, squeezed the turquoise with one hand and with the other, he rattled the letterbox. Rat a *tat* tat tat tat ta ta ta ta *tat*. *Don't you never turn a stranger from your door.* And they don't come any stranger than me, he muttered.

His ears were radar scanners: someone behind the door was

frozen to the spot. Loud footsteps and the rattle of a chain. The door was flung open and there stood Eleanor Crumsty, glaring at him, a pickaxe handle in her raised fist. The fierce little woman with the trolley – the one who'd told him to *grow more*.

'Hello,' he said, apologetically. 'Bonjour. Guten Abend. I'm sorry to bother you. It's just that I live – more or less – downstairs. It's not that I'm complaining, believe me, it's a relief to break the monotony, but I thought I should mention it to you. I seem to have noticed some rather impressive carrots which appear to be growing through my living room ceiling. I may well have eaten of the insane root and my reason may be clapped in irons somewhere, but they seem real enough. They have shadows, even. I could show you if you like.'

Her ears thrilled at this stream of words – Rangoon used to rattle on like this. She jerked her head.

'You'd better come in,' she said, as the wind blew Callum's blonde curls around like apple blossom on a gusty summer morning.

She went ahead, he followed her, and the passage walls were covered with leaves. He was so high on dope and hunger that he thought for a moment he was back in his own flat.

'Through here,' she glowered at him.

His fingertips told him that these plants were real, where his were *trompe-l'oeil*, perfect apart from where Gerth had kicked a hole in the plaster.

'Real,' he said. 'My dear, a fardel of flora, a garden in Garstone, I'm very impressed.'

She looked at him, frowning. Somewhere in his eyes was a shadow of Rangoon, only Rangoon never looked so pale, apart from when he was in Silvertown Infirmary. And this man was so much younger. Rangoon's eyes were clear blue where Callum's were misty, like a steamy mirror, shattered.

'Naturally, they're real,' she said. 'What else? Come through and sit down. You're white as a ghost, and I can't have you fainting on this hard floor. Pass out in the passage! Concussion at the very least and where would we be.'

He tottered into the room and sat where she pointed, a spasm of cramp tearing at his guts. These days, his legs were as much use as pipe-cleaners. Best to keep his eyes shut, that way he couldn't see the walls undulating above the roller-coaster floor. Windows were the worst: they bellied like clear sails in the wind as if tons of water surged behind them. His throat constricted like a man drowning.

'Tea?' she said.

'Thank you. Three sugars, please,' he said, 'if you don't mind.'

She made tea, her head whirling to hear words like these again, even if they came from this wraith, this spectre who claimed to live so close.

'Here you are,' she said, but he didn't seem to hear.

That was better, thought Callum, hot china at his lips, hot sugary liquid scalding his mouth until his teeth ached. Heat gave him a spine again, a spine and arms and hands that held the cup. Soon his guts would feel the anaesthetic and the veins in his legs would fill with blood again.

'Thank you,' he said, risking a chink of light through one half-open eye. Bless you, he thought, for she'd drawn the curtains and the monstrous ocean was safely outside. Her curtains were dark, studded with random dots of light, and he realised he was looking at the night sky. His saviour squatted on the floor in a carpet of soft green. Oh, yes, the carrots.

'I thought I'd lost you there,' she said. 'You've been asleep all day. I thought it was a coma, but no-one can drink tea in a coma, not that I've heard of. Can you?'

'All day?' Callum said. 'I feel so soothed.'

His voice surprised him: for so long words had come out shrill, gabbled, accusing, and he forgot what he was saying in the middle of a sentence. And then he would founder, fielding frightened or angry looks from strangers, feeling bereft at the automatic wide berth people give loonies. Now, in a perfect stranger's flat, for the first time since he could remember, he was talking normal. Relatively normal.

'I feel soothed,' he said again, for the sheer pleasure of

hearing it. 'The balm of your presence. The calm of your something. I've been asleep all day?'

'Yes,' she said, watching him like a hawk.

'I'm sorry,' he said, apologising for his being with a wave of the hand. 'I don't always remember.'

'Ha ha. Ha,' she said. 'I know that one.'

Know that one? If you don't remember, what can you be sure of? She knew that no-one's life begins lying fully clothed in a pile of stinking rubbish in a back alley in East London. That was always where her memory began. She'd been so thirsty. And then Rangoon had come and everything had started to happen; it had been wonderful. They had tramped the highways and byways and found a place she called Summerland and she still had a pebble to prove it.

And then there was no more Rangoon after Silvertown and everything telescoped away into broken nights and days until an angel gave her a banana. Len, that was his name. Then a bus and a lot of fuss, boys in blue – men in white and women in pink and questions questions questions until she came here and they left her alone. To this day she felt Rangoon must be somewhere around the corner, if only she could find the right corner.

But now there was an emaciated young man on her sofa, with curly hair like a cherub and his words were an echo of Rangoon. She'd talked to him on and off all day and sometimes his eyes were open and empty, sometimes shut and grey.

'You came about the carrots,' she offered.

'Carrots.'

Callum looked at her blank ceiling then at the feathery green stepping stones on the floor.

'Yes,' he said. 'They're growing through my ceiling. A heavenly harvest, I don't mind or anything, but I thought I'd see if you knew anything about them.'

She patted the soft green carpet around her.

'Carrot tops,' she said. 'Curly furly feathery carrot tops. All mine. I didn't know anyone was down there, you know, after the eviction. I hid on the balcony. I put seeds in between the floorboards. And Growmore.'

She noticed Callum's amazement. Gawping like a . . .

'Codfish! It's the dirt from the basement,' she said sharply. 'It seems anything will grow anywhere I sprinkle it. Must have green fingers, Rangoon said that. I told you about the basement? And Rangoon? You may have been asleep while I told you. I used to live in a basement and things just grew. And Rangoon, he – well, nemind that for now.'

Callum sat and counted his fingers. The basement. Rangoon. Things just grew.

'It must be a change, being up so high,' he said, cocktail-party bright. 'Half-way to paradise, I always used to think. And you are even halfer than me. The land where the bong tree grows. Growmore, of course.'

She opened her mouth to speak, then shut it tight. Just who was he, this raggle taggle angel?

'Tea?' she said.

'Three sugars,' he said, 'please. If you don't mind.'

'What did you say before?' she asked him suddenly.

'Heavens, I don't know,' he said.

'Heaven,' she said, 'that was part of it. And a land?'

'Where the bong tree grows,' he said, nodding. 'You must think I'm silly.'

'Must I?' she said, laughing. 'Well, we'll see. Have you been there? The land where the bong tree grows?'

'Many times,' he said, laughing. 'In a beautiful pea-green airship, singing to a small guitar.'

'A boat,' she said. 'Do you sing?'

'Oh, that as well,' he said. 'Many a time and oft.'

'He always wanted to go there,' she said. 'Rangoon.'

'Burma,' Callum said. 'Burma? Isn't Rangoon in Burma?'

'No,' she said, what was the matter with him. 'The land where the bong tree grows. Rangoon.'

Callum closed his eyes.

'Sail away for a year and a day,' he said.

'Yes,' she said. 'That's it.'

'When I was a child,' Callum said, his eyes clearing. 'I thought as a child, and now I am a man, I fear I'll never think as clear again.'

'Yes,' she said, 'yes.'

'The Duchess! The Duchess! Oh my dear paws! Oh my fur and whiskers!' Callum cried.

'Go on!' she said, her eyes alight and alive.

'Curiouser and curiouser,' he said. 'Heavens to Betsy! You do some.'

'I don't know, I mean,' she said, 'maybe – I saw an aged aged man, a-sitting on a gate. Um. I sometimes dig for buttered rolls, in any municipal bin, one day I found a lone sardine, concealed inside a tin. There! That was Rangoon. Did you know Mr Lewis Carroll Dodgson?'

'Many years ago,' Callum said. 'A very dear friend.'

'Then I wonder,' she said. 'I wonder.'

'What do you wonder?' Callum said.

She put her head on her knees. Her head was spinning with it all. She breathed deep and looked up at him. His cheeks were almost pink and she got up and looked out of the window.

''Twas brillig,' she said, not daring to look at him, 'and the something. Well?'

'And the slithy toves,' Callum said, giggling, 'did gyre and gimble in the wabe. All mimsy were the borogroves, and the mome raths outgrabe.'

'That's it!' she said. Who was he, this angel? 'That's very it. Could you write it down for me, could you, I've been wanting to hear that ever since . . . nemind. Look, I've got a pencil, never know when it might come in handy and now you're here. Put it on the wall. Big. Please.'

'I'd love to,' Callum said, and the letters flowed on to the plaster with curls and flourishes.

'It's good here,' she said, pacing up and down, almost skipping, her hands dancing with joy. 'I always used to look at the pavements, you know, in London, after Rangoon. Pavements and gratings and drains and rubbish. That's how they look at you if you're me, rubbish. Chin down, shoulders forward, old Crum, shuffle like a shadow. Ha ha. Then here, well, now, I look up. At the skies above. People say hello here sometimes, they say, nice day, pet.'

'Lovely day, pet,' Callum said, adding a cartoon caterpillar to the poem. 'Hello. I'm Callum, by the way.'

'Hello, Callum,' she said, shaking his hand. 'I'm Eleanor Crumsty. For what it's what's in a name, anyway? More tea?'

'The cup that cheers,' he said. 'I'd like that, Eleanor. Thank you. Three sugars, if you don't mind.'

'I know,' she said. 'And I couldn't mind less.'

51

'Tell me what you were saying – when I was dozing, I'm sorry about that,' Callum said, amazed that he really wanted to know. 'You said – about a basement. About a friend of yours. Rangoon. Please tell me.'

It was a long time since any face had come into focus, or the sound of any voice separated itself into words, let alone words that interested him. This fierce ferretty madwoman was the only living being – except Wolf – who'd come clear through the fog of his daily existence.

'Ah, Rangoon!' Eleanor said. 'He was a prince among men. I'd be dead without him. Picked me up in a back alley, Callum, put me on my feet and walked me all over. Talk talk talk, that was Rangoon, never a dull moment. A gentleman, you understand.'

Callum wondered what had happened to him, but he guessed she'd tell him if she wanted to. She fell silent.

'And the carrots,' he prompted. 'Forgive me for sleeping, I've been very ill for a long time.'

She refilled his tea-cup and her eyes bored into him.

'How old would you say I am, there's the rub,' she said.

'Old as the hills,' Callum said. 'Younger than springtime, I don't know.'

'You do it,' she said, smiling blissfully. 'You talk like he did. I like it, talk some more.'

'After you tell me about the basement,' he said, his eyes huge. 'I did ask first.'

'Hoity toity!' she said, wheezing a laugh. 'Well, let's see. I was looking for Rangoon, you see, he'd been ill in Silvertown

Infirmary and one day when I went, he'd gone. They didn't know where. No forwarding address, and he never had one, so it was back to the highways and byways for me. I'd leaned on him, you see, totally, he did everything for me, money, food, where we slept, everything.'

Callum nodded.

'I once had a gentleman friend who did pretty much the same,' he said.

'Yes!' she cried. 'And after they go, well, you don't know what to do, where to begin even. I was frightened on the streets, and the hostels, well, dirty dossers and carbolic, young man, I haven't the time for it. Then I remembered, Rangoon had said four walls and a roof for a lady in winter. I found a basement and it's a good job I did, for three days later, there was a hurricane. Right in the middle of London, a hurricane! Freak weather, I loved the wind, and as soon as it dropped I went out with my trolley to see what I could see.'

'There was a storm the day after,' Callum said dreamily. 'I wanted lightning to strike me, but I wasn't tall enough.'

She hadn't heard him, miles and years away.

'Whole roofs had been lifted off,' she said, cackling, waving her hands wildly. 'Slates dealt to the four winds like a deck of cards! There was a café nearby with geraniums on the windowsill, and the pots were scattered and smashed, so I took the geraniums. I remember a man standing by his car. There was a tree right across the roof and he was just standing with his mouth open. Everyone was moving slowly; they thought it was awful, but I felt alive, you know, alive like I was with Rangoon. He'd talked about judgement falling on the cities, you see, and now it had. That trolley there – that's where I put all the treasure after the storm.'

Callum looked where she pointed – an old navy shopping trolley, handles and seams thick with black tape.

'Yes,' she said. 'Yes. Now I liked my basement, but it was dark and I didn't like to burn a candle too often. People see lights, and that just means gid aht of it sooner or later. I'd been thinking how to get light down there.'

She nodded and poured Callum more tea. It was stone cold, but he didn't care. She stayed silent until he said, gently:

'Light?'

She looked at him as if puzzled.

'Light,' she said. 'Oh yes. Well, I was going up the High Road and I saw a piece of paper in the chemist's shop window, you know, it said "Life Begins at Forty With Regina Royal Jelly". The window was half-smashed, but I noticed that. Further on there was a dress shop and the wind had blown its windows in completely. All the mannequins were lying on the floor, on the pavement, heads off, arms loose, all their clothes anyhow. And I was looking and I heard someone say *"They can't help it, her sort, laugh at anything, poor soul."* It was me laughing, you get used to people talking like you're not there.'

Callum nodded. As the Ragga-Vagabond, he knew this very well.

'And I was laughing,' she said, 'because there it was – the light – my answer. Hundreds of pieces of broken mirror that no-one wanted. Except me. Except me.'

She stood up and started to pace the floor, avoiding the feathery green carrot-tops.

'Yes,' she said. 'Cut a long story short, Callum. I could tell you. Cut it short, I filled the basement with mirrors and the light came in and got trapped. The geraniums grew again. I got marigolds out of the park. How old do you think I am?'

Callum shrugged.

'As old as you feel,' he said.

'And I'd been feeling a hundred,' she said excitedly. 'So old after Rangoon went, old and tired and give it all up. But one day – one day – I've never told anyone this, mind, one day I caught sight of something in the mirrors and it wasn't the flowers. It was me. I had flesh, you know, just like anyone else, and I'd thought it would be grey and wrinkled and baggy. Well, it wasn't. It was mucky. Dirt's good camouflage, Rangoon said. Keeps them away, the cleanliness and Godliness brigade. Ha! My flesh was a bit wrinkled, but not a hundred years' worth. And my hair, well, I'd thought it was wild as fireweed, tangled like an old witch. But it wasn't! There was grey, yes, and white, but it was dark brown too, with enough red in it that I knew why Rangoon had called me Ginger sometimes. He liked to dance on the beach, Rangoon.'

'I'll take you sand-dancing,' Callum said. 'I love it.'

'What fun!' she said. 'You see, I'd been told. Life begins at forty with Regina Royal Jelly. That day I decided I was forty and I've never felt better. And after that, everything just grew for me, wherever I was. I started plants here, you know, after the demolition. They couldn't find me, never thought of looking on the balcony roof!'

'I just went in the cupboard,' Callum said. 'It was easy.'

'I'll make more tea,' she said. 'There's the heel of a loaf and a scrape of butter. That'll do.'

'And what about Rangoon?' Callum called, feeling awake and alert for the first time in ages.

'I'll find him, the sly old bugger,' she said. 'You can help me, if you want to. Anyone can do anything they want, you know, if they really want to.'

'Really?' Callum said, his eyes begging her to tell him it was true.

'Really,' she said firmly, handing him a hunk of bread. 'You've got to really want it, though. No half measures.'

'Of course not,' he said, sighing.

'I mean that!' she said urgently. 'Half measures lead to a mish-mash and I don't want that. Do you?'

'No half measures,' he said, holding his hand out.

She looked surprised, but she took and shook it, and it felt to Callum like a pact between them – as important and strong as when he'd first shared blood with Wol.

52

Eleanor Crumsty's crow-black coat hung in the wardrobe, sprouting slow spores of lichen. Her black vagrant skirt grew soft bands of moss. She opened the door one day, looking for shoes. Her eyes found no shoes, but later she was troubled by the image of a thick green velvet skirt.

'I've never had a velvet skirt,' she said out loud. 'As far as I can remember.'

She stowed it at the back of her mind along with all the other things she could picture but not place. A window, a tree with the sweetest, most elusive scent in the world, a clean white bed and angels. Sometime she'd had a wad of notes that she buried and the rats ate them. Something ate them. She couldn't find them. And further forward in her mind, Rangoon, always Rangoon, twinkling eyes and pipe-smoke, Rangoon laying out a feast on his coat on the beach in Summerland.

The green velvet skirt gave her a warm ache. Soon she dreamed of herself as a child skipping down a street somewhere, her thin legs cloaked in folds of green velvet. Maybe she'd been the child of a rich family, maybe her mother had once been well-to-do and the skirt was cut down to fit her. Or else her mother had been lucky at the rag shop or a rummage sale. Or maybe it was something Rangoon had said about a sister somewhere.

Callum said it was probably past lives.

'Don't try and make sense of it,' he told her. 'You'll use

what you know in this life and, I mean, what would a bus stop be doing, say, in ancient China?'

'China? I was Chinese?' He lost her a lot of the time, but so had Rangoon and she felt comfortable with that.

'You might have been,' Callum said. 'You might have been an empress or an emperor. Or a farmer. Or a geisha girl.'

He draped a scarf along his shoulders and flirted with his eyelashes.

Eleanor laughed.

'You'd have been a geisha girl,' she said. 'I was probably a doctor. A bad doctor and these aching bones of mine are sent to teach me a lesson.'

Callum sighed.

'You see?' he said. 'Hung up on guilt and crime and punishment. This life as a penance for your last – it's not that simple.'

'Tea,' said Eleanor, sensing a story coming.

She liked his stories. She liked him. His questions were all right. Never a word about what did you do, where did you come from: she'd spent years evading that sort of thing in police stations and Credsworth and the benefit office and the hospital. Callum had no curiosity like that, although he asked a lot of questions.

Did you see that shooting star this morning?

Cup of tea?

Shall we take the bus to the hills?

Shall we take the train to the coast?

Did you dream last night?

Isn't it a lovely day?

He sang as well. Not all trained and operatic, but as natural as a bird, a few notes dropped into a sentence.

'Isn't it a lovely day *for a walk in the rain?*'

She took their tea into the living room and listened to him.

'It seems to me,' Callum said, 'that every life you live teaches you something, well, lots of things. Once upon a time you were a servant and you learned how to serve. Another time, maybe you were an employer, but you'd understand your servants better and treat them right. You have to experience everything and learn from it, otherwise you just do the same thing over and over. Out there in eternity, when you're out of the body, you look at all the lives you can lead, like picking a holiday from a brochure.'

'You're telling me I chose this?' Eleanor sneered.

'Yes,' Callum said. 'That's where *déjà vu* comes in. Whenever you get a sense of *déjà vu*, you know you're in the right place. Look how you felt about the view from these windows – the bridge, the sun on the river, the pleasure boat cruising along at night. That was part of your life package deal. And you see it as it is, so it can't be past lives. You've been meant to come here. It's taken whatever you've done before to get you here. It's all meant.'

'I've learned how to live with nothing,' she said. 'I woke with nothing until Rangoon found me. He cracked me open like a nut and oh, life was sweet with him. I was nothing and then I mattered. He said I was a delight, can you imagine it, Callum, me, a delight? And all the basement years – I must have been a troglodyte many lives ago and that's how I survived with nothing in the city of plenty. And now I live higher than anyone else in another city, higher than the tree-tops.'

'You are a delight. A troglodyte delight. And we are merely the stars' tennis balls, struck and bandied which way pleases them. But look at Gerth,' Callum said, and the room shivered on his sorrow. 'I saw him and I knew him as my destiny. He saw me and it was the same. But he was so frightened to be other than the crowd. We had all the love in the world and he left me. His destiny was with me, jeered at, reviled, but living in love. He chickened out for money and power and the safety of the herd. He'll think of himself as happy, but it will be a shadow of ecstasy and I sometimes wonder if he'll wake up at night and go to the bathroom and sit on the toilet and cry because he's thrown it all away.'

'Fear,' Eleanor said. 'In my life – as far as I can remember, there was no way to escape from fear. No chance of melting into a crowd. No herd to tell me I was doing all right. Just Rangoon and he was a law unto himself, and to me. But the skirt, Callum – the window and the beautiful tree, a bed, I think it was my bed? If that was in this life, where did it go? So many pretty places. As if I lived in the country.'

'Maybe you did,' Callum said. 'Maybe you're an eccentric aristocrat who got struck by amnesia one day, like a bolt of lightning burning your memory away. Maybe you have a grieving family who comb the police reports to this day.'

'I hardly think so,' she said stiffly. 'These days it's almost impossible to lose people, what with computers and social security numbers. Unless you want to lose them. Maybe that's it. Maybe they left me somewhere, me and my blank mind, and never came back for me. Maybe they're all six foot under, keeping a place for me.'

'Do you think so?' Callum said. 'Well, maybe. If my true love can leave me and never even bother to find out if I'm alive and well, then anything's possible. But it's cruel.'

'You're not cruel,' she told him. 'And I'm not cruel. And Rangoon was never cruel. I don't know why he went, sometimes people just go and you never find them again. Or find out why.'

'Sometimes we are very cruel,' he said, 'but only to ourselves. But maybe this is the next thing to learn. To be kind to ourselves. Is the kitty up to a bus ride to the sea?'

'Yes,' she said. 'Let's go to the sea and have ice-cream. It isn't Summerland, but it's lovely . . . I'll have to go back to Summerland with you some day, if I can only think of the way.'

53

Callum could always be kind to Eleanor and she to him. Planning treats for someone else means enjoying the treat yourself. Callum did picnics and they'd get on any bus painted green and get off as soon as it was pretty. The hills, a lake, the sea, a forest.

Eleanor found tuppenny ha'penny plates in the junk shop beside the post office where magic turns an emergency giro into cash. And there were saucepans, cutlery even, cleared from a dead person's flat. She found a jar of horseradish sauce in the supermarket. She made dinners.

There was another shop where you bought everything in scoops. The Weighing Machine. It sold cake mixtures, lemon, orange, chocolate, coffee, strawberry, vanilla and cherry. Simply add water. She felt inspired as she scooped up pink cherry cake mix and bright red sticky cherries.

'There's an offer on icing, pet,' said the woman at the till. 'White, yellow, pink, blue, whatever you like.'

Eleanor made a cake and had a tea-party for Callum.

Callum cried when he saw the pink cake and ran downstairs for candles. He had a candle that played Happy Birthday when you lit it.

'Your birthday?'

'No,' he said. 'Is it yours?'

'Maybe,' she said. 'I don't know.'

He sang 'Happy Birthday' for her. Happy Birthday, Happy Cakeday. After a while, she joined in.

Not that they spent every day together. Some days she didn't answer her door, and some days he didn't. She had to be alone to grip the sliding edge of reality, sweating with fear. He had to lie on the floor and cry for Gerth. She could hear him through the letterbox, and stomped around her flat snarling at his demons. He could sense her lonely terror through the unanswered door and tiptoed away to light a candle to keep her bright. After a day apart, their meeting was anxious. Have you changed – have *you*?

A pot of tea, a cigarette, and no you haven't, and another pot of tea and plans for the time to spend together.

One night, they'd even gone to the Turk's Head for a sing-along. No-one raised an eyebrow at the pair of them, though both had been refused drinks many times when they tried it alone. But Callum told Eleanor, before they went out, that she didn't need to take so many bags with her, just the trolley, if she must. He said that her sandals looked better than her boots. He also said her best hat was too dressy for a pub and she grumbled as she unskewered its battered felt and cherries from her hair.

Then she looked at him and shook her head.

'No,' she said. 'That shawl, no. And no earrings for you if I can't have my hat.'

'But I feel so plain,' Callum said. 'And my hands, I play with the fringes on my shawl.'

'Use your pockets,' she said. 'Put on your jeans. Use my boots.'

And they passed through doors that had always been closed to them, and some people thought they were mother and son, brother and sister, nephew and auntie. A man who'd shouted 'poof' and 'bender' at Callum three years before made room for them at the bar. Only last week he'd crossed the street, calling Eleanor a bloody alky.

The Turk's Head was a pub where poor people go and drink halves slowly, thumb and fingers rolling coins inside ragged pocket linings. A place where people nip off the lit end of their cigarettes and smoke them in two halves. If you got there early, there were peanuts and pickled onions on the bar. You could see people ducking their glasses under the table to pour tots from small bottles they'd sneaked in themselves. A toothless old lady threw her skirts up on her birthday and did the can-can in flesh-pink nylon bloomers and everyone clapped.

And everyone sang. Someone said to Callum, here, you should get up and sing, you, you look like you've got a lovely voice, doesn't he? Leave him be, said someone else, he'll give us a tune when he's good and ready, divven pay him no mind, mister, ye enjoy yersel, ye and yer friend.

'Oh, I'll sing,' Callum said. 'Do you know "The Man I Love"?'

Sotto voce to Eleanor, he murmured: *cuz if you do, I wish you'd introduce us!*

She laughed into the warm froth on her Guinness.

'He's a way with his voice that brings tears to me eyes,' someone said while Callum stood and sang his heart out.

For an encore he sang 'The Boy I Love is up in the Gallery' and Ganzie Tom, the oldest of all the old people there, smiled and sang with him, remembering the music hall and a time when there was plenty of nothing and life could only get better. Long ago and far away when he was young and the next oyster was sure to hold a pearl.

The second time they went, people said 'Hello, how have you been?' Ganzie Tom roared at Callum to save his coppers and have a drink wi' him, a proper drink, mind, a short, owt he wanted, him and his lady friend and all. Callum sang 'Lover Man' and 'Somewhere over the Rainbow' and someone said he should get himself an outfit and go in for the Talent Spot down at The Fox and Parrot.

'Forst prize is twenty-five pund, man, ye'll walk it!'

Callum winked when he called Eleanor his lady friend, and people nudged each other and said, ee, ye knaa, he dotes on her, ye can tell. So that became their Saturday night, dressing down for going out.

54

'I can see your point,' the woman said doubt-fully, 'but there isn't really anything we can do, Mr Harking.'

'Oh,' Wol said, itching for a cigarette. He hated offices, grey rooms like this with 'No Smoking' signs everywhere and this lah-di-dah woman with her expensive voice sitting behind a desk as wide as a main road, with her name in front of her on a steel plate. Mrs Myra Bannister. He felt like an alien. And from what she was saying he could have walked in all public school and Armani and it wouldn't have made any difference.

'Sorry,' he said automatically. 'It's just it's a lot to take in. I've been travelling a long time, you see. I suppose I'm just tired. Could you go through it again? Would you mind?'

Mrs Myra Bannister looked patient.

'It won't change the fundamental position, Mr Harking,' she said.

She's got me down as cracked, Wol thought. Here comes the careful enunciation like what one uses with the mentally deficient lower classes, don't y'know! Never mind, maybe she'd explain it better this time.

'You've given me a name and a date of birth,' she said, holding up the slip of paper as if it were a urine sample. 'You say that you are this little boy's father. I've looked through his file and his mother Christine didn't register you as his father. Father unknown – I've shown you that piece of paper.'

'I am,' Wol said, 'his dad. She told me.'

'Mr Harking,' she said. 'It is not unusual for young women who have to – however regretfully – give up their babies for adoption, to be, shall we say, less than a hundred per cent certain of who the father is. Whether this is true of Christine, I wouldn't like to guess. On paper, that is, in the eyes of the law, this child did not have a father. Do you understand that? In the eyes of the law you are in no way related to this child. Have you discussed your present searches with Christine?'

'Chrissy's dead,' Wol said. 'She died ten years ago.'

'I'm very sorry,' she said. 'I have to tell you also, that even if she had named you as the boy's father, I wouldn't be able to help you very much at this stage.'

Was that supposed to make him feel better?

'What,' he said, 'if Chrissy had put me down all legal – you still couldn't do anything?'

'No,' she said. 'Mr Harking, with adoption, we are in a very sensitive position. There are moves to open it all up a great deal more, but that is only at the stage of discussion. It is a very delicate and complicated issue. The position is that this child has been living with a family he knows as his own for thirteen years. They are his parents and he is only just thirteen years old. It was felt, and has been built into law, that the sudden appearance of someone like yourself would provide stress and distress. It could provoke quarrels and insecurity. It could easily lead to family breakdown: especially for a young teenager, which as we know, is the most difficult and challenging time in any family. And one must consider the adoptive parents – the people the child calls mother and father. A child they have brought up as their own suddenly confronted with a father or mother who he has never known? Very traumatic.'

'I can see that,' Wol said. 'I wouldn't go barging in or anything. I suppose I just wanted to see him. Know he's all right. You know?'

'I do know,' Mrs Bannister said. 'Let me get you some coffee.'

While she was out of the room, Wol wondered about diving across the desk and rifling through the file and to hell with the consequences. The worst she could do was throw him out.

But she came back before he'd had time to finish even the thought.

'It is very nice for me,' she said, 'to find a young man who is interested in his child even at this late date. It seems a pity that things broke down between Christine and yourself before the child was born.'

She sounded less severe now, more school nurse than lady magistrate. Wol had told her very little about Chrissy and himself. Maybe he should? Only it sounded so tacky.

'I didn't want it to,' he said. 'I wanted to marry her. Only she was already married and her husband was a real hard man. He was in gaol. She came down here so no-one would know. She told me about the baby when she came back, then she said it wasn't true. Then she said it might be. Then she said I'd never know. Then she was dead. It's been on my mind, just wanting to know. You know, I'd have been all right if there wasn't a baby, I just had to know the truth.'

'You would be surprised,' Mrs Bannister said, 'very surprised to find out how common this sort of thing is. You're not the only young man who's been rejected in this way. Sometimes the husband is a sailor, or travels abroad on business. Sometimes, as with your Chrissy, he's serving time. Women get lonely and turn to someone else for comfort. And suddenly the husband's coming back and the mother goes into a panic of fear and just wants to be rid of the child and its father and everything to do with that lonely time when her husband was away. Often, years later, she regrets it. My advice to the mothers, and to you, is to get on with your own life and rest assured that we have done our utmost to find this child the best family available.'

'So there's nothing I can do?' Wol held her eyes.

'The only thing you can do, Mr Harking,' she said, 'is wait until this child is eighteen and put your name on the National Adoption Contact Register.'

'What does that do?' Wol gulped his coffee.

'It's a list of the names of the natural parents of adopted children. By registering, you're saying that you would like to be in touch with your child. If the child, once he or she has reached eighteen, wishes to contact you, there you are. It's very successful.'

'How do you mean, successful?' Wol's head was buzzing.

'Well,' she said patiently, 'suppose you are an adopted child and at the age of eighteen you decide to trace your natural parents. You will feel very ambivalent about this. Are you being disloyal to your adoptive parents? Will your natural parents want you to contact them? They gave you away, after all. Any adoptive child who decides to go ahead is referred, in the first place, to the register. If they find their parent's name already there, they know that at least one of their fears is unfounded.'

'I see,' Wol said. 'Can I do that then? It's a start.'

'You can,' Mrs Bannister said, 'when your son – or, I must stress – the child you believe to be your son – is eighteen years old. Prior to that, you see, suppose someone else looks at the register and passes on the information to a child or a young teenager – that's a risk we can't take.'

'It's very complicated,' Wol said. 'I mean, I can see why and everything. You've been a big help, Mrs Bannister.'

'I'm sorry I can't do more,' she said, 'but I hope the position is now clearer to you?'

'Yeah,' Wol said. 'Yeah. So I ring you in five years' time and we see what happens, eh?'

'Yes,' she said. 'If you still feel the same in five years' time, that is exactly what you do.'

'Right,' Wol said, standing up. 'Right then. Thank you.'

Mrs Bannister looked at the polaroid photo of Wayne Tyrone Boone, aged three weeks. Lots of babies have blue eyes and blond curls, but all the same . . . She wrote a sheet of notes and clipped it into the file.

55

Camomile tea-bags for calm, coffee blended from mocha mysore and continental roast for kicks, Aqua Libra, bread studded with sesame and sunflower seeds, a tub of Virgin Olio, jars of olives, capers, hummus, sticky buns with icing and cherries, a six-pack of poison-blue bottles of Babycham – the usual pink-cross parcel designed for Callum.

Wol went through the neglected stairwells and corridors of Garstone Towers, praying that Callum would still be there. It had occurred to him as he drove back from Oxford that Callum might easily be dead – starvation, mugging, or by his own hand. When they'd last met, his state of mind could only be described as go-to-hell – all aimed at himself, of course. Callum couldn't hurt a fly.

Wol felt guilty and selfish for leaving him, and wondered: if he'd found his child, if he'd met his child, even more if there was any hope of definite contact, would he still feel this way? He could only imagine what it would have been like, and no – he wouldn't have a shred of guilt, he'd feel elated, full of it, mission accomplished. There would be no room for thoughts and fears about Callum's death.

The last few months seemed like a pie in the sky piece of self-indulgence that any fool would have set down and thought out and decided against. But not this fool!

But Wol was glad he'd gone – meeting Gloria and Ricky had given him a sense of happiness. He hadn't been the only one ever to love Chrissy: even though she'd driven Gloria round the twist, she'd still loved her enough to let her be there all the time the baby was growing.

Life, Wol thought, is a weird number.

If he'd been more together, if Gloria had been with Ricky, if Chrissy's old man had been down for decades rather than years – well then, little Wayne would be living in a whole family linked by blood. He knew that in the eyes of society none of them would be considered suitable parents or relatives: he couldn't imagine Myra Bannister cheerfully handing a child over to any of them. He imagined Wayne in a 'normal' household – how could a child mixed from the crazy job-lot of genes pooled between him and Chrissy fit in? There was nothing he could do about it anyway. Maybe Wayne was better off with his new name and his adopted family: it would be all he knew, after all. Maybe he'd be in touch after he was eighteen and need to meet his dad . . .

If and maybe. Wol tried to switch off the aimless stream.

Right now, Callum was the needy one and Wol gritted his teeth as he started along the balcony. My brother, he thought, my blood brother, for God's sake let your heart still be beating.

Elvis Presley belted through the door, 'You Were Always on My Mind', and Wol relaxed. Wolf barked up a storm when he knocked and leapt up at him as the door opened. He fussed the dog and looked up with a smile at a woman he'd never seen before. She had a needle and thread clamped between her lips and yards of velvet bundled in her arms. Her face was any age, kicked to bits and so effing what; eyes that had been around quite some and a mouth that wouldn't waste words on a stranger.

'Is Callum in?' he said. 'I'm Wol.'

'Wol the wanderer,' her voice was gritty and amused. 'You pick your moments. Cal – your friend's here.'

'Bring him in!' Callum cried, a flourish in his voice.

The woman jerked her head and he went past her into the sitting room. There was a sea of clothes strewn over the floor and Callum was dabbing on foundation, a wreath of dusty lilies in his hair. He dropped the sponge when he saw Wol and looked at him in the mirror for a full minute before he turned. He looked like the apple blossom fairy.

'I've seen you come in just like this so often,' he said. 'Through the looking glass. So glad this time is real. Welcome to Wonderland, brother. Well, sister of mercy! Never fear, I know how bad it's been, but I can assure you – the phoenix is drying his wings and will shortly emerge in a blaze of glory!'

He held Wol close and when he drew away he was crying.

'This is the best way to *ruin* my mascara,' he said. 'I'm so glad you're back. Let's make some tea.'

'Mate,' Wol said, 'oh, mate, you're looking great!'

'That,' Callum said, sweeping his arm graciously towards the door, 'is largely due to Eleanor, my woman upstairs who does – practically anything!'

He swung Wol round with a pixie smile.

'Eleanor, this is Wol,' he said, his voice warm and gentle on each name. 'My blood brother, meet my fairy godmother. Wol was my partner all those heady years ago when we were Ms Cogan and the Divine Miss M.'

'That's nice,' Eleanor said. 'And what perfect timing too – it's a tea-break.'

'She is such a slave-driver!' Callum rolled his eyes. 'Come through to the kitchen, brother, and then I can tell you all about her.'

'All about me?' Eleanor half-smiled from where she sat with her sewing. 'That should be interesting. Do feel free to fill me in on the details, Cal. I would be so grateful. And remember, two sugars, stirred not shaken. Please.'

56

'She has amnesia,' Callum said cheerfully, filling the kettle. 'She woke up *sans* shoes or i.d. in a back lane in the East End of London with no idea of her name or age or how she'd got there. A hobo angel came along and saved her; his name was Rangoon. Then one day he disappeared. We have lovely chats about the lost men in our lives. This was all some years ago – she's not good at chronology. She has, since then, been a rather chic bag lady, a frustrating psychiatric patient, imagine, Wol, she's a graduate from our own dear Alma Mater, Credsworth the knacker house! And, in her current manifestation, she is an angel of mercy to me.'

'How did you meet her?' Wol asked.

'She lives upstairs,' Callum said lightly. 'Another evictee who wasn't. Carrots, Wol, carrots.'

He laughed at Wol's puzzlement until he was breathless.

'Talk to her about gardening sometime,' he said. 'Rather, about growing things. Along the way, she developed fingers as green as the fields of Mother Ireland. Any plant any time any place – you'll be astonished. I have even thought of introducing her to my billionaire brother and compost crazy papa, but she wasn't taken with the idea. And I simply couldn't face any of them. She said she'd be too jealous of meeting my family, since she probably hasn't got one, or at least one that could be bothered to find her. And even if she had, she wouldn't have a clue who they were.'

'Like Wayne,' Wol said, grinning.

'Wayne?' Callum arched his eyebrows. 'What a hunky name

– is it for real? Is he the reason for your prolonged absence from my *bijou* kasbah? *Do* tell!'

'I don't know if you remember,' Wol said. 'You know. It was ages ago I told you. About Chrissy?'

'Chrissy?'

'The one woman in my life. My young life.'

'You did tell me about a woman – and a baby – your baby, your maybe baby,' Callum said softly. 'Of course I remember.'

'Well, that's Wayne,' Wol said.

'So he was real! Did you find him?'

'Yes and no,' Wol said. 'I found out he's alive, well, he was born, anyway, and his name's Wayne Tyrone. And he was adopted so he's probably not Wayne Tyrone any more, and there, as they say, the trail disappears into an iceberg of bureaucracy. There's nothing I can do until he's eighteen. And not a lot even then.'

Callum put one hand on his arm.

'You must tell me everything,' he said. 'I know I've been – out to lunch? Impaled on the arrows of heartbreak like a latter-day Saint Sebastian? Performing an emotional suttee? I *love* that word Mr Corbett, I do. Well, my dear Wol, the suttee is done, I decided it was high time to sweep away the ashes of the Love of my Life. The queen is in residence, as they say. Put out more flags!'

'Welcome back to Planet Earth,' Wol said. 'So when did Eleanor turn up?'

'My dear, I haven't a clue,' Callum said. 'It must have been a week or so after you went. Maybe a month, *qui'en sabe*. I thought I was the only squatter in the gaping catacombs of Garstone Towers.'

'Just how long does it take to make tea or explain me?' Eleanor shouted from the next room.

'Ten minutes. For ever,' Callum called. 'You're *so* bossy!'

He loaded a tray and half-bowed Wol ahead of him.

'We've been ever so busy, haven't we?' he said, handing tea to Eleanor. 'We started going to the pub and discovered talent nights, Wol. Tax-free riches for a little warble or two! So far

I've won twenty-five quid, that was at The Fox and Parrot. Then I won a crate of lager – where was that?'

'Lil Peacock's Cellar,' Eleanor said. 'And six months worth of Gallagher's Finest Bakery Products. That was at Garstone Social Club. He's so talented.'

'We've been wallowing in Belgian buns and stotty cakes,' Callum said, brushing the praise aside. 'Macaroons and rum truffles and cream doughnuts! Kiddies' party time every day! We have sandwiches and pies too. It's wonderful!'

'Is this what all this is in aid of?' Wol said, waving his hand at the fabric strewn all over the floor.

'This is the big one,' Callum said. 'A mystery holiday destination for two courtesy of The Frog and Nightgown. I'm dreaming of Sardinia and Madeira and Crete. Madam here says it's Bognor or Torquay on a coach.'

'Brilliant,' Wol said. 'What numbers are you doing?'

'Stevie Wonder,' Callum said, ' "I Just Called to Say I Love You"; Elvis, "American Trilogy"; and The Righteous Brothers, "Unchained Melody". What do you think?'

' "Unchained Melody" – mega,' Wol said briskly. 'Everyone knows it, everyone loves it. Same with Stevie Wonder. But I'm not sure about Elvis. It's sort of sacrilege, isn't it, the King? I know people do him all the time, but no-one's as good as him, and they don't sort of take it seriously. You know. The Jarrow Elvis? The Prudhoe Elvis? It's – well, dodgy.'

He didn't notice Eleanor glaring at him.

Walks in here after months, she thought, *and starts pouring cold water on us right away. Gid aht of it by default! Holiday for two – and I can just see which two it's going to be. Bye bye, old Crum! Upsi-bloody-daisy!*

'I mean, it's none of my business, right?' Wol said. 'But you can do anyone, you. What about something totally different?'

Knock him down why don't you? Eleanor bristled. She felt like a mother wolf around Callum.

Callum's shoulders sagged.

'Can't you see, Sister Morphine, I'm not that strong?' he

said. 'Don't ask me to think, Wol, I'm living on massive infusions of pastry and adrenalin at the moment.'

'What would you suggest?' Eleanor was curt, 'since you seem to be one of life's natural managers?'

'It's only an idea,' Wol floundered in the wave of hostility. 'But you know when we were doing our act? Yeah? You wanted to do Noël Coward and I said no, not for Benny Hartmann.'

'Oh,' Callum said. 'You may have something. I couldn't change a hair of me, of course, without my manageress's express permission, but let me find the tape, Eleanor, see what you think.'

Two minutes transformed him into a twenties dandy and he mimed a cigarette holder.

'Could be,' Eleanor said, grudgingly. 'Five weeks of toughening you up for Elvis down the Swannee, but nemind.'

'I'm much more convincing as a lounge lizard than I ever could be as an ex-truck driver turned international sex god,' Callum said.

Eleanor picked up the cassette case.

' "World Weary",' she said. 'That's the one playing now? OK. I like that line . . . "*an ocean view, some great big trees, a bird's eye view of the Pyrenees*". It's got something. Rangoon would have loved it. What else?'

'Do you know his songs?' Wol said.

Eleanor laughed.

'Maybe,' she said, 'maybe not. I'm the last person to ask. Rangoon would know them, he knew everything.'

'The question direct,' Callum frowned. 'Miz Eleanor finds such things discommodin'.'

'Sorry,' Wol said.

'You get used to it after a while,' she said. 'Can't say I have, but you learn to live with it.'

'I've said she should write a book,' Callum said. 'Call it *Don't Ask Me, I Only Lived It*.'

57

'ELVIS IS DEAD' said the red sprawling graffiti beside the bus stop.

'How tacky,' Callum said, clutching his holdall. 'Wol, can't we do something to improve the view?'

Wol took a can from inside his jacket and sprayed a dayglo pink 'NOT' between 'IS' and 'DEAD'.

'Better?' he asked.

'Much,' Callum said. 'And here's the 13. The omens are looking rather good tonight.'

'I thought Elvis was dead,' Eleanor said, once they were upstairs.

'Someone like Elvis never dies,' Callum told her. 'You're only dead when there's no-one alive who remembers you. Watch this!'

He stood up and shouted down the bus.

'Who's Elvis?'

A raucous chorus came back at once.

'He's the King!'

'He's the greatest!'

'He's working in Woolworth's in the Metro centre, man!'

'Howay, he's not, I've seen him in Burger King. Does a great bag of chips these days, Elvis!'

'You see?' Callum sat down again. 'Everybody knows who Elvis is. Even people who weren't born when he left this planet.'

'Where is he, though,' Eleanor said, 'if not on this planet?'

'Elvis is one of the Immortals,' Callum said. 'And when we

slough off this flesh, we shall join him. It's absurd to think that this is all there is. What would be the point?'

Eleanor considered. It was a nice idea, that dying only meant shedding your body. Rangoon had told her that's what snakes did, simply shed their skins and had a brand-new set of scales shimmering underneath. He'd found snakes' skins discarded all over the place in Burma one dry season; he said they were brittle, thin as orange papers. She wondered if Rangoon was dead – he was old when she'd met him and he coughed on damp mornings and got exasperated by the way his joints ached. And the last time she'd seen him, in Silvertown Infirmary, he was pale as wax.

'What happens when people die, then?' she asked Callum.

'My dear,' Callum said. 'I'd love to talk about it, but we're seven stops short of The Frog and Nightgown and the phrase "to die" is not one I wish to dwell on when contemplating a live performance. Should I have done Elvis, oh God, Wol, triple something when we get there, my nerves, dear, I thought I'd packed them off to boarding school, but here they are home for half-term. Oh dear.'

Callum was singing seventh – another good omen, he said. After a couple of drinks he relaxed.

'That's the thing about competitions,' he said. 'If you win, you've got something and if you don't, well, you haven't lost anything.'

'Oh, professor, I must write that down!' Wol jeered.

Someone with a streak of mischief must have told the first singer he looked like Cliff Richard, to go by the sub-aviator glasses and a somewhat streaky tan that stopped short of his white polo neck. He had a way of bobbing his head so that the mike caught the gasps for breath rather than the song. Wol shuddered as he greased his hair back into a quiff and pelvic-thrust his way – out of time – through 'Living Doll'. Inevitably he finished with 'Summer Holiday', pushing up his hair and glasses and grinning against the spotlight.

'No competition,' Eleanor said.

'Rather fond of himself,' Wol said. 'But don't count your travellers' cheques quite yet. Or, indeed, do! Look at this!'

It wasn't the Jarrow Elvis, it wasn't the Prudhoe Elvis, but it certainly had sideburns and an ill-fitting white body suit.

Haaaaar yew lonesung tew-naaaht!

Callum winked at them both and went off to change.

Pseudo-Elvis pseudo-sang 'Blue Suede Shoes'.

'Hooley Moses, I am dying,' Wol said. 'There's a cat upon the wall! If he doesn't stop his crying, I'll stick my finger up his HOOOOly Moses I am dying . . .'

A Gary Glitter lookalike who corpsed when one of his platforms snapped – *stand clear of the doors*, Wol sniggered.

A pleasant enough young man in a cream blazer salvaged Cliff's reputation with 'The Young Ones', only to torpedo it to extinction with 'Congratulations'.

'Too too Eurovision,' Wol said. 'Luxembourg, nul point!'

'Radio Luxembourg,' Eleanor said. 'Rockin' and a rollin' on the royal ball for y'all tonight, my friends.'

'Oh, I adored Luxembourg,' Wol said. 'I've got some tapes of it somewhere.'

'You have?' she almost shouted.

'Shush!'

'One more till Callum,' Wol said, 'Keep your fingers crossed.'

'I have plaited my toes,' Eleanor told him. Wol grasped her hand.

It wasn't fair to stick a three-foot mane of red curls on a perfectly nice young woman, dress her out in a basque and stilettoes and tell her she's Cher. But someone had, and the same someone had forgotten to point out that Cher never blushes.

'Oh, someone lend her a frock, for heaven's sake,' Wol said. 'She's got me all embarrassed.'

The emcee leapt on to the stage for the last gasp of 'The Shoop Shoop Song': she-who-would-be-Cher ran off without waiting for applause.

'Whey, what a lot of talent there is on Tyneside,' the emcee bellowed. 'Time to throw your giros over the bar and get the doubles in, folks, and we'll be back in twenty minutes.'

'Thank you!' Wol shot his fist into the air. 'The Angels are with us, Eleanor, Cal's opening the second half!'

'Is that good?' she asked.

'Wondrous,' Wol assured her. 'By the time Cal comes on, everyone'll have forgotten that shambolic first half and had a couple of drinks and be in the mood for entertainment. Not that he needs anything extra – he's head and shoulders above this lot. But – as he would say – it's yet another omen.'

'I'll get you a drink,' she said, amazed by how easy it was to simply stand up and go to the bar, how no-one gave her a sideways glance. She understood the decimal now and took a delight in counting out the right change, earning herself a *bless you, pet*, from the harassed barmaid.

Callum swirled on to the stage and stood eyeing them all with a wicked twinkle. He bit a puff of smoke from his cigarette holder and exhaled. He played the whole of 'Mrs Worthington' to a family party half-way back and Eleanor felt the whole room curl up comfortably in the palm of his elegant hand. There was a growing ripple of applause and he tossed his jacket on to the chair and moved straight into 'World Weary', letting rip with camp disdain.

He sang 'Unchained Melody' unaccompanied and in the stunned silence which followed he gave everything he had of Marie Lloyd and Noël Coward to 'I'll Be Seeing You'. Just as Eleanor had predicted, people joined in and tethered him to the stage, clapping until their hands were sore.

'*Fait accompli*,' Wol told him when he slipped back to their table – the audience scarcely bothered to whisper during the last acts. The father of the family Callum had wooed with 'Mrs Worthington' came over and bought them a round of drinks and shook all their hands.

Accepting the trophy and the sealed envelope was a delightful formality.

'Either I'm dreaming or I'm practising for the Oscars,' Callum said, tearing the envelope open. 'Oh my God!'

'Where's yer holiday, bonny lad?' shouted from the audience.

'A beautiful island where time stands still only if you let it,' Callum read. 'Sample the fun-filled nightlife – my dear! or go back in time to a warm and friendly people who have kept their simple joyous lifestyle unspoiled in glorious sunshine.'

'Never mind the slaver, man, where?'

'Sairanac,' Callum said, 'This voucher valid for twelve months. Sairanac. Where on earth is Sairanac?'

'You'll have to find out and come back and tell us,' the emcee said, flourishing him off stage. 'Let's have a big hand for our winner, folks.'

Part six

···························

Wonderland

58

The bus from Sairanac's only airport dropped Callum and Eleanor and Wol in a deserted square at about half-past eleven. The driver nodded enthusiastically – they'd find somewhere to stay, *si*, hotel, no problem, bed, *si, si*, don't worry, apartamento, what you like, plenty of everything, no hassle! Wol wondered, looking round the shuttered houses, how true this was, or whether the driver just wanted to get rid of them and get home.

'Isn't it wonderful,' Callum said, as he turned to see the bright stars in new places above them, the jagged silhouette of palm trees against the clear navy sky.

'I feel like I'm floating,' Eleanor said, for the air was soft and warm on her skin.

The night tantalised her with a kaleidoscope of viridian scents. In Garstone Towers she had a herb garden, a patchwork of leaves, each yielding a tangy and wholly individual savour when she rubbed them between finger and thumb. Callum's perfume was a deep forest green. In the fields of summer Rangoon had shown her how to choose flavoursome leaves by their shape and particular shade of green. She thought of summer in the city, when parks breathed the bittersweet scent of marigolds and roses.

And in Summerland – all those years and miles away – in Summerland the salt air was alive with the bouquet of sunny days and hot sand and blue-green dune grass, sea pinks and thistles and the tang of the ocean itself. Ah, Rangoon!

The air of the night-time square held all of this: only more alive and vivid than she'd ever dreamed of. There was an added zest to every drifting aroma, for here in Sairanac, on the other side of the Equator, midnight was as warm as midday in the height of an English summer. Green, she thought, I can smell forty shades of green.

'You can always get a place to stay in a port,' Wol quoted Callum's breezy optimism in the plane. 'Well, maestro?'

'We're not in the port proper,' Callum said. 'Not that we'd be proper anywhere, but you know what I mean.'

'We can stay here,' Eleanor said. 'I don't want a roof and four walls and a door somewhere in a place like this. There's benches. And trees if it rains. And it won't rain.'

'True,' Callum said. 'Only it's better to be in the country-side if you're staying out of doors.'

'That's what Rangoon said,' she cried. 'Snoopy droopy civvy street, gid aht of it, public nuisance.'

'Follow me,' Wol said. 'I have ears like a bat! My eyes are sharp as an owl's, and I have the nesting instincts of a cuckoo.'

Eleanor's trolley rattled along the cobbled street and Wol led them with confidence: a left turn down an alley, a right turn through a street that curved along past a fountain stilled for the night. At the end of the curve, cobblestones swept down to a jetty. Music and talk came from an open doorway and a golden light spilled out right to the edge of the waves.

'Let's drink to your super senses,' Callum said.

They went into Dorabella's Bar. There was a momentary silence as the fishermen looked them over and the *padron* paused half-way through polishing a flawless glass.

'It has to be fizzy!' Callum said. 'Spanish of course, but I prefer it. Chameleons feed on light and air, but we shall thrive on tapas and champagne!'

Dorabella herself brought their bottle over, its frosted glass run aground on a heap of ice-pebbles in a crystal bucket. Wol popped the cork and the clientele raised their glasses, calling *salut!*

'*Viva la vida!*' Wol cried, raising his glass.

'Every bubble in champagne holds a genie,' Callum said.

'Look at them dancing – look at the candle flame through your glass, Eleanor – isn't it lovely?'

It was. Dorabella's Bar was warm like the night outside and Eleanor could smell candle wax melting, beeswax from every pore of the table, wine and sweet liqueurs and beer and cigarettes and pipe tobacco, clothes and boots stiff with the sea.

Dorabella was pleased whenever new people came in, it broke the familiar dialogue, her mother-in-law's grumbling litany, the fishermen's routine of flirting and her husband Arturo's protestations of proud ownership. She took another bottle of champagne over to the table and paused for a second until Callum asked her to join them – as she knew he would.

She sat down and lit a cigarette.

'Holidays?' she asked. '*Vacances*? German? French?'

'Holidays indeed,' Callum said. 'Only we're English.'

He wondered if that was OK, you could never tell what ancient feuds lurked in the blood all over the globe. In Corsica he'd been amazed to find that they hated the Italians. The Portuguese hated Moroccans, the French hated everybody.

'English,' she said, nodding. 'I go to England when I am a girl. In a hotel. Making beds and cleaning. Earl's Court. Very dirty place.'

'Vile,' Callum agreed.

'Vile?' she wrinkled her brow.

'Nasty,' he said. 'Bad people.'

'It is,' she said. 'I go to Brighton. How I love Brighton! You know Brighton? You are from London?'

'Newcastle,' he said, 'in the north.'

'Oh, geordie,' she said, laughing. 'I have a boyfriend who is geordie – don't tell Arturo – my husband – after twenty years he's still jealous. Andy Foster was the geordie – you know him?'

'No,' Wol said, 'It's a big place.'

'He said,' Dorabella nodded, blushing like a teenager, 'Newcastle is a big place, the best place. He called me – pet? Hinney? Andy, he was such fun. He said he was a foreigner in London, no-one understands him nor me. He said he would teach me to talk geordie and I would always be a foreigner. He made me laugh a lot, Andy Foster. Almost I married with him, but then my mother is ill and I have to come home. You know.'

Callum filled her glass. She chinked it with each of them.

'Holidays?' she asked again.

'He won a competition,' Eleanor said.

'*Concurso*,' Wol said. 'He won and the prize was a holiday here.'

'*Un ganador*,' Dorabella said. 'That's good. Here it's quiet a lot, ten years ago, everywhere tourists. What *concurso* to get here?'

'It was a singing comp – *concurso*,' Eleanor said proudly. 'He sings beautifully.'

'A singer?' Dorabella said.

'Callum *canta como un* angel,' Wol said.

'Oh pull-ease!' Callum said. 'So do you, Wol.'

Dorabella smiled.

'So sing for us,' she said. 'Just for your first night. Please? There's a piano.'

She stood and told the whole bar that they had two singers in, musicians, people who had won a national competition in England and the first prize was this holiday. Everyone whistled and clapped. She indicated the piano with a regal sweep of her arm.

'Oh heavens,' Callum said, 'and I wanted to be incognito, an international queen of mystery.'

'Did I do wrong?' Eleanor said anxiously.

'Angel, you couldn't,' Callum told her. 'I'm thrilled to bits, dear, just playing hard to get.'

'What shall we do?' Wol asked him.

'The Divine Miss M rides again?' Callum said. 'Break a stiletto, darling! Make with the keys, Saint Winifred. What do you think, Miss Crumsty, as our roving liver-lipped manageress?'

'Give 'em hell, tiger!' Eleanor said, her eyes sparkling like the bubbles in her glass.

59

The next day, Callum and Wol and Eleanor shared a bus with a crate of hysterical chickens, a bunch of indignant ducks tied by the feet, a small angry pig on a lead and an aisle full of ratty ali baba baskets piled with vegetables and smoked meat. By the time they reached the market, Callum had bought all the livestock.

'I know sentimentality is a privilege of the supermarket society,' he said, 'but Dorabella could use the eggs. I cannot bear cruelty.'

The previous owners of ducks and hens felt a little deflated: no haggling, full price! – an empty day ahead, but one blessed with full pockets. Callum organised his little flock into a shaded pen next to the dry fountain. Loco, this gringo, but what the hell.

The dust shifted as they walked, heat haze had them floating into the riot of the market. Eleanor was amazed: here, dazzling bright flowers burst from dry ditches and swarmed over clumps of dusty rock. In England, these flowers were exotic but here a donkey chewed at them with an expression of disdain. A tiny desiccated woman switched at his threadbare rump, and he took as much notice as if she were a beached root wrapped in black cloth.

They came across an old man dancing to a wind-up gramophone. It played a sad love song: '*Povo que lavas no rio*,' one of three scratchy vinyl EPs which were his repertoire. His shaking hands sketched heartbreak, his feet moved in a dying shuffle and his ancient latex face formed a mask of tragedy. When the record slowed half-way through, he shuffled to the handle and jerked it round, spitting a curse when the needle jumped and skated.

Eleanor stared at him: his eyes twinkled like Rangoon's, and his flying fingers were like Rangoon's stories, extravagant, ironic. She tossed a coin into his greasy cap.

'My God,' Wol said, through the shouting and hustling, 'look!'

He moved as if mesmerised towards an open-air tattoo artist sweating over the bleeding chest of a young man sitting in the chair opposite him. The young man swigged neat tequila and drew so deep on his cigarette that his movie-star cheeks became skeletal. His skin was bleeding from a fresh crown of roses and a pennant where the needle was writing 'ROSA'. It must be Rosa standing beside him, humming to the wind-up gramophone and twisting a gold ring with an ant's eye of diamond chip on the third finger of her left hand. *Mi prometido, mi prometida.*

Rosa looked away when she saw the three of them staring at the raw flesh. What, me, with him?

The air was alive with music, from the bars, from cheap cassette players on the stalls. Music and the smell of food: tortillas, frying fish, roasting peppers. On one stall a man dropped balls of dough into fat the colour of gravy and flipped them around until they were crisp. He tossed them in coarse sugar and tonged them into paper cones and swapped them for small sweaty coins from small dirty children.

Callum bought a bright pink water-ice and it stained his lips. Eleanor's turned orange, Wol's a carnival yellow.

They watched an old lady stabbing a cushion to make lace fine as gossamer, coathangers swathed with lace hanging at her back; a hoop with bright ribbons hung high above her head like a rare jellyfish, its ribbons sifting the breeze like tentacles sifting salt water: the whole market floated between dust and the ocean of cloudless sky.

A tired young woman nursing a baby sat beside a blanket heaped with vegetables. A bowling-alley rack of melons, a pyramid of potatoes, turnips with limp green leaves shrivelling in the sun.

'It makes me want to buy everything,' Callum said. 'Oh to be rich and just give it away!'

In the solid shadow of a canopy, the young men sat like statues, fingertips twitching a cigarette, a thick glass of thin beer. Blue smoke rose around their blue-black hair like incense. On the wall behind them the painted words read 'BAR PARADISO'.

Young women walked along, arms linked for safety against the unblinking male stares and the uncertainty of white stiletto heels.

Eleanor sat on the rim of a well, drinking it all in.

Everywhere children: hoarse urgent screams as they ducked under the stalls and their bare heels scuffed on jagged crates. A boy stood cursing the day he was born, tears running into his angry mouth; he cursed the cruelty and shame of a mother who will not buy sugared doughballs, a plastic aeroplane, a plastic wristwatch: she will not even buy the grey plastic hand-cuffs with silver keys that will turn him into Arnold Schwarz-enegger, and how is he to hold his head up when his mother treats the birds in the fields and the dogs in the street better than her own flesh and blood?

They sauntered on, and found an Indian sitting cross-legged beside wooden bowls of spice and powders, jars with roots like foetuses, herbs like fossilised sea-creatures. One bowl held scaly scarlet pods spiked like dried scorpions.

Wol talked to him and came back to tell Eleanor and Callum: 'He'll mix you a love-potion, a hate-potion, he can blend powders to make you potent as a bull or weak as a kitten. Not a man to be on the wrong side of.'

'Handy,' Callum said. '*Do* get his phone number!'

Eleanor realised with a start that she'd left her trolley in the attic room at Dorabella's, and a lump of panic filled her throat and made her dizzy. But Callum was so happy, light dancing through his turquoise cotton shirt, Wol was a mad angel with the sun painting his curls, and she made herself stop and breathe. *Deep and slow, that's my girl!*

Almost at once, she felt her feet floating with every step; her body was elastic, weightless, like a balloon. Turn somersaults and do cartwheels? *Fly through the air with the greatest of ease?* She could do anything under the dazzling sun in this bright market.

60

'I have a friend,' Dorabella said to them. 'I don't know, but I'll ask you anyway.'

It was two days after their arrival: they had two rooms squirrelled away above the café and Dorabella wouldn't take money from them, just singing. They sang.

Dorabella leaned back against the wall, her head framed by geraniums. This had been her bedroom when she was a little girl and she liked these crazy hippies being here now.

'Ask away, Reina Dorabella,' Callum said.

'Thank you so much, Principe Azul,' she mocked. 'Now. How do I tell you bout this friend of mine? Another crazy woman, only an American. She makes pottery – everything you see in the bar is hers. You know how you love those bowls with the mermaids swimming in them? That's Mercedes. Every shop sells her work – the tourists think they are buying the work of native peasants and it's my friend Mercedes. The American. They're happy, she's happy. Anyway, what else about her? She has second sight – you'll like that. People get freaked because she can see the dead and talk with them.'

'I like her so far,' Wol said.

'Wol, you'll love her,' Dorabella said. 'Well, this crazy woman came to Sairanac – sheesh – only three years ago. Believe me, no-one comes here very much. Not like it used to be. And she found herself a man, a Sairanacian, Gabriel Jesus, and got married to him. Now what do you think has happened to my friend?'

'She wants singers, dear,' Callum said.

'Maybe that as well, but no. You?' Dorabella looked at Wol.

'She's coming to visit and you need the rooms,' Wol said.

'*Pesimista*!' Dorabella drawled. 'And far out, man, you're far out. You?'

'She's having a baby,' Eleanor said.

'Listen!' Dorabella laughed. 'This is the one with the truth – almost. Another one with a second sight. A baby? You don't know Mercedes. She has had a baby, only not one but three. She makes a joke and says that's her family all come at once and she can get on with her work. She's *loca*, this Mercedes, I love her. And tomorrow these babies have their – *bautizo*? They make a big party for this and I would like you to come with me and my husband and his mother. Unless, God willing, she's not able to travel. God forgive me, but I could do with a day off. A year. A life.'

'Oh,' Callum said, 'I love parties.'

'Then you'll come?' Dorabella said. 'I thought so. Anyway, you have to see where she lives, my God, it's *extraño* – crazy place, you know, it's . . . You have to see. They call it Santa Marlita del Río Mildunas. Look and see if it's in your book.'

Dorabella loved their *Rough Guide to Sairanac*; she got them to read about her bar over and over. 'Dorabella's Bar wouldn't be out of place in Casablanca, and the lady herself will welcome you with a rare mix of kitsch and glamour, and watch out for the cocktails after midnight!'

'Here it is,' Callum said. 'Santa Marlita del Río Mildunas is off the beaten track – its name means the river of a thousand beaches. Time has passed it by, as has the new mountain road, so you have some desert trekking to get there. The village revolves around a shrine to Santa Marlita, whose bones were found in a cave nearby, and her prophecy that "One day there will be shade and green covering the desert like springtime in an easier land." There's an astonishing collection of cacti growing there and a bar that, like the rest of Santa Marlita, has seen better days. Worth trying to talk to Anna Consuela, the awesome matriarch of the village. No-one knows how old she is, but she knows the history of the village going back centuries.'

Dorabella laughed.

'Anna Consuela is Gabriel Jesus's grandmother,' she said, shaking one hand. 'She's a wild old woman, she gave Mercedes a hell of a time up there at first. Now, with the great grand-children she's OK. And the bar – well, Gabriel Jesus has taken it over and it's unrecognisable. That book of your doesn't tell the half of it. Anyway, would you come?'

'Love to,' Callum said. 'Yes?'

'I like the bit about shade and green covering the desert,' Eleanor said. 'Rangoon said something like that. Yes.'

'We'll go very early, it takes a time to get there,' Dorabella smiled. 'You'll like it.'

'We'll dress up,' Callum said.

'And not the bloody Carmen Miranda,' she said. 'My God, my husband nearly faints himself, he is saying, is this one a woman or a man, what's happening, Dorabella? I say him, these are artistes, they are actors and singers, don't worry yourself. Count the money. He's a happy man.'

She winked at them.

'She knows, you know,' Wol said.

'Can't imagine how,' Callum lisped, tossing back his curls.

'You boys!' Dorabella laughed. 'Wait till you meet Mercedes!'

61

Mercedes's first view of Santa Marlita had been less than inspiring – a miserable clutch of *chozas* cringing at the foot of an extinct volcano. To get there, they'd driven up a crumbling hairpin road through the clouds and into the blazing heat of a mountain-top desert.

Home? Home is where the heart is, and she'd given hers to Gabriel Jesus and if the days were arid, their nights were alive with the burning affirmation of flesh and heart and spirit.

Dust and decay and an air of despair permeated the place. Anna Consuela, Gabriel Jesus's grandmother, ignored her for months, passing her daily on her way to tend the cactus garden, where each plant was named for someone born in the village. Gabriel Jesus, for example, was represented by a Medusa tangle of luscious green. Those in favour with Anna Consuela thrived on fresh water, those out of favour she sprinkled with piss. Since his marriage, she'd ignored Gabriel Jesus's cactus, but it grew like a triffid in spite of her.

Mercedes's own dead grandmother hovered around Santa Marlita like an angel and one day she brought with her a wiry bare woman, who grinned like a lizard. This was the woman whose bones lay in the cave under the name of Santa Marlita, and she'd lived here thousands of years ago when the volcano was still alive. She found it very funny that she was now a saint for a white-bearded God who didn't exist.

Once Anna Consuela had overheard Mercedes talking with the lizard woman, she softened: only a wise woman could see the dead and speak to them, so maybe this foreign grand-daughter-in-law could be an ally.

After all, Mercedes had brought her grandson home to live: he had stormed out of the village after a row and gone away through the clouds. Most people who went away through the clouds were never seen again. Her heart leapt when he came back – Gabriel Jesus was her first-born grandchild and her favourite. Since he'd deprived her of a proper wedding, she fretted about great-grandchildren, inspecting the glistening cactus in the garden daily, but there were no buds.

'What of children?' she asked one day, abruptly.

'Oh, you know, one day,' Mercedes said. 'Grandmother, there's a lot I want to do before that.'

'A lot?'

It turned out that Mercedes wanted to build a statue. Not just life-size, like a saint or the Blessed Virgin. She wanted her statue to rise above the village like a colossus; there would be stairs in the legs and rooms in the belly, and the breasts and head.

Anna Consuela couldn't imagine it, but she gave it a grudging blessing, so long as Mercedes would then get down to the proper business of producing a fourth generation.

Just to make sure, one day when Gabriel Jesus and Mercedes had gone through the clouds to the town to deliver pots, Anna Consuela rummaged around in their house until she found their sinful packets of prophylactics. She ran her needle through each one three times. If they were going to fly in the face of God and Nature, then Nature and God could use a helping hand.

She crossed herself against the cackling laughter of the lizard woman, and muttered a rosary against this naked dancing old devil. The lizard woman followed her home and sat on the end of her bed all night, clear as day even in the darkness.

62

No sooner had Mercedes laid the foundations for her statue than she suspected she was pregnant. She had just finished one of the mighty feet when she had a spasm of cramp and was violently sick.

'Goddamn it!' she said, rinsing her mouth out and feeling her belly. 'Not now!'

'Now,' the lizard woman said, sitting cross-legged above her on the smallest toe.

'I mean,' Mercedes said, climbing up to sit beside her on the dusty surface, 'I want a baby, but later.'

'Babies come when they're ready,' the lizard woman said, 'and you'll have three.'

'Wonderful,' Mercedes snarled, lighting a cigarette, 'I just hope they come quickly. Three goddamn years out of my life. Give me a break!'

'Oh, they come quickly,' the lizard woman said, rocking with laughter.

'Hold on,' Mercedes said. 'Am I missing something here?'

'Three babies,' the lizard woman said, dancing along the foot. 'Three little babies like peas in a pod.'

Mercedes closed her eyes.

'You mean? You do. Oh, Christ.'

Her grandmother appeared next to the lizard woman.

'Mercedes,' she said, 'my little jewel. Wash your mouth out! I wish I could just wrap my arms around all four of you.'

'I'm glad someone's pleased,' Mercedes shouted and slid off the toe.

Anna Consuela was sitting on her stone by the cactus garden

of life when the lizard woman came to her. She crossed herself and when the figure wouldn't go away, she closed her eyes and gripped her rosary beads and the magic leather pouch around her neck.

'You will have three great-grandchildren,' the lizard woman said. 'Don't pretend you don't see me and hear me.'

Anna Consuela opened one eye. God forgive her – it was the naked devil she'd tried so hard to get away from!

'That's better,' the devil said. 'This is important. And I'm not a devil. Your heart would explode with the truth if I told you who I am, but believe me, the same God who made you made me.'

Now Anna Consuela knew she was damned. But the devil had spoken the holy name and she was still standing there in her awful nakedness. Maybe she was an angel? Maybe it was a test of her faith? *Es alucinante!* Anna Consuela opened her other eye.

'Now we're talking,' the devil/angel/lizard woman said, 'I'm here to tell you about your great-grandchildren. Do you want to know?'

'Oh, yes,' Anna Consuela said, her eyes filling with tears. 'Tell me. I've prayed for this ever since Gabriel Jesus came back.'

'You've done more than pray,' the lizard woman cackled. 'You're a dab hand with a needle, Anna Consuela. Don't waste time worrying, it's done and it's for the best. Look!'

Anna Consuela blushed and looked where she pointed. There in the garden of the children were three new green shoots. As she watched they shimmered out of sight. She stood and walked dreamily to the wild growth that meant Gabriel Jesus and Mercedes and the spiked green stems glittered with spiders' webs. In the heart of their tangled embrace, she saw three tiny pale buds.

'See?' the angel danced in front of her. 'There's your proof. But I have to warn you. Mercedes must stop working at the end of the fourth month. Up till then it's good, this statue she's making, it's wonderful. After that, she must rest. You must see to it. Get your grandson moving, Anna Consuela, this is the making or breaking of him.'

'My grandson will be a man,' Anna Consuela said, her eyes flashing. 'I'll whip the hide off his back if I have to.'

But she didn't have to say anything at first.

The minute Mercedes told Gabriel Jesus, he was a man transformed. He wouldn't let her lift a finger, until she screamed at him that she was pregnant not terminally ill. He stopped going to the bar and stood around nagging and fretting while she insisted on working on her statue far into the night.

Then Anna Consuela spoke to him.

'She mustn't work beyond the fourth month, Gabriel, or I'll kill you,' she said. 'Sooner if she wants to. And what are you going to do to give these children a father to be proud of?'

'Children?' he gasped. 'What do you mean?'

'Women know these things,' she said. 'Men are fools. Mercedes is having more than one child.'

He went pale.

'So?' she said.

He shook his head and went away, dithering by the bar, but deciding no, he needed to think clearly. And he couldn't bear to let Mercedes out of his sight for long.

'My grandmother says it's more than one,' he told her, rubbing her belly with coconut oil the way Anna Consuela had told him.

'It's three,' she said, laughing hysterically. 'Three.'

'What shall we call them?' he said: he'd dreamed about holding his baby close to his chest in his strong arms, this baby he'd die for, but he couldn't imagine how you picked up three of them.

'How about Sue, Durex and Today?' she said. 'Huey, Dewey and Louie? I don't know if it's boys or girls or a mix. They won't tell me.'

'Who won't tell you?' he said.

'Oh, I'm raving,' she said. 'And I won't be able to do much

more on the statue. Already I can feel it's not good for them. I've turned into a baby carrier, I don't matter any more, just them.'

'You matter more than anything,' he said, kissing her belly.

'Soon all I'll be able to do is lie here like a beached whale,' she said. 'Will you still love me?'

'For ever,' he said, 'and after that another for ever.'

'That'll do,' she said.

63

In the fifth month of her pregnancy, Mercedes got depressed. She looked at her statue, two legs and a belly rising to the navel, it felt as if it would never be finished.

Anna Consuela spent long hours in the garden of life talking with the lizard woman. One afternoon she came to see Mercedes and her eyes were bright. She put one broad palm on her Mercedes's enormous belly and muttered a prayer.

'Let me tell you a story,' she said, putting water on to boil.

Her great-granddaughter-in-law shifted her body upwards against the pillows and nodded.

'*Érase una vez*,' Anna Consuela began, the way all good stories start. 'My grandfather was *un alfareiro*, a potter like you.'

He wasn't, but the lizard woman had told her that some lies are good lies, especially if you're dealing with someone as stubborn as Mercedes.

'He was a master potter,' Anna Consuela added. 'A genius. A poet with clay and glazes. A magician at the wheel. Strong as a horse, with the eyes of an artist. Such a potter is rare.'

Mercedes bristled.

'You have the same gift,' the old woman grudged. 'But all gifts must be worked with. And you work hard.'

'I did,' Mercedes said. 'Can you imagine me trying to get close to my wheel now?'

'Well, forget the wheel. My grandfather had a vision one time. He'd been to Catalunya, fighting as men must, and he came back with this vision.'

'She's lying,' Mercedes thought, and laughed at the way Anna Consuela couldn't even look her in the eye. She wanted something, and it must be important to give it such a build-up.

'He had seen palaces and churches in Catalunya,' Anna Consuela went on. 'Only now he had lost one leg.'

'One leg,' Mercedes repeated solemnly. That was a nice authentic touch.

'And these wonderful buildings had inspired him,' the old woman said firmly. 'Their walls and roofs shone in the sunshine like the streets of heaven. Even the huts of peasants gleamed – you know why? I'll tell you. The people of Catalunya are poor, but they make their homes beautiful.'

She's trying to turn me into a housewife, Mercedes thought.

'They make tiles, you know, painted with flowers and trees and animals. Some of them just glazed in one colour. They put them on the roofs and set them in the walls and the meanest *choza* becomes fit for a king. There will be a roof tiled with stripes of green and gold and brown, shining like candy at a fiesta, my grandfather said. A roof where one tile is white and the next black like a chequerboard.'

'That was his vision?' Mercedes said; she could see it and was fascinated despite herself. 'Did he do it?'

'Unfortunately, he died,' Anna Consuela said, God forgive the easy lies tripping from her tongue! 'But I always remember him talking about it.'

'I thought he was as strong as a horse,' Mercedes said. 'How did he die?'

'Oh, fever, gangrene, I don't know,' the old woman said. 'I was a child. What does it matter? But I never forgot the story. That's what matters.'

And *you* never forget a birth or a death, you old fox, Mercedes thought.

'Go on,' she said, keeping her voice light.

'Now I was thinking,' Anna Consuela said carefully. 'Soon there will be three new lives here and that makes you look at things. We've let our village get old and tired. No place for children. Your children. My great-grandchildren. God has granted us a few months to put it right. What if we made my grandfather's vision be real? What do you think?'

'I could do it,' Mercedes said. 'I'd have done it already if I'd thought of it. You've got me.'

'You need a vision sometimes,' Anna Consuela said, her eyes suddenly fixed on Mercedes. 'You mustn't try with that statue of yours until after the children come. But you're not someone who can be idle.'

Mercedes stretched. Anything to keep her still until the children came. Well, why not?

'OK, grandmother,' she said – she'd walked right into this one! – 'What would you have on your roof?'

'Well now,' Anna Consuela leaned forwards and her eyes gleamed with mischief.

This is how the rebirth of Santa Marlita began.

64

'Arturo's not happy about leaving his car here,' Dorabella said, while her husband checked the locks on the doors again and glared up and down the empty road.

'It'll be fine,' Wol said. 'Tell him I'll put a spell of protection on it.'

'Oh, now you're a magician?' Dorabella laughed at Wol's unblinking *yes*, and shouted to her husband. He came over and stood frowning. Wol chanted solemnly, bowed to the four points of the compass, and waved his hand.

'It's done,' he said, resisting the urge to laugh as Arturo crossed himself.

'And if you think this is bad,' Dorabella said, looping her arm through her Arturo's elbow, 'Remember that these *pasaderas* – stepping stones – were only put down this year.'

She led the way from one smooth disc of stone to the next.

'What did you do to the car?' Eleanor asked.

'I made it invisible to any wicked eyes,' Wol said. 'It's a spell from the third dynasty. The court magician, Wu Li, won many a battle without any loss of life through his spells. It's very useful.'

'You'll have to teach me,' Eleanor said.

'Madame Crumsty,' Wol said. 'You have magic dripping from your fingertips.'

'Do I?' she said. 'Do I really?'

'You do,' he said.

'And I've been worrying,' she said, 'about these gifts for these babies, and their mother and father, it's so kind of them to ask us when they don't even know us. Will they be all right?'

'Oh, don't worry,' Callum said. 'We've brought what we can, in our role as the three wise persons.'

All five of them stopped at the rise before the village and Dorabella lit a cigarette.

'I'd never have believed it,' Arturo said. 'Santa Marlita del Río Mildunas – well, it's always been a joke. Either a joke or something you threaten your kids with to make them behave. And look at it now!'

'You three won't know,' Dorabella added, 'it's always been like Siberia for us, on Sairanac. A place of ghosts. A place people tell terrible stories about, so far away from civilisation that God himself has forgotten about it. I came here once when I was a teenager and it gave me the creeps. My mother brought me to see the holy relics of Santa Marlita and, tell you the truth, I thought I'd die here. I was never so glad to be away from anywhere. I couldn't believe when Mercedes settled here, I thought she'd take one look and head straight back to America, love or no love.'

While she was talking, Callum and Wol gazed ahead of them. The gaudy rooftops of the village floated in a heat haze, shiny as buttercups. Here and there the sunbeams burned a blind spot, and Callum tried to focus past the glare. There was a vast shape towering in the distance. It almost seemed to be a giant figure severed at the waist – but that was impossible.

Wasn't it?

Arturo started to walk on.

'Now you've seen a ghost,' Dorabella laughed at Callum. 'That's Mercedes's statue. She's going to finish it now the babies are born and when it's finished, she's going to live there.'

'She's crazy,' Arturo called over his shoulder.

'Live in a statue?' Callum was intrigued.

'Yes,' Dorabella said, leaning on his arm. 'There will be a bedroom in each breast, with the nipple as a window. A studio in the head with the eyes as windows. The legs hold a curving staircase like a church tower. A kitchen in the belly. What Arturo doesn't know is that Mercedes wants me to live there too. She's asked me.'

'Are you going to?' Callum said, his eyes dancing.

'Maybe,' Dorabella said. 'Maybe just weekends, maybe holidays if God decides I'm allowed holidays. Or if I do.'

Eleanor was looking all around at everything. She had already found a dozen places where she could hide, well, that was automatic. In her mind she saw the sand turned to earth with a carpet of grass and dark pools of shade cast by trees and bushes. The sun burned down on her head as she stood in the still air of this desert. All at once she felt a light green breeze rich with the scent of flowers, and every pore of her body thrilled to its touch. She knew that this breeze was yet to come and somehow she was part of it.

'All right?' Wol asked her. 'You're miles away.'

'Yes,' she said, 'I'm all right. I'm here. It's not so much miles away as – time. Goodness, what am I babbling about? Sun stroke, Wol. It's not, it's just that I love it here. It's what Callum calls *déjà vu*, only I feel it's yet to come? Oh dear, I've even lost myself.'

'Don't worry about it,' Wol said. 'The path of unknowing leads to truth.'

'Does it?' she asked. 'Really?'

'It does and it doesn't,' he said. 'The only important thing is to keep searching.'

Their eyes met: it had happened before, talking got them so far and then feelings beyond words took over and all they could say came through their eyes. Callum called it a moment of true knowledge.

Now his eyes joined them and instinctively they all held hands.

'Come on, crazies,' Dorabella said. 'Enough witchcraft! We're on our way to a *bautizo*. And me and my stilettoes need a manly arm to support us. You'll do.'

She walked the last hundred yards to the village, arm in arm with Callum. Wol followed with Eleanor.

'Ever so proper,' Callum called, 'like a school crocodile.'

'What's that?' Dorabella said, alarmed.

'Oh, you don't know about English schools, do you?' Callum said, straight-faced. 'Well . . .'

65

Mercedes hugged Dorabella close for a long time. Every woman needs a friend to confide in, someone who'll listen and never judge. Someone who gives time freely and offers a glass of wine or a cup of tea sooner than trot out a parallel anecdote laced with home-grown psychology. Someone who hears everything, even the bits that make you feel lower than shit on a snake's belly. Such a friend listens to the times when you walked hand in hand with the devil down his rotten twisted paths until you were crawling: a friend never changes towards you. In your heart, this friend is closer than a lover: someone who will stay for ever while lovers come and go.

For Mercedes, this someone was Dorabella. The only real friend she'd had since she was at school. She told her everything. The cruel fanatacism of her parents and the priest, the drug busts, broken dreams and dangers that had led her to Sairanac. That's life, said Dorabella, give me your glass.

She felt the same. Mercedes knew all about Dorabella's year in England, and the place she kept in her heart for Andy Foster. She knew about the lost babies and the discreet string of affairs and the secret bank accounts and separate beds. She knew too, of her friend's plans to leave Arturo, not because she hated him, but because there was no love between them any more, just the business. And she knew that Dorabella's indifference was born the day she learned about Arturo's mistress. Ain't life peculiar, Mercedes said, have a cigarette.

Many hours of talking had built their friendship into a solid living thing.

And now they held each other close, until, laughing and crying, they drew apart and their kicked-to-bits eyes met and confirmed it all.

'I brought these three. Tourists, but then again, not tourists,' Dorabella said. 'The boys sing in my bar. They're famous in Newcastle, these two. And this is Eleanor, their friend.'

'In Newcastle?' Mercedes grinned. 'They say the best things come from Newcastle.'

Dorabella laughed and kissed her cheek.

'Thank you for having us,' Eleanor said, a little anxiously. 'We've brought you some little things for the babies. We didn't really know . . .'

'That's kind,' Mercedes said, taking her arm. 'You didn't have to. Come and join the party.'

Something about Eleanor reminded her of her grandmother; she was like a wild bird, an exquisitely polite sparrow who'll sing its heart out for crumbs and a kind word. Yet she was wiry and don't-give-a-damn like the lizard woman as well. Mercedes smiled as they drew near the throng of people: the lizard woman was dancing among them and diving through people, laughing like a drain every time she did.

'This place is full of spirits,' Anna Consuela said smoothly, when yet another guest shivered momentarily in the blazing sunshine. How could she say anything to stop the irreverent ghost/demon/angel without everyone noticing her talking to thin air, and nudging each other?

Most of all, the lizard woman hovered round the babies in their lacy white gowns, propped in a nest of white satin, while everyone cooed and paid homage to their newness. They smiled toothless smiles at her and lifted their hands towards her million-year-old eyes.

But the lizard woman stopped when she saw Eleanor and Mercedes and her face was alight.

'This is the beginning of it,' she told Mercedes, stroking Eleanor's cheek with one invisible hand. 'This one here, she doesn't know it, but this is when it all begins. Oh, enjoy your party, I'll tell you later!'

She scandalised Anna Consuela by thumbing her nose at the priest and turning naked cartwheels along the makeshift altar. The old lady almost burst out laughing, but decorum prevailed.

Wol and Callum squatted next to the three babies. Wol's heart swelled with tenderness. One baby grasped his outstretched finger, another made a grab for Callum's mad fluffy hair. The third just pointed at them and laughed.

'Well, you've got our number,' Callum said.

Eleanor rooted through her trolley.

'These,' she said to Mercedes, 'they're trees. Well, they will be. If I'd known sooner I could have done more. The birth of a baby is so important. And three – well, it's miraculous. Callum says the spirits of your ancestors come back to a living plant and watch over you. You may think that's a bit, well, I don't know, silly, but . . .'

'I don't,' Mercedes said, taking the three pots from her. Each one held a tough little spike, like a fossil, with a hint of green at its tip.

'They're dragon trees,' Eleanor said. 'We got them in the port yesterday. Wol said they were very important to the *guanches* – do you know about the *guanches*?'

'Yes,' Mercedes said, 'I do. These are the trees with sap the colour of blood and it heals all illnesses?'

'That's what they say,' Eleanor said.

'Thank you,' Mercedes kissed her on both cheeks and nodded.

Anna Consuela and the lizard woman came up to them. Anna Consuela was trying hard to ignore the skipping grinning figure but she wouldn't simply vanish, oh no, she was here for the party and that was that. And what was she saying now?

'One of those used to grow here. It was old when I was young, but like everything, the river of fire destroyed it.'

Anna Consuela crossed herself when she saw the embryonic trees.

'God bless you,' she said to Eleanor. Friend of Dorabella she might be, but whoever she was, this pale nervous stranger had brought a wonderful living thing to Santa Marlita. A thing only ever spoken of by the women who had passed on the leather pouch and its precious contents. The dragon tree!

She had seen them arrive, Callum and Wol and Eleanor and that scandalous blonde, Dorabella, and despaired that her granddaughter-in-law made friends of such people. Now, she asked God to forgive her unkindness. For on her deathbed, the last wise woman had told her that the dragon tree must grow in Santa Marlita before the prophecy would begin to be true. Anna Consuela had buried the words in her heart, trying to dismiss them as the ravings of a dying woman. Now she knew it was true – and all the other things she had heard came flooding back. The time was here.

'Come,' she said to Eleanor, 'there's something I must show you.'

Mercedes watched her taking Eleanor away from the party, towards the garden of life. She was pointing even beyond there, and Mercedes knew she was going to the cave where the lizard woman had drawn her last breath. Curiouser and curiouser, she thought.

Then the babies saw her and called out 'mamma, mamma,' and she sprawled among them on their white satin throne, knowing she had never been happier.

66

Eleanor walked with Anna Consuela. She knew she was going somewhere special, but where? This was adventure and the thought came to her – what if I never get back? She felt like Gretel in the woods. The old woman talked all the time as they went through the weird and wonderful cacti; she said names for each one and stopped at a thick tangle of spikes and buds. She bent close and Eleanor crouched beside her.

'*Mi nieto*, Gabriel Jesus,' said Anna Consuela. 'Mercedes, *su esposa. Los bisnietos.*'

Her voice caressed the words and her broad fingertips traced three golden flowers.

'Yes,' Eleanor said. '*Si*, I mean. Your family.'

'*Mi familia*,' Anna Consuela said, nodding as she straightened up. 'Me – *bisabuelita*. Great-granny. You?'

'No,' Eleanor said, shaking her head. 'Me – no family.'

Anna Consuela leaned on her arm as they walked further.

'You – family,' she said.

They walked round a mound of rocks and the ground rose ahead of them. Sand dragged at their feet and Eleanor was sweating before they stopped. She looked where Anna Consuela pointed and then the old woman pushed her gently onwards.

She had to duck to get into the cave, but then the rocks rose above her and she looked up at its high dark roof. The cave glowed with luminous streaks and a fern grew where a pencil-thin sunbeam touched the rocks. She went deeper towards the sound of trickling water. At the back of the cave, a spring, bubbling from the bare floor, ran along a funnel of rock and disappeared into darkness. In the rock face above it, she saw shapes so delicate that a master must have carved them – spiral shells, a many-legged creature – a jewel-perfect seahorse.

She knelt, and heard Anna Consuela gasp as she cupped her hands in the flow and drank.

'*Bueno?*' the old woman's voice echoed in the gloom.

'Very good,' she said. The water was ice-cold.

'You,' Anna Consuela said firmly, 'very good. You – here.'

'Me here?' Eleanor said.

The old woman nodded and bent down to fill a small bottle from the clear spring.

'Come,' she said and they went back into blinding daylight.

Back in the village, Arturo was playing his violin and she could hear Callum and Wol singing hymns with the uncles and brothers. The priest smiled and told Mercedes that it was marvellous to find foreigners who believed in the true God. She smiled back, for her grandmother stood beside him and said he wasn't so bad for a priest, at least he really believed the mumbo-jumbo.

'Yes,' Dorabella said to Gabriel Jesus. 'They're very good, those two. Our place is packed every night since they came. I tell you, man, you could use them here. Come on, get me a drink and I'll show you what I mean.'

No-one noticed Anna Consuela swap her bottle of water for the priest's. It wasn't the first time: everyone in Santa Marlita had been baptised with water from the cave. But then she saw the lizard woman and her bright knowing eyes, and she shook her head. The lizard woman just laughed and pulled her face into grotesque distortions of horror and mirth.

Worse, when the priest was intoning the sacred words, she danced through the crowd with her five naked children and they all kissed the babies and clapped their hands as the incense rose and the priest's pale hands dashed water on their brows. Anna Consuela clutched her rosary in one hand, while the other smoothed her leather pouch.

The atmosphere changed when the priest left, escorted across the stepping stones by Gabriel Jesus. Now the violins played music for dancing and Old Simeon's accordion wheezed along with them. Dorabella improvised a drum from an empty oil can and Mercedes waltzed through the crowd with an armful of shrieking giggling babies.

Gabriel Jesus came running through the dunes and cut the cords of three red balloons. Everyone watched them fly free until they were dots over the snowy peak of the dead volcano.

Night came late and swift in Santa Marlita. One minute the sky was heavenly blue, with a golden glow on the horizon. Then the sun went down, out like a candle flame in a pool of wax. Now the sky was a navy zeppelin tethered to the horizon, pricked with stars. The gleaming crescent of the moon appeared, and they lit torches all along the street.

'I have to talk with you,' Gabriel Jesus said to Callum and Wol. 'Come and drink with me – and Dorabella.'

Anna Consuela sat and watched it all, her lined face beautiful in the torchlight. One hand rested on Eleanor's shoulder, and everyone who came up to congratulate the mountainous matriarch greeted her with the same reverence.

She didn't know all of what Anna Consuela was saying, but she heard the name Elena and realised that she was being talked about with a warmth she'd never experienced before. As far as she could remember. She giggled at the thought. Here, her lack of memory didn't matter. That damn fool doctor said she had a defective hippocampus, well! She'd found a perfect hippocampus on the rock face in the cave and that would just have to do.

Gabriel Jesus came over to his grandmother and knelt in front of her. Anna Consuela ruffled his hair and whispered to him. He leapt to his feet and offered Eleanor his hand. She took it.

Suddenly she was dancing, her feet flying, her whole body whirling along the street. She saw Callum and Wol clapping and heard this new father talking urgently into her ear.

'Never before,' he said. 'My grandmother likes you, Elena.

She's hoping you'll stay. She says you're magic. Are you magic?'

His eyes were dancing as the music stopped and she looked at him. Then another man took her arm and swept her away into the bright crowd.

67

'There's no reason why we shouldn't stay,' Wol said. 'I've got bugger all in England for another few years. Even then, Wayne might not be interested. And if he is, he could come out here. A long-lost dad who's a cabaret artiste in Sairanac is a hell of a sight more exciting than a dole queue hippy in Fenham. There's nothing grey here.'

He waved his hand at the sparkling ocean, the geraniums cascading from every balcony, the cloudless blue sky.

'There's Wolf,' Callum said. 'But I'm sure young Hannah could be persuaded to bring him over. Having boarded him with her already, I owe her a holiday. I mean, we've got everything here. They know we're off our trolleys, but they seem to like it. It feels OK being me. God, that's so sixties, but you know what I mean.'

'I thought of going back,' Eleanor said, 'just to have a look for Rangoon. But where would I begin? I have a feeling he's dead. I'd like to know for sure. But they all seem to want me here, you know, up in the village, and it feels lovely.'

'And I think I am finally over Gerth,' Callum said. 'According to Trish, he's married the boss's divorced daughter.'

'That would fit,' Wol said.

'Who's Gerth?' Eleanor said. 'You've told me, but . . .'

'Bless your amnesia,' Callum said, laughing. 'He's nobody – nobody to worry our pretty little heads about.'

They were walking along to the square where the bus had first dropped them.

'Let's have a coffee,' Wol said. 'And a think. And decide.

This is it. We will have decided in half an hour. No going back, we stick with it.'

'Shall we try that café through the archway?' Callum said. 'The one with the white lacy tables and the fountain? Lili Marlene's? Since we are – at least – temporarily employed and this is rather a life decision.'

They walked into the cool shadow of the archway. Lili Marlene's was set in an open courtyard with wooden balconies rising on all sides. A staircase rose from the courtyard in twin curves, and flowers burgeoned at every step. Beyond these stairs a hibiscus spread a canopy of leaves and gold-spiked purple flowers. Overhead hung canopies striped yellow and white, and a passion-flower vine grew up the pillars and along the carved balustrades. Camellias filled Grecian urns and deco jardinières overflowed with pink geraniums like lace. Callum ordered *café con leches* and iced water and they lazed in the perfumed air.

Eleanor felt drawn to the curving stairs; the purple-hazed tree was a magnet and she got up and went towards it as if she was floating.

First the hibiscus tree. Then a fig tree, every branch a fistful of green fruit. She ducked under its branches, and as she straightened up her heartbeat went into overdrive and she froze.

If this was dreaming, she never wanted to wake up. For there in front of her – only footsteps away – was *her* tree, more glorious than she'd remembered it. The tree she'd chased through dreams like a child after a rainbow, the tree she'd wished for and hoped so much to show Rangoon. Proof that there had been something real before the alley in East London where he'd found her.

She drank it in. Elegantly curved branches sure as a swirl of ink on silk, leaves waxy green and still, and the palest of pink flowers. She tiptoed towards it and then came the elusive scent, faint and unmistakable.

She reached out and touched one of the blooms and her fingertips thrilled with memory.

Her mind was made up. Let it be.

She walked right round the spreading branches and then backed away. It didn't vanish – she could still see it through the hibiscus and the fig from the top of the stairs.

One day, when she had somewhere to put it, somewhere so close she could see it every day, she'd tell Callum and he'd find a way of spiriting one of the branches into her trolley and she'd plant it and it would grow. She felt superstitious about it; something stopped her simply blurting it all out when she sat down with them again.

'You've seen a vision,' Callum said. 'Share it?'

She gulped her coffee and nodded.

'Just the most beautiful tree,' she said, forcing her voice to be light. 'I don't know what it is, but it's just past the fig tree.'

Callum went up the stairs.

'It is lovely,' he said. 'Like a geisha girl. Or a dowager empress who managed to avoid the footbinder. It's a magnolia.'

'Magnolia,' she repeated. 'Of course, I knew. My memory! A magnolia!'

'We have thirteen minutes to make our decisions,' Wol reminded them, his eyes laughing at them. 'Those who wish to stay may order a cocktail.'

Callum and Eleanor grabbed the cocktail menu.

'By the way, mine's a Blue Moon,' Wol said.

'Mine's a Blue Lagoon,' Callum said, 'in honour of Miss Anderson, among others.'

'I'm not sure,' Eleanor said.

They both looked at her. Wol crossed his fingers and Callum rubbed the turquoise pendant at his throat. She had become as necessary to them as breathing.

'I don't know if I like vodka,' she said, frowning at the card, 'but why not. Yes. I think I'll try Blue Heaven.'

68

At sunset, the rocks above the cave cast a shadow like the fingers of an outstretched hand. Elena unwrapped the magnolia branch from layers of plastic and wet newspaper. She'd waited a long time for this, there had been so much to do before she could think of her own dream. Three of her birthdays and three for Callum and Wol. Many bright candles of Mercedes's babies, and two hectic holidays with Hannah . . . yards of red tape to bring Wolf and his wild tail home to Callum . . . Eventually, last week, she'd been down through the clouds, drinking coffee in Lili Marlene's and finally the moment was there and she spoke to Callum as casually as she dared.

Today was the day.

She dug her fist into the sand and poured water from the spring to stop it all sliding back in. The next bit she had done so many times, but now it mattered so much that she was anxious and her hand shook as she took a pinch of the basement dirt and dropped it into the hole.

Now for the magnolia, and she looked at its dark bark and curled leaves with such love that in another world it would have burst into bloom at once.

She put it in the hole and rolled the sand back round it to hold it firm.

Time for sleep.

Her dreams were full of running, calling, voices calling a name for her and it wasn't Eleanor and it wasn't Elena but she couldn't quite catch it no matter how hard she ran towards it, crying, wait, please, wait. In the dream, when she stopped, the voice came from behind her and she turned and ran again until she was breathless.

She woke up exhausted.

For a moment she thought she was in the hut in Summerland, for the roof of the cave was curved stone and she was about to leap up and shout for Rangoon and tell him her dreams so he'd make it all better . . .

Nothing in your dreams is bigger or more powerful than you, none of it can destroy you.

Then she remembered – there was no Rangoon, at least, nowhere she could find him. It's OK, she told herself, it's OK. There was a village outside, bright as a fairground, square huts with roofs like gleaming slabs of toffee and absurd chimneys like Dutch coffee pots painted with hieroglyphs. There was Anna Consuela and her three bright-eyed great-grandchildren and the way she had of making Elena feel utterly at home. You've been adopted, Wol said. She liked being adopted. Even the different words Anna Consuela used didn't matter, Elena understood her and, more wonderfully, she was understood. And Anna Consuela's hut had a roof like a chessboard carved from virgin marble and lapis lazuli.

Elena started to relax into the new day.

A bird came and visited her every morning while she ate breakfast: it waited for crumbs, almost tapping its delicate foot with impatience. It was a mustard-yellow creature and it sang to her. Sometimes its singing was like laughter.

She liked the woman Mercedes, the one who called her *la jardinera*, who said that her spirit lived in her eyes and so she would always be at the beginning of her life. Mercedes could see the past and the future, she could read palms and cards and tea-leaves, but she'd shrugged when Elena said she couldn't remember how her life began and just told her she was lucky.

She enjoyed the half-conversations she had with the old men in Santa Marlita. They searched for English words and their old brown hands drew pictures in the air to show her what they meant. They were slow and she felt good with that. One of them, Carlos, nodded like a maniac when she said

Rangoon: he mimed a rifle at his shoulder and drew his finger across his throat. He rolled his sleeves up and showed her deep scars still white on his wrists and shook his head.

'Boorr-ma!' he said. 'Very bad.'

Then he put one finger across his lips and crossed himself and wouldn't be drawn any further. But some afternoons she'd sit with him and he'd chink his glass with hers and whisper *Rangoon* and wink at her as if it was their secret.

And Anna Consuela's great-grandchildren, well, she loved them. Blaise and Antonio and Anna. They worshipped their mother, and Mercedes treated them like puppies. They followed her when she went to work on the statue and stood in a wide-eyed line as she hauled herself up with ropes and pulleys. Their mother could fly, their mother worked half-way to heaven, and they gazed up the colossal thighs and belly of the statue, squinting against the sun while Mercedes worked on the smiling head.

Anna Consuela would call to them, and they scampered back to her wide skirts, and played while she filled their head with stories and gave them names for everything in sight and everything they could dream of.

For them, Gabriel Jesus was a climbing frame, a horse, a king, a pirate, a cowboy. They ran into his bar, L'Alfareria Magia, and the old men showed them pocket knives and buttons and keys and made faces for them to laugh at and paper kites and aeroplanes for them to fly. Their father poured lemonade out of a silver nozzle like a gun.

And then they could bounce from auntie to uncle to auntie like pinballs. There was Tia Dorabella who lived up the narrow twisting stairs in the statue, and she always had sweets for them and sparkly clothes to dress up in. Tio Wol and Tio Callum came every week and painted their giggling faces and taught them how to dance and sing, t'ai chi and tango in the great statue's shadow.

And she was Tia Lena, their auntie who lived in a cave and made flowers grow by magic.

Elena's only sadness was that Rangoon wasn't there to be

part of it all, although often she heard him, smelt his pipe tobacco, turned quick as a flash and almost saw him. Sometimes. Ah well.

And today – Elena's heart skipped a beat.

Magnolia! Magnolia! The tree outside her window from God alone knows when and where – today her magnolia tree would be growing outside her cave.

Should she wait until Callum and Wol came? No, they were singing in L'Alfareria Magia tonight and Gabriel Jesus would pour drinks while his eyes worshipped Mercedes and his three children. Wol's fingers would be flying over the old piano, the children sitting on high stools with their great-grandmother regally enthroned beside them. Callum would sing 'La Bamba' and love songs from every film ever made.

The excursion bus would fill the bar and the cash-register would ring like church bells at Christmas until it was Cinderella time. The tourists were guided back to their bus along Mercedes's stepping stones, starlight and the young men of the village with flaming torches to light the way. And then the village would draw close round the piano, and the singing went on until sunrise.

Right now Callum and Wol would be taking off wigs and make-up, hanging up sequins and net and falling gratefully into bed in the little flat over Dorabella's bar hundreds of feet below the clouds. *Goodnight, babies, the milkman's on his way.*

She rolled over and went out into the brilliant sunshine.

Oh dear God, oh no.

The magnolia twig stood in the sand exactly where she'd put it. The only change in it from yesterday was that the leaves had shrivelled.

She crouched beside it, her eyes searching the dark bark for traces of buds – even one bud.

There was nothing.

69

Callum and Wolf found her there hours later, her tanned face streaked with dried salt.

'Darling,' he said, falling to his knees beside her, 'whatever's wrong?'

Wolf licked her face.

'Look,' she said, pointing at the twig.

'Oh, divine madness and magnolia magic!' Callum said. 'But why has my *prestidigitadora loca* been crying? Your eyes are made for tears of joy, too too beautiful tears – yes! But these are sad and sad. I don't understand.'

'The magnolia,' she said, 'the branches you pinched for me, you know, I said I liked it, but it's more than that.'

'Come and sit in the shade,' he said maternally. 'Can't have your brains totally fried. Now tell Auntie Callum everything.'

She started crying again.

'I told you about the window,' she said, 'and the tree. Only I didn't know what tree it was until we saw it. Magnolia. I couldn't believe it, and there it was up the stairs behind the fig tree in Lili Marlene's and I knew it was mine. That's when I ordered Blue Heaven. And then I've been so busy since I got adopted – this crazy found family of mine and the prophecy and everything. And you two are all over the island. But yesterday it seemed right to tell you. Time to make my dream happen. I thought if I let you know how important it is, then somehow it wouldn't work. And I was right, you see. It doesn't. Here goes nothing, Cal.'

'Maybe it's the sand,' he said.

'Don't be silly,' she said. 'It's worked on plaster, it's worked on stone, good God, there's poppies growing on bare rock here now. It's not the sand. Look at Anna Consuela's cactus garden, all the grass and the dragon trees beside Mercedes's statue. Look at the walls of the huts, for goodness's sake! It's just . . . I don't want to say, it sounds so stupid.'

'I would rather listen to you than sit at the feet of Plato,' Callum said. 'Nothing from your lips is stupid. Tell me.'

He put his arm round her and Wolf licked her arm as if it was a frightened puppy.

'I wanted it to grow for him, he would have loved it,' she said. 'I thought if I could make it grow, maybe he'd come back; he was so brave and he was so tired. He must have had rheumatism and been in such pain in all those cold wet places in England. If he was here, he'd get well again. And I could have shown him something from before I met him, something real.'

No need to ask who *he* was.

'That's not stupid,' Callum said. 'Give it a bit of time.'

'It's never needed time before,' she said.

Callum looked at the twig. She was right.

And she was crying again.

'Now come on,' he said. 'I shall start bawling any minute now, and ruin my mascara. What would Rangoon say if he saw you in a heap like this?'

'Rangoon?' she said shakily. 'Ah, Rangoon!'

'No, what would he say?' Callum persisted.

'Oh,' she said, 'have a good cry, he'd say, for it's jolly old Saturday, mad-as-a-hatter-day, nothing-much-matter-day-night!'

'Well, there you are,' Callum said. 'Weep no more, my lady – no-one can take Rangoon away from you. What else would he say?'

She sniffed.

'Something about I'd rather you eyed my blessed pipe than piped your blessed eye, dear Crum. Why sit still and weep, while others dance and play? He always talked me out of it, Rangoon.'

'You've got him in your heart,' Callum said, 'and that's the only place that matters.'

'Rangoon,' she cried. 'Sometimes I listen to you and it's him. Oh, be Rangoon for me, Cal, I miss him every minute.'

'Bless you,' Callum said, 'I'd be honoured.'

She stared. Callum followed her eyes. Five bright new leaves were uncurling from the dry twig. As they watched, a slender twig stretched like a newly woken animal before their very eyes. Wolf beat his tail against the sand.

'I've a neater sweeter maiden in a cleaner greener land,' she whispered intently. 'Where are you? Rangoon?'

'He's here,' Callum said. 'He'll always be right here beside you. Just like me.'

A bud swelled from the new branch, the colour of candle-wax, the shape of a flame.

'Rangoon?' her voice challenged the air.

Callum squeezed her hand.

The bud sprung open and a soft and exquisite fragrance drifted towards them.